WHERE THE JACKALS HOWL

AND OTHER STORIES

BOOKS BY AMOS OZ

FICTION
Where the Jackals Howl
Elsewhere, Perhaps
My Michael
Unto Death
Touch the Water, Touch the Wind
The Hill of Evil Counsel
A Perfect Peace
Black Box
To Know a Woman
Fima
Don't Call It Night
The Same Sea
Rhyming Life and Death
Scenes from Village Life

NONFICTION
Under This Blazing Light
In the Land of Israel
The Slopes of Lebanon
Israel, Palestine and Peace
The Story Begins
A Tale of Love and Darkness
How to Cure a Fanatic

FOR CHILDREN
Soumchi
Panther in the Basement
Suddenly in the Depths of the Forest

The Amos Oz Reader

Amos Oz

Where the Jackals Howl

AND OTHER STORIES

TRANSLATED FROM THE HEBREW BY
Nicholas de Lange and Philip Simpson

MARINER BOOKS
HOUGHTON MIFFLIN HARCOURT
Boston • New York
2012

First Mariner Books edition 2012

Copyright © 1965 by Amos Oz and Massada Ltd.

Copyright © 1980, 1976 by Amos Oz and Am Oved Publishers Ltd.

English translation copyright © 1981, 1976, 1973 by Amos Oz

Revised translation of *Artsot ha-tan*

www.hmhbooks.com

Library of Congress Cataloging-in-Publication Data
Oz, Amos.
[Artsot ha-tan. English]
Where the jackals howl and other stories / Amos Oz ; translated from the Hebrew by Nicholas de Lange and Philip Simpson.
p. cm.
ISBN 978-0-547-74718-7
1. Jews — Social life and customs — Fiction. 2. Short stories, Hebrew — Translations into English. I. De Lange, N. R. M. (Nicholas Robert Michael), date. II. Simpson, Philip. III. Title.
PJ5054.O9A8713 2012
892.4'36 — dc23   2012015524

Book design by Melissa Lotfy

DOC 10 9 8 7 6 5 4 3 2 1

"Nomad and Viper," "The Way of the Wind," "A Hollow Stone," and "Upon This Evil Earth" were translated by Nicholas de Lange. The other stories were translated by Philip Simpson.
The translations are based on a revised edition published 1976 in Hebrew. The dates given at the end of each story refer to the year when they were first written. The author revised them extensively for this volume.

To Nily

CONTENTS

WHERE THE JACKALS HOWL

AND OTHER STORIES

Where the Jackals Howl

1

AT LAST the heat wave abated.

A blast of wind from the sea pierced the massive density of the *khamsin,* opening up cracks to let in the cold. First came light, hesitant breezes, and the tops of the cypresses shuddered lasciviously, as if a current had passed through them, rising from the roots and shaking the trunk.

Toward evening the wind freshened from the west. The *khamsin* fled eastward, from the coastal plain to the Judean hills and from the Judean hills to the rift of Jericho, from there to the deserts of the scorpion that lie to the east of Jordan. It seemed that we had seen the last *khamsin.* Autumn was drawing near.

Yelling stridently, the children of the kibbutz came streaming out onto the lawns. Their parents carried deck chairs from the verandas to the gardens. "It is the exception that proves the rule," Sashka is fond of saying. This time it was Sashka who made himself the exception, sitting alone in his room and adding a new chapter to his book about problems facing the kibbutz in times of change.

Sashka is one of the founders of our kibbutz and an active, prominent member. Squarely built, florid and bespectacled, with a handsome and sensitive face and an expression of fatherly assurance. A man of bustling energy. So fresh was the evening breeze passing through the room that he was obliged to lay a heavy ash-tray on a pile of rebellious papers. A spirited straightforwardness animated him, giving a trim edge to his sentences. Changing times, said Sashka to himself, changing times require changing ideas. Above all, let us not mark time, let us not turn back upon ourselves, let us be vigorous and alert.

The walls of the houses, the tin roofs of the huts, the stack of steel pipes beside the smithy, all began to exhale the heat accumulated in them during the days of the *khamsin*.

Galila, daughter of Sashka and Tanya, stood under the cold shower, her hands clasped behind her neck, her elbows pushed back. It was dark in the shower room. Even the blond hair lying wet and heavy on her shoulders looked dark. If there was a big mirror here, I could stand in front of it and look myself over. Slowly, calmly. Like watching the sea wind that's blowing outside.

But the cubicle was small, like a square cell, and there was no big mirror, nor could there have been. So her movements were hasty and irritable. Impatiently she dried herself and put on clean clothes. What does Matityahu Damkov want of me? He asked me to go to his room after supper. When we were children we used to love watching him and his horses. But to waste the evening in some sweaty bachelor's room, that's asking too much. True, he did promise to give me some paints from abroad. On the other hand, the evening is short and we don't have any other free time. We are working girls.

How awkward and confused Matityahu Damkov looked when he stopped me on the path and told me I should come to his room after supper. And that hand in the air, waving, gesticulating, trying to pluck words out of the hot wind, gasping like a fish out of water, not finding the words he was looking for. "This evening. Worth your while to drop in for a few minutes," he said. "Just wait and see, it will be interesting. Just for a while. And quite . . . er . . . important. You won't regret it. Real canvases and the kind of paints professional artists use, as well. Actually, I got all these things from my cousin Leon who lives in South America. I don't need paints or canvases. I . . . er . . . and there's a pattern as well. It's all for you, just make sure that you come."

As she remembered these words, Galila was filled with nausea and amusement. She thought of the fascinating ugliness of Matityahu Damkov, who had chosen to order canvases and paints for her. Well, I suppose I should go along and see what happens and discover why I am the one. But I won't stay in his room more than five minutes.

2

IN THE mountains the sunset is sudden and decisive. Our kibbutz lies on the plain, and the plain reduces the sunset, lessens its impact. Slowly, like a tired bird of passage, darkness descends on the land surface. First to grow dark are the barns and the windowless storerooms. The coming of the darkness does not hurt them, for it has never really left them. Next it is the turn of the houses. A timer sets the generator in motion. Its throbbing echoes down the slope like a beating heart, a distant drum. Veins of electricity awake into life and a hidden current passes through our thin walls. At that moment the lights spring up in all the windows of the veterans' quarters. The metal fittings on the top of the water tower catch the fading rays of daylight, hold them for a long moment. Last to be hidden in the darkness is the iron rod of the lightning conductor on the summit of the tower.

The old people of the kibbutz are still at rest in their deck chairs. They are like lifeless objects, allowing the darkness to cover them and offering no resistance.

Shortly before seven o'clock the kibbutz begins to stir, a slow movement toward the dining hall. Some are discussing what has happened today, others discuss what is to be done tomorrow, and there are a few who are silent. It is time for Matityahu Damkov to emerge from his lair and become a part of society. He locks the door of his room, leaving behind him the sterile silence, and goes to join the bustling life of the dining hall.

3

MATITYAHU DAMKOV is a small man, thin and dark, all bone and sinew. His eyes are narrow and sunken, his cheekbones slightly curved, an expression of "I told you so" is fixed upon his face. He joined our kibbutz immediately after World War II. Originally he was from Bulgaria. Where he has been and what he has done, Damkov does not tell. And we do not demand chapter and verse. However, we know that he has spent some time in South America. He has a mustache as well.

Matityahu Damkov's body is a cunning piece of craftsmanship. His torso is lean, boyish, strong, almost unnaturally agile. What impression does such a body make on women? In men it arouses a sense of nervous discomfort.

His left hand shows a thumb and a little finger. Between them is an empty space. "In time of war," says Matityahu Damkov, "men have suffered greater losses than three fingers."

In the daytime he works in the smithy, stripped to the waist and gleaming with sweat, muscles dancing beneath the taut skin like steel springs. He solders together metal fittings, welds pipes, hammers out bent tools, beats worn-out implements into scrap metal. His right hand or his left, each by itself is strong enough to lift the heavy sledgehammer and bring it down with controlled ferocity on the face of the unprotesting metal.

Many years ago Matityahu Damkov used to shoe the kibbutz horses, with fascinating skill. When he lived in Bulgaria it seems that his business was horsebreeding. Sometimes he would speak solemnly of some hazy distinction between stud horses and work horses, and tell the children gathered around him that he and his partner or his cousin Leon used to raise the most valuable horses between the Danube and the Aegean.

Once the kibbutz stopped using horses, Matityahu Damkov's craftsmanship was forgotten. Some of the girls collected redundant horseshoes and used them to decorate their rooms. Only the children who used to watch the shoeing, only they remember sometimes. The skill. The pain. The intoxicating smell. The agility. Galila used to chew a lock of blond hair and stare at him from a distance with gray, wide-open eyes, her mother's eyes, not her father's.

She won't come.

I don't believe her promises.

She's afraid of me. She's as wary as her father and as clever as her mother. She won't come. And if she does come, I won't tell her. If I tell her, she won't believe me. She'll go and tell Sashka everything. Words achieve nothing. But here there are people and light: supper time.

On every table gleamed cutlery, steel jugs and trays of bread.

"This knife needs sharpening," Matityahu Damkov said to his neighbors at the table. He cut his onions and tomatoes into thin slices and sprinkled them with salt, vinegar and olive oil. "In the winter, when there's not so much work to be done, I shall sharpen all the dining-room knives and repair the gutter as well. In fact, the winter isn't so far away. This *khamsin* was the last, I think. So there it is. The winter will catch us this year before we're ready for it."

At the end of the dining room, next to the boiler room and the kitchen, a group of bony veterans, some bald, some white-haired, are gathered around an evening paper. The paper is taken apart and the sections passed around in turn to the readers who have "reserved" them. Meanwhile there are some who offer interpretations of their own and there are others who stare at the pundits with the eyes of weary, good-humored old age. And there are those who listen in silence, with quiet sadness on their faces. These, according to Sashka, are the truest of the true. It is they who have endured the true suffering of the labor movement.

While the men are gathered around the paper discussing politics, the women are besieging the work organizer's table. Tanya is raising her voice in protest. Her face is wrinkled, her eyes harassed and weary. She is clutching a tin ashtray, beating it against the table to the rhythm of her complaints. She leans over the work sheets as if bending beneath the burden of injustice that has been laid or is about to be laid on her. Her hair is gray. Matityahu Damkov hears her voice but misses her words. Apparently the work organizer is trying to retreat with dignity in the face of Tanya's anger. And now she casually picks up the fruits of victory, straightens up and makes her way to Matityahu Damkov's table.

"Now it's your turn. You know I've got a lot of patience, but there are limits to everything. And if that lock isn't welded by ten o'clock tomorrow morning, I shall raise the roof. There is a limit, Matityahu Damkov. Well?"

The man contorted the muscles of his face so that his ugliness intensified and became repulsive beyond bearing, like a clown's mask, a nightmare figure.

"Really," he said mildly, "there's no need to get so excited. Your lock has been welded for days now, and you haven't come to collect it. Come tomorrow. Come whenever you like. There's no need to hurry me along."

"Hurry you? Me? Never in my life have I dared harass a working man. Forgive me. I'm sure you're not offended."

"I'm not offended," said Matityahu. "On the contrary. I'm an easygoing type. Good night to you."

With these words the business of the dining room is concluded. Time to go back to the room, to put on the light, to sit on the bed and wait quietly. And what else do I need? Yes. Cigarettes. Matches. Ashtray.

4

THE ELECTRIC current pulses in twining veins and sheds a weary light upon everything: our little red-roofed houses, our gardens, the pitted concrete paths, the fences and the scrap iron, the silence. Dim, weak puddles of light. An elderly light.

Searchlights are mounted on wooden posts set out at regular intervals along the perimeter fence. These beacons strive to light up the fields and the valleys that stretch away to the foothills of the mountains. A small circle of plowed land is swamped by the lights on the fence. Beyond this circle lies the night and the silence. Autumn nights are not black. Not here. Our nights are gray. A gray radiance rising over the fields, the plantations, and the orchards. The orchards have already begun to turn yellow. The soft gray light embraces the treetops with great tenderness, blurring their sharp edges, bridging the gap between lifeless and living. It is the way of the night light to distort the appearance of inanimate things and to infuse them with life, cold and sinister, vibrant with venom. At the same time it slows down the living things of the night, softening their movements, disguising their elusive presence. Thus it is that we cannot see the jackals as they spring out from their hiding places. Inevitably we miss the sight of their soft noses sniffing the air, their paws gliding over the turf, scarcely touching the ground.

The dogs of the kibbutz, they alone understand this enchanted motion. That is why they howl at night in jealousy, menace, and rage. That is why they paw at the ground, straining at their chains till their necks are on the point of breaking.

An adult jackal would have kept clear of the trap. This one was a cub, sleek, soft, and bristling, and he was drawn to the smell of blood and flesh. True, it was not outright folly that led him into the trap. He simply followed the scent and glided to his destruction with careful, mincing steps. At times he stopped, feeling some obscure warning signal in his veins. Beside the snare he paused, froze where he stood, silent, as gray as the earth and as patient. He pricked up his ears in vague apprehension and heard not a sound. The smells got the better of him.

Was it really a matter of chance? It is commonly said that chance is blind; we say that chance peers out at us with a thousand eyes. The jackal was young, and if he felt the thousand eyes fixed upon him, he could not understand their meaning.

A wall of old, dusty cypresses surrounds the plantation. What is it, the hidden thread that joins the lifeless to the living? In despair, rage, and contortion we search for the end of this thread, biting lips till we draw blood, eyes contorted in frenzy. The jackals know this thread. Sensuous, pulsating currents are alive in it, flowing from body to body, being to being, vibration to vibration. And rest and peace are there.

At last the creature bowed his head and brought his nose close to the flesh of the bait. There was the smell of blood and the smell of sap. The tip of his muzzle was moist and twitching, his saliva was running, his hide bristling, his delicate sinews throbbed. Soft as a vapor, his paw approached the forbidden fruit.

Then came the moment of cold steel. With a metallic click, light and precise, the trap snapped shut.

The animal froze like stone. Perhaps he thought he could outwit the trap, pretending to be lifeless. No sound, no movement. For a long moment jackal and trap lay still, testing each other's strength. Slowly, painfully, the living awoke and came back to life.

And silently the cypresses swayed, bowing and rising, bending and floating. He opened his muzzle wide, baring little teeth that dripped foam.

Suddenly despair seized him.

With a frantic leap he tried to tear himself free, to cheat the hangman.

Pain ripped through his body.

He lay flat upon the earth and panted.

Then the child opened his mouth and began to cry. The sound of his wailing rose and filled the night.

5

AT THIS twilight hour our world is made up of circles within circles. On the outside is the circle of the autumn darkness, far from here, in the mountains and the great deserts. Sealed and enclosed within it is the circle of our night landscape, vineyards and orchards and plantations. A dim lake astir with whispering voices. Our lands betray us in the night. Now they are no longer familiar and submissive, crisscrossed with irrigation pipes and dirt tracks. Now our fields have gone over to the enemy's camp. They send out to us waves of alien scents. At night we see them bristling in a miasma of threat and hostility and returning to their former state, as they were before we came to this place.

The inner circle, the circle of lights, keeps guard over our houses and over us, against the accumulated menace outside. But it is an ineffective wall, it cannot keep out the smells of the foe and his voices. At night the voices and the smells touch our skin like tooth and claw.

And inside, in the innermost circle of all, in the heart of our illuminated world, stands Sashka's writing desk. The table lamp sheds a calm circle of brightness and banishes the shadows from the stacks of papers. The pen in his hand darts to and fro and the words take shape. "There is no stand more noble than that of the few against the many," Sashka is fond of saying. His daughter stares wide-eyed and curious at the face of Matityahu Damkov. You're ugly and you're not one of us. It's good that you have no children and one day those dull mongoloid eyes will close and you'll be dead. And you won't leave behind anyone like you. I wish I wasn't here, but before I go I want to know what it is you want of me and why you told me to come. It's so stuffy in your room and there's an old bachelor smell that's like the smell of oil used for frying too many times.

"You may sit down," said Matityahu from the shadows. The shabby stillness that filled the room deepened his voice and made it sound remote.

"I'm in a bit of a hurry."

"There'll be coffee as well. The real thing. From Brazil. My cousin Leon sends me coffee too, he seems to think a kibbutz is a kind of kolkhoz. A kolkhoz labor camp. A collective farm in Russia, that's what a kolkhoz is."

"Black without sugar for me, please," said Galila, and these words surprised even her.

What is this ugly man doing to me? What does he want of me?

"You said you were going to show me some canvases, and some paints, didn't you?"

"All in good time."

"I didn't expect you to go to the trouble of getting coffee and cakes, I thought I'd only be here for a moment."

"You are fair," the man said, breathing heavily, "you are fair-haired, but I'm not mistaken. There is doubt. There has to be. But it is so. What I mean is, you'll drink your coffee, nice and slow, and I'll give you a cigarette too, an American one, from Virginia. In the meantime, have a look at this box. The brushes. The special oil too. And the canvases. And all the tubes. It's all for you. First of all drink. Take your time."

"But I still don't understand," said Galila.

A man pacing about his room in an undershirt on a summer night is not a strange sight. But the monkeylike body of Matityahu Damkov set something stirring inside her. Panic seized her. She put down the coffee cup on the brass tray, jumped up from the chair and stood behind it, clutching the chair as if it were a barricade.

The transparent, frightened gesture delighted her host. He spoke patiently, almost mockingly:

"Just like your mother. I have something to tell you when the moment's right, something that I'm positive you don't know, about your mother's wickedness."

Now, at the scent of danger, Galila was filled with cold malice:

"You're mad, Matityahu Damkov. Everybody says that you're mad."

There was tender austerity in her face, an expression both secretive and passionate.

"You're mad, and get out of my way and let me pass. I want to get out of here. Yes. Now. Out of my way."

The man retreated a little, still staring at her intently. Suddenly he sprang onto his bed and sat there, his back to the wall, and laughed a long, happy laugh.

"Steady, daughter, why all the haste? Steady. We've only just begun. Patience. Don't get so excited. Don't waste your energy."

Galila hastily weighed up the two possibilities, the safe and the fascinating, and said:

"Please tell me what you want of me."

"Actually," said Matityahu Damkov, "actually, the kettle's boiling again. Let's take a short break and have some more coffee. You won't deny, I'm sure, that you've never drunk coffee like this."

"Without milk or sugar for me. I told you before."

6

THE SMELL of coffee drove away all other smells: a strong, sharp, pleasant smell, almost piercing. Galila watched Matityahu Damkov closely, observing his manners, the docile muscles beneath his string shirt, his sterile ugliness. When he spoke again, she clutched the cup tightly between her fingers and a momentary peace descended on her.

"If you like, I can tell you something in the meantime. About horses. About the farm that we used to have in Bulgaria, maybe fifty-seven kilometers from the port of Varna, a stud farm. It belonged to me and my cousin Leon. There were two branches that we specialized in: work horses and stud horses, in other words, castration and covering. Which would you like to hear about first?"

Galila relaxed, leaning back in the chair and crossing her legs, ready to hear a story. In her childhood she had always loved the moments before the start of a bedtime story.

"I remember," she said, "how when we were children we used to come and watch you shoeing the horses. It was beautiful and strange and so . . . were you."

"Preparing for successful mating," said Matityahu, passing her a plate of crackers, "is a job for professionals. It takes expertise and intuition as well. First, the stallion must be kept in confinement for a long time. To drive him mad. It improves his seed. He's kept apart from the mares for several months, from the stallions too. In his frustration he may even attack another male. Not every stallion is suitable for stud, perhaps one in a hundred. One stud horse to a hundred work horses. You need a lot of experience and keen observation to pick out the right horse. A stupid, unruly horse is the best. But it isn't all that easy to find the most stupid horse."

"Why must he be stupid?" asked Galila, swallowing spittle.

"It's a question of madness. It isn't always the biggest, most handsome stallion that produces the best foals. In fact a mediocre horse can be full of energy and have the right kind of nervous temperament. After the candidate had been kept in confinement for a few months, we used to put wine in his trough, half a bottle. That was my cousin Leon's idea. To get the horse a bit drunk. Then we'd fix it so he could take a look at the mares through the bars and get a whiff of their smell. Then he starts going mad. Butting like a bull. Rolling on his back and kicking his legs in the air. Scratching himself, rubbing himself, trying desperately to ejaculate. He screams and starts biting in all directions. When the stallion starts to bite, then we know that the time has come. We open the gate. The mare is waiting for him. And just for a moment, the stallion hesitates. Trembling and panting. Like a coiled spring."

Galila winced, staring entranced at Matityahu Damkov's lips.

"Yes," she said.

"And then it happens. As if the law of gravity had suddenly been revoked. The stallion doesn't run, he flies through the air. Like a cannon ball. Like a spring suddenly released. The mare bows and lowers her head and he thrusts into her, blow after blow. His eyes are full of blood. There's not enough air for him to breathe and he gasps and chokes as if he's dying. His mouth hangs open and he pours saliva and foam on her head. Suddenly he starts to roar and howl. Like a dog. Like a wolf. Writhing and screaming. In that moment there is no telling pleasure from pain. And mating is very much like castration."

"Enough, Matityahu, for God's sake, enough."

"Now let's relax. Or perhaps you'd like to hear how a horse is castrated?"

"Please, enough, no more," Galila pleaded.

Slowly Matityahu raised his maimed hand. The compassion in his voice was strange, almost fatherly:

"Just like your mother. About that," he said, "about the fingers and about castration as well, we'll talk some other time. Enough now. Don't be afraid now. Now we can rest and relax. I've got a drop of cognac somewhere. No? No. Vermouth then. There's vermouth too. Here's to my cousin Leon. Drink. Relax. Enough."

7

THE COLD light of the distant stars spreads a reddish crust upon the fields. In the last weeks of the summer the land has all been turned over. Now it stands ready for the winter sowing. Twisting dirt tracks cross the plain, here and there are the dark masses of plantations, fenced in by walls of cypress trees.

For the first time in many months our lands feel the first tentative fingers of the cold. The irrigation pipes, the taps, the metal fittings, they are the first to capitulate to any conqueror, summer's heat or autumn's chill. And now they are the first to surrender to the cool moisture.

In the past, forty years ago, the founders of the kibbutz entrenched themselves in this land, digging their pale fingernails into the earth. Some were fair-haired, like Sashka, others, like Tanya, were brazen and scowling. In the long, burning hours of the day they used to curse the earth scorched by the fires of the sun, curse it in despair, in anger, in longing for rivers and forests. But in the darkness, when night fell, they composed sweet love songs to the earth, forgetful of time and place. At night forgetfulness gave taste to life. In the angry darkness oblivion enfolded them in a mother's embrace. "There," they used to sing, not "Here."

> *There in the land our fathers loved,*
> *There all our hopes shall be fulfilled.*
> *There we shall live and there a life*
> *Of health and freedom we shall build ...*

People like Sashka were forged in fury, in longing and in dedication. Matityahu Damkov, and the latter-day fugitives like him, know nothing of the longing that burns and the dedication that draws blood from the lips. That is why they seek to break into the inner circle. They make advances to the women. They use words similar to ours. But theirs is a different sorrow, they do not belong to us, they are extras, on the outside, and so they shall be until the day they die.

The captive jackal cub was seized by weariness. The tip of his right paw was held fast in the teeth of the trap. He sprawled flat on the turf as if reconciled to his fate.

First he licked his fur, slowly, like a cat. Then he stretched out his neck and began licking the smooth, shining metal. As if lavishing warmth and love upon the silent foe. Love and hate, they both breed surrender. He threaded his free paw beneath the trap, groped slowly for the meat of the bait, withdrew the paw carefully and licked off the savor that had clung to it.

Finally, the others appeared.

Jackals, huge, emaciated, filthy and swollen-bellied. Some with running sores, others stinking of putrid carrion. One by one they came together from all their distant hiding places, summoned to the gruesome ritual. They formed themselves into a circle and fixed pitying eyes upon the captive innocent. Malicious joy striving hard to disguise itself as compassion, triumphant evil breaking through the mask of mourning. The unseen signal was given, the marauders of the night began slowly moving in a circle as in a dance, with mincing, gliding steps. When the excitement exploded into mirth the rhythm was shattered, the ritual broken, and the jackals cavorted madly like rabid dogs. Then the despairing voices rose into the night, sorrow and rage and envy and triumph, bestial laughter and a choking wail of supplication, angry, threatening, rising to a scream of terror and fading again into submission, lament, and silence.

After midnight they ceased. Perhaps the jackals despaired of their helpless child. Quietly they dispersed to their own sorrows. Night, the patient gatherer, took them up in his arms and wiped away all the traces.

8

MATITYAHU DAMKOV was enjoying the interlude. Nor did Galila try to hasten the course of events. It was night. The girl unfolded the canvases that Matityahu Damkov had received from his cousin Leon and examined the tubes of paint. It was good quality material, the type used by professionals. Until now she had painted on oiled sackcloth or cheap mass-produced canvases with paints borrowed from the kindergarten. She's so young, thought Matityahu Damkov, she's a little girl, slender and spoiled. I'm going to smash her to pieces. Slowly. For a moment he was tempted to tell her the truth outright, like a bolt from the blue, but he thought better of it. The night was slow.

In oblivion and delight, compulsively, Galila fingered the fine brush, lightly touching the orange paint, lightly stroking the canvas with the hairs of the brush, an unconscious caress, like fingertips on the hairs of the neck. Innocence flowed from her body to his, his body responded with waves of desire.

Afterward Galila lay without moving, as if asleep, on the oily, paint-splashed tiles, canvases and tubes of paint scattered about her. Matityahu lay back on his single bed, closed his eyes and summoned a dream.

At his bidding they come to him, quiet dreams and wild dreams. They come and play before him. This time he chose to summon the dream of the flood, one of the severest in his repertoire.

First to appear is a mass of ravines descending the mountain slopes, scores of teeming watercourses, crisscrossing and zigzagging.

In a flash the throngs of tiny people appear in the gullies. Like little black ants they swarm and trickle from their hiding places in the crevices of the mountain, sweeping down like a cataract. Hordes of thin dark people streaming down the slopes, rolling like an avalanche of stone and plunging in a headlong torrent to the levels of the plain. Here they split into a thousand columns, racing westward in furious spate. Now they are so close that their shapes can be seen: a dark, disgusting, emaciated mass, crawling with lice and fleas, stinking. Hunger and hatred distort their faces. Their eyes blaze with madness. In full flood they swoop upon the fertile valleys, racing over the ruins of deserted villages without a moment's check. In their rush toward the sea they drag with them all that lies in their path, uprooting posts, ravaging fields, mowing down fences, trampling the gardens and stripping the orchards, pillaging homesteads, crawling through huts and stables, clambering over walls like demented apes, onward, westward, to the sands of the sea.

And suddenly you too are surrounded, besieged, paralyzed with fear. You see their eyes ablaze with primeval hatred, mouths hanging open, teeth yellow and rotten, curved daggers gleaming in their hands. They curse you in clipped tones, voices choking with rage or with dark desire. Now their hands are groping at your flesh. A knife and a scream. With the last spark of your life you extinguish the vision and almost breathe freely again.

"Come on," said Matityahu Damkov, shaking the girl with his right hand, while the maimed hand, his left, caressed her neck. "Come on. Let's get away from here. Tonight. In the morning. I shall save you. We'll run away together to South America, to my cousin Leon. I'll take care of you. I'll always take care of you."

"Leave me alone, don't touch me," she said.

He clasped her in a powerful and silent embrace.

"My father will kill you tomorrow. I told you to leave me alone."

"Your father will take care of you now and he'll always take care of you," Matityahu Damkov replied softly. He let her go. The girl stood up, buttoning her skirt, smoothing back her blond hair.

"That isn't what I want. I didn't want to come here at all. You're taking advantage of me and doing things to me that I don't want and saying all kinds of things because you're mad and everyone knows you're mad, ask anyone you like."

Matityahu Damkov's lips broadened into a smile.

"I won't come to you again, not ever, And I don't want your paints. You're dangerous. You're as ugly as a monkey. And you're mad."

"I can tell you about your mother, if you want to hear. And if you want to hate and curse, then it's her you should hate, not me."

The girl turned hurriedly to the window, flung it open with a desperate movement and leaned out into the empty night. Now she's going to scream, thought Matityahu Damkov in alarm, she'll scream and the opportunity won't come again. Blood filled his eyes. He swooped upon her, clapped his hand over her mouth, dragged her back inside the room, buried his lips in her hair, probed with his lips for her ear, found it, and told her.

9

SHARP WAVES of chill autumn air clung to the outer walls of the houses, seeking entry. From the yard on the slope of the hill came the sounds of cattle lowing and herdsmen cursing. A cow having difficulty giving birth perhaps, the big torch throwing light on the blood and the mire. Matityahu Damkov knelt on the floor and gathered up the paints and the brushes that his guest had left scattered there. Galila still stood beside the open window, her back to the room and her face to the darkness. Then she spoke, still with her back to the man.

"It's doubtful," she said. "It's almost impossible, it isn't even logical, it can't be proved, and it's crazy. Absolutely."

Matityahu Damkov stared at her back with his mongoloid eyes. Now his ugliness was complete, a concentrated, penetrating ugliness.

"I won't force you. Please. I shall say nothing. Perhaps just laugh to myself quietly. For all I care you can be Sashka's daughter or even Ben-Gurion's daughter. I shall say nothing. Like my cousin Leon I shall say nothing. He loved his Christian son and never said I love you, only when this son of his had killed eleven policemen and himself did he remember to tell him in his grave, I love you. Please."

Suddenly, without warning, Galila burst into laughter:

"You fool, you little fool, look at me, I'm blond, look!"

Matityahu said nothing.

"I'm not yours, I'm sure of it because I'm blond, I'm not yours or Leon's either, I'm blond and it's all right! Come on!"

The man leaped at her, panting, groaning, groping his way blindly. In his rush he overturned the coffee table, he shuddered violently and the girl shuddered with him.

And then she recoiled from him, fled to the far wall. He pushed aside the coffee table. He kicked it. His eyes were shot with blood, and a sound like gargling came from his lips. She suddenly remembered her mother's face and the trembling of her lips and her tears, and she pushed the man from her with a dreamy hand. As if struck, they both retreated, staring at each other, eyes wide open.

"Father," said Galila in surprise, as if waking on the first morning of winter at the end of a long summer, looking outside and saying, rain.

10

THE SUN rises without dignity in our part of the world. With a cheap sentimentality it appears over the peaks of the eastern mountains and touches our lands with tentative rays. No glory, no complicated tricks of light. A purely conventional beauty, more like a picture postcard than a real landscape.

But this will be one of the last sunrises. Autumn will soon be here. A few more days and we shall wake in the morning to the sound of rain. There may be hail too. The sun will rise behind a screen of dirty gray clouds. Early risers will wrap themselves in overcoats and emerge from their houses fortified against the daggers of the wind.

The path of the seasons is well trodden. Autumn, winter, spring, summer, autumn. Things are as they have always been. Whoever seeks a fixed point in the current of time and the seasons would do well to listen to the sounds of the night that never change. They come to us from out there.

1963

Nomad and Viper

1

THE FAMINE brought them.

They fled north from the horrors of famine, together with their dusty flocks. From September to April the desert had not known a moment's relief from drought. The loess was pounded to dust. Famine had spread through the nomads' encampments and wrought havoc among their flocks.

The military authorities gave the situation their urgent attention. Despite certain hesitations, they decided to open the roads leading north to the Bedouins. A whole population — men, women, and children — could not simply be abandoned to the horrors of starvation.

Dark, sinuous, and wiry, the desert tribesmen trickled along the dirt paths, and with them came their emaciated flocks. They meandered along gullies hidden from town dwellers' eyes. A persistent stream pressed northward, circling the scattered settlements, staring wide-eyed at the sights of the settled land. The dark flocks spread into the fields of golden stubble, tearing and chewing with strong, vengeful teeth. The nomads' bearing was stealthy and subdued; they shrank from watchful eyes. They took pains to avoid encounters. Tried to conceal their presence.

If you passed them on a noisy tractor and set billows of dust loose on them, they would courteously gather their scattered flocks and give you a wide passage, wider by far than was necessary. They stared at you from a distance, frozen like statues. The scorching atmosphere blurred their appearance and gave a uniform look to their features: a shepherd with his staff, a woman with her babes, an old man with his eyes sunk deep in their sockets. Some were half-blind, or perhaps feigned half-blindness from some vague alms-gathering motive. Inscrutable to the likes of you.

How unlike our well-tended sheep were their miserable specimens: knots of small, skinny beasts huddling into a dark, seething mass, silent and subdued, humble as their dumb keepers.

The camels alone spurn meekness. From atop tall necks they fix you with tired eyes brimming with scornful sorrow. The wisdom of age seems to lurk in their eyes, and a nameless tremor runs often through their skin.

Sometimes you manage to catch them unawares. Crossing a field on foot, you may suddenly happen on an indolent flock standing motionless, noon-struck, their feet apparently rooted in the parched soil. Among them lies the shepherd, fast asleep, dark as a block of basalt. You approach and cover him with a harsh shadow. You are startled to find his eyes wide open. He bares most of his teeth in a placatory smile. Some of them are gleaming, others decayed. His smell hits you. You grimace. Your grimace hits him like a punch in the face. Daintily he picks himself up, trunk erect, shoulders hunched. You fix him with a cold blue eye. He broadens his smile and utters a guttural syllable. His garb is a compromise: a short, patched European jacket over a white desert robe. He cocks his head to one side. An appeased gleam crosses his face. If you do not upbraid him, he suddenly extends his left hand and asks for a cigarette in rapid Hebrew. His voice has a silken quality, like that of a shy woman. If your mood is generous, you put a cigarette to your lips and toss another into his wrinkled palm. To your surprise, he snatches a gilt lighter from the recesses of his robe and offers a furtive flame. The smile never leaves his lips. His smile lasts too long, is unconvincing. A flash of sunlight darts off the thick gold ring adorning his finger and pierces your squinting eyes.

Eventually you turn your back on the nomad and continue on your way. After a hundred, two hundred paces, you may turn your head and see him standing just as he was, his gaze stabbing your back. You could swear that he is still smiling, that he will go on smiling for a long while to come.

And then, their singing in the night. A long-drawn-out, dolorous wail drifts on the night air from sunset until the early hours. The voices penetrate to the gardens and pathways of the kibbutz and charge our nights with an uneasy heaviness. No sooner have you settled down to sleep than a distant drumbeat sets the rhythm of your slumber like the pounding of an obdurate heart. Hot are the nights, and vapor-laden. Stray clouds caress the moon like a train of gentle camels, camels without any bells.

The nomads' tents are made up of dark drapes. Stray women drift around at night, barefoot and noiseless. Lean, vicious nomad hounds dart out of the camp to challenge the moon all night long. Their barking drives our kibbutz dogs insane. Our finest dog went mad one night, broke into the henhouse, and massacred the young chicks. It was not out of savagery that the watchmen shot him. There was no alternative. Any reasonable man would justify their action.

2

YOU MIGHT imagine that the nomad incursion enriched our heat-prostrated nights with a dimension of poetry. This may have been the case for some of our unattached girls. But we cannot refrain from mentioning a whole string of prosaic, indeed unaesthetic disturbances, such as foot-and-mouth disease, crop damage, and an epidemic of petty thefts.

The foot-and-mouth disease came out of the desert, carried by their livestock, which had never been subjected to any proper medical inspection. Although we took various early precautions, the virus infected our sheep and cattle, severely reducing the milk yield and killing off a number of animals.

As for the damage to the crops, we had to admit that we had never managed to catch one of the nomads in the act. All we ever found were the tracks of men and animals among the rows of vegetables, in the hayfields, and deep inside the carefully fenced orchards. And wrecked irrigation pipes, plot markers, farming implements left out in the fields, and other objects.

We are not the kind to take such things lying down. We are no believers in forbearance or vegetarianism. This is especially true of our younger men. Among the veteran founders there are a few adherents of Tolstoyan ideas and such like. Decency constrains me not to dwell in detail on certain isolated and exceptional acts of reprisal conducted by some of the youngsters whose patience had expired, such as cattle rustling, stoning a nomad boy, or beating one of the shepherds senseless. In defense of the perpetrators of the last-mentioned act of retaliation I must state clearly that the shepherd in question had an infuriatingly sly face. He was blind in one eye, broken-nosed, drooling; and his mouth — on this the men responsible were unanimous — was set with long, curved fangs like a fox's. A man with such an appearance was capable of anything. And the Bedouins would certainly not forget this lesson.

The pilfering was the most worrisome aspect of all. They laid hands on the unripe fruit in our orchards, pocketed the faucets, whittled away piles of empty sacks in the fields, stole into the henhouses, and even made away with the modest valuables from our little houses.

The very darkness was their accomplice. Elusive as the wind, they passed through the settlement, evading both the guards we had posted and the extra guards we had added. Sometimes you would set out on a tractor or a battered jeep toward midnight to turn off the irrigation faucets in an outlying field and your headlights would trap fleeting shadows, a man or a night beast. An irritable guard decided one night to open fire, and in the dark he managed to kill a stray jackal.

Needless to say, the kibbutz secretariat did not remain silent. Several times Etkin, the secretary, called in the police, but their tracking dogs betrayed or failed them. Having led their handlers a few paces outside the kibbutz fence, they raised their black noses, uttered a savage howl, and stared foolishly ahead:

Spot raids on the tattered tents revealed nothing. It was as if the very earth had decided to cover up the plunder and brazenly outstare the victims. Eventually the elder of the tribe was brought to the kibbutz office, flanked by a pair of inscrutable nomads. The short-tempered policemen pushed them forward with repeated cries of "Yallah, yallah."

We, the members of the secretariat, received the elder and his men politely and respectfully. We invited them to sit down on the bench, smiled at them, and offered them steaming coffee prepared by Geula at Etkin's special request. The old man responded with elaborate courtesies, favoring us with a smile which he kept up from the beginning of the interview till its conclusion. He phrased his remarks in careful, formal Hebrew.

It was true that some of the youngsters of his tribe had laid hands on our property. Why should he deny it. Boys would be boys, and the world was getting steadily worse. He had the honor of begging our pardon and restoring the stolen property. Stolen property fastens its teeth in the flesh of the thief, as the proverb says. That was the way of it. What could one do about the hotheadedness of youth? He deeply regretted the trouble and distress we had been caused.

So saying, he put his hand into the folds of his robe and drew out a few screws, some gleaming, some rusty, a pair of pruning hooks, a stray knife-blade, a pocket flashlight, a broken hammer, and three grubby bank notes, as a recompense for our loss and worry.

Etkin spread his hands in embarrassment. For reasons best

known to himself, he chose to ignore our guest's Hebrew and to reply in broken Arabic, the residue of his studies during the time of the riots and the siege. He opened his remarks with a frank and clear statement about the brotherhood of nations — the cornerstone of our ideology — and about the quality of neighborliness of which the peoples of the East had long been justly proud, and never more so than in these days of bloodshed and groundless hatred.

To Etkin's credit, let it be said that he did not shrink in the slightest from reciting a full and detailed list of the acts of theft, damage, and sabotage that our guest — as the result of oversight, no doubt — had refrained from mentioning in his apology. If all the stolen property were returned and the vandalism stopped once and for all, we would be wholeheartedly willing to open a new page in the relations of our two neighboring communities. Our children would doubtless enjoy and profit from an educational courtesy visit to the Bedouin encampment, the kind of visit that broadens horizons. And it went without saying that the tribe's children would pay a return visit to our kibbutz home, in the interest of deepening mutual understanding.

The old man neither relaxed nor broadened his smile, but kept it sternly at its former level as he remarked with an abundance of polite phrases that the gentlemen of the kibbutz would be able to prove no further thefts beyond those he had already admitted and for which he had sought our forgiveness.

He concluded with elaborate benedictions, wished us health and long life, posterity and plenty, then took his leave and departed, accompanied by his two barefooted companions wrapped in their dark robes. They were soon swallowed up by the wadi that lay outside the kibbutz fence.

Since the police had proved ineffectual — and had indeed abandoned the investigation — some of our young men suggested making an excursion one night to teach the savages a lesson in a language they would really understand.

Etkin rejected their suggestion with disgust and with reasonable arguments. The young men, in turn, applied to Etkin a number of epithets that decency obliges me to pass over in silence. Strangely enough, Etkin ignored their insults and reluctantly agreed to put their suggestion before the kibbutz secretariat. Perhaps he was afraid that they might take matters into their own hands.

Toward evening, Etkin went around from room to room and invited the committee to an urgent meeting at eight-thirty. When he came to Geula, he told her about the young men's ideas and the undemocratic pressure to which he was being subjected, and asked her to bring along to the meeting a pot of black coffee and a lot of good will. Geula responded with an acid smile. Her eyes were bleary because Etkin had awakened her from a troubled sleep. As she changed her clothes, the night fell, damp and hot and close.

3

DAMP AND close and hot the night fell on the kibbutz, tangled in the dust-laden cypresses, oppressed the lawns and ornamental shrubs. Sprinklers scattered water onto the thirsty lawn, but it was swallowed up at once: perhaps it evaporated even before it touched the grass. An irritable phone rang vainly in the locked office. The walls of the houses gave out a damp vapor. From the kitchen chimney a stiff column of smoke rose like an arrow into the heart of the sky, because there was no breeze. From the greasy sinks came a shout. A dish had been broken and somebody was bleeding. A fat house-cat had killed a lizard or a snake and dragged its prey onto the baking concrete path to toy with it lazily in the dense evening sunlight. An ancient tractor started to rumble in one of the sheds, choked, belched a stench of oil, roared, spluttered, and finally managed to set out to deliver an evening meal to the second shift, who were toiling in an outlying field. Near the Persian lilac Geula saw a bottle dirty with the remains of a greasy liquid. She kicked at it repeatedly, but instead of shattering, the bottle rolled heavily among the rosebushes. She picked up a big stone. She tried to hit the bottle. She longed to smash it. The stone missed. The girl began to whistle a vague tune.

Geula was a short, energetic girl of twenty-nine or so. Although she had not yet found a husband, none of us would deny her good qualities, such as the dedication she lavished on local social and cultural activities. Her face was pale and thin. No one could rival her in brewing strong coffee — coffee to raise the dead, we called it. A pair of bitter lines were etched at the corners of her mouth.

On summer evenings, when the rest of us would lounge in a group on a rug spread on one of the lawns and launch jokes and bursts of cheerful song heavenward, accompanied by clouds of cigarette smoke, Geula would shut herself up in her room and not join us until she had prepared the pot of scalding, strong coffee. She it was, too, who always took pains to ensure that there was no shortage of biscuits.

What had passed between Geula and me is not relevant here, and I shall make do with a hint or two. Long ago we used to stroll together to the orchards in the evening and talk. It was all a long time ago, and it is a long time since it ended. We would exchange unconventional political ideas or argue about the latest books. Geula was a stern and sometimes merciless critic: I was covered in confusion. She did not like my stories, because of the extreme polarity of situations, scenery, and characters, with no intermediate shades between black and white. I would utter an apology or a denial, but Geula always had ready proofs and she was a very methodical thinker. Sometimes I would dare to rest a conciliatory hand on her neck, and wait for her to calm down. But she never relaxed completely. If once or twice she leaned against me, she always blamed her broken sandal or her aching head. And so we drifted apart. To this day she still cuts my stories out of the periodicals, and arranges them in a cardboard box kept in a special drawer devoted to them alone.

I always buy her a new book of poems for her birthday. I creep into her room when she is out and leave the book on her table, without any inscription or dedication. Sometimes we happen to sit together in the dining hall. I avoid her glance, so as not to have to face her mocking sadness. On hot days, when faces are covered in sweat, the acne on her cheeks reddens and she seems to have no hope. When the cool of autumn comes, I sometimes find her pretty and attractive from a distance. On such days Geula likes to walk to the orchards in the early evening. She goes alone and comes back alone. Some of the youngsters come and ask me what she is looking for there, and they have a malicious snicker on their faces. I tell them that I don't know. And I really don't.

4

VICIOUSLY GEULA picked up another stone to hurl at the bottle. This time she did not miss, but she still failed to hear the shattering sound she craved. The stone grazed the bottle, which tinkled faintly and disappeared under one of the bushes. A third stone, bigger and heavier than the other two, was launched from ridiculously close range: the girl trampled on the loose soil of the flower bed and stood right over the bottle. This time there was a harsh, dry explosion, which brought no relief. Must get out.

Damp and close and hot the night fell, its heat pricking the skin like broken glass. Geula retraced her steps, passed the balcony of her room, tossed her sandals inside, and walked down barefoot onto the dirt path.

The clods of earth tickled the soles of her feet. There was a rough friction, and her nerve endings quivered with flickers of vague excitement. Beyond the rocky hill the shadows were waiting for her: the orchard in the last of the light. With determined hands she widened the gap in the fence and slipped through. At that moment a slight evening breeze began to stir. It was a warmish summer breeze with no definite direction. An old sun rolled westward, trying to be sucked up by the dusty horizon. A last tractor climbed back to the depot, panting along the dirt road from the outlying plots. No doubt it was the tractor that had taken the second-shift workers their supper. It seemed shrouded in smoke or summer haze.

Geula bent down and picked some pebbles out of the dust. Absently she began to throw them back again, one by one. There were lines of poetry on her lips, some by the young poets she was fond of, others her own. By the irrigation pipe she paused, bent down, and drank as though kissing the faucet. But the faucet was rusty, the pipe was still hot, and the water was tepid and foul. Nevertheless she bent her head and let the water pour over her face and neck and into her shirt. A sharp taste of rust and wet dust filled her throat. She closed her eyes and stood in silence. No relief. Perhaps a cup of coffee. But only after the orchard. Must go now.

5

THE ORCHARDS were heavily laden and fragrant. The branches intertwined, converging above the rows of trunks to form a shadowy dome. Underfoot the irrigated soil retained a hidden dampness. Shadows upon shadows at the foot of those gnarled trunks. Geula picked a plum, sniffed and crushed it. Sticky juice dripped from it. The sight made her feel dizzy. And the smell. She crushed a second plum. She picked another and rubbed it on her cheek till she was spattered with juice. Then, on her knees, she picked up a dry stick and scratched shapes in the dust. Aimless lines and curves. Sharp angles. Domes. A distant bleating invaded the orchard. Dimly she became aware of a sound of bells. She was far away. The nomad stopped behind Geula's back, as silent as a phantom. He dug at the dust with his big toe, and his shadow fell in front of him. But the girl was blinded by a flood of sounds. She saw and heard nothing. For a long time she continued to kneel on the ground and draw shapes in the dust with her twig. The nomad waited patiently in total silence. From time to time he closed his good eye and stared ahead of him with the other, the blind one. Finally he reached out and bestowed a long caress on the air. His obedient shadow moved in the dust. Geula stared, leapt to her feet, and leaned against the nearest tree, letting out a low sound. The nomad let his shoulders drop and put on a faint smile. Geula raised her arm and stabbed the air with her twig. The nomad continued to smile. His gaze dropped to her bare feet. His voice was hushed, and the Hebrew he spoke exuded a rare gentleness:

"What time is it?"

Geula inhaled to her lungs' full capacity. Her features grew sharp, her glance cold. Clearly and dryly she replied:

"It is half past six. Precisely."

The Arab broadened his smile and bowed slightly, as if to acknowledge a great kindness.

"Thank you very much, miss."

His bare toe had dug deep into the damp soil, and the clods of earth crawled at his feet as if there were a startled mole burrowing underneath them.

Geula fastened the top button of her blouse. There were large perspiration stains on her shirt, drawing attention to her armpits. She could smell the sweat on her body, and her nostrils widened. The nomad closed his blind eye and looked up. His good eye blinked. His skin was very dark; it was alive and warm. Creases were etched in his cheeks. He was unlike any man Geula had ever known, and his smell and color and breathing were also strange. His nose was long and narrow, and a shadow of a mustache showed beneath it. His cheeks seemed to be sunk into his mouth cavity. His lips were thin and fine, much finer than her own. But the chin was strong, almost expressing contempt or rebellion.

The man was repulsively handsome, Geula decided to herself. Unconsciously she responded with a mocking half-smile to the nomad's persistent grin. The Bedouin drew two crumpled cigarettes from a hidden pocket in his belt, laid them on his dark, outstretched palm, and held them out to her as though proffering crumbs to a sparrow. Geula dropped her smile, nodded twice, and accepted one. She ran the cigarette through her fingers, slowly,

dreamily, ironing out the creases, straightening it, and only then
did she put it to her lips. Quick as lightning, before she realized the
purpose of the man's sudden movement, a tiny flame was dancing in
front of her. Geula shielded the lighter with her hand even though
there was no breeze in the orchard, sucked in the flame, closed her
eyes. The nomad lit his own cigarette and bowed politely.

"Thank you very much," he said in his velvety voice.

"Thanks," Geula replied. "Thank you."

"You from the kibbutz?"

Geula nodded.

"Goo-d." An elongated syllable escaped from between his
gleaming teeth. "That's goo-d."

The girl eyed his desert robe.

"Aren't you hot in that thing?"

The man gave an embarrassed, guilty smile, as if he had been
caught red-handed. He took a slight step backward.

"Heaven forbid, it's not hot. Really not. Why? There's air, there's
water . . ." And he fell silent.

The treetops were already growing darker. A first jackal sniffed
the oncoming night and let out a tired howl. The orchard filled
with a scurry of small, busy feet. All of a sudden Geula became
aware of the throngs of black goats intruding in search of their master. They swirled silently in and out of the fruit trees. Geula pursed
her lips and let out a short whistle of surprise.

"What are you doing here, anyway? Stealing?"

The nomad cowered as though a stone had been thrown at him.
His hand beat a hollow tattoo on his chest.

"No, not stealing, heaven forbid, really not." He added a lengthy
oath in his own language and resumed his silent smile. His blind
eye winked nervously. Meanwhile an emaciated goat darted forward and rubbed against his leg. He kicked it away and continued
to swear with passion:

"Not steal, truly, by Allah not steal. Forbidden to steal."

"Forbidden in the Bible," Geula replied with a dry, cruel smile.

"Forbidden to steal, forbidden to kill, forbidden to covet, and forbidden to commit adultery. The righteous are above suspicion."

The Arab cowered before the onslaught of words and looked down at the ground. Shamefaced. Guilty. His foot continued to kick restlessly at the loose earth. He was trying to ingratiate himself. His blind eye narrowed. Geula was momentarily alarmed: surely it was a wink. The smile left his lips. He spoke in a soft, drawn-out whisper, as though uttering a prayer.

"Beautiful girl, truly very beautiful girl. Me, I got no girl yet. Me still young. No girl yet. Yaaa," he concluded with a guttural yell directed at an impudent goat that had rested its forelegs against a tree trunk and was munching hungrily at the foliage. The animal cast a pensive, skeptical glance at its master, shook its beard, and solemnly resumed its munching.

Without warning, and with amazing agility, the shepherd leapt through the air and seized the beast by the hindquarters, lifted it above his head, let out a terrifying, savage screech, and flung it ruthlessly to the ground. Then he spat and turned to the girl.

"Beast," he apologized. "Beast. What to do. No brains. No manners."

The girl let go of the tree trunk against which she had been resting and leaned toward the nomad. A sweet shudder ran down her back. Her voice was still firm and cool.

"Another cigarette?" she asked. "Have you got another cigarette?"

The Bedouin replied with a look of anguish, almost of despair. He apologized. He explained at length that he had no more cigarettes, not even one, not even a little one. No more. All gone. What a pity. He would gladly, very gladly, have given her one. None left. All gone.

The beaten goat was getting shakily to its feet. Treading circumspectly, it returned to the tree trunk, disingenuously observing its master out of the corner of its eye. The shepherd watched it without moving. The goat reached up, rested its front hoofs on the tree, and calmly continued munching. The Arab picked up a heavy stone and swung his arm wildly. Geula seized his arm and restrained him.

"Leave it. Why. Let it be. It doesn't understand. It's only a beast. No brains, no manners."

The nomad obeyed. In total submission he let the stone drop. Then Geula let go of his arm. Once again the man drew the lighter out of his belt. With thin, pensive fingers he toyed with it. He accidentally lit a small flame, and hastily blew at it. The flame widened slightly, slanted, and died. Nearby a jackal broke into a loud, piercing wail. The rest of the goats, meanwhile, had followed the example of the first and were absorbed in rapid, almost angry munching.

A vague wail came from the nomad encampment away to the south, the dim drum beating time to its languorous call. The dusky men were sitting around their campfires, sending skyward their single-noted song. The night took up the strain and answered with dismal cricket-chirp. Last glimmers of light were dying away in the far west. The orchard stood in darkness. Sounds gathered all around, the wind's whispering, the goats' sniffing, the rustle of ravished leaves. Geula pursed her lips and whistled an old tune. The nomad listened to her with rapt attention, his head cocked to one side in surprise, his mouth hanging slightly open. She glanced at her watch. The hands winked back at her with a malign, phosphorescent glint, but said nothing. Night.

The Arab turned his back on Geula, dropped to his knees, touched his forehead on the ground, and began mumbling fervently.

"You've got no girl yet," Geula broke into his prayer. "You're still too young." Her voice was loud and strange. Her hands were on her hips, her breathing still even. The man stopped praying, turned his dark face toward her, and muttered a phrase in Arabic. He was still crouched on all fours, but his pose suggested a certain suppressed joy.

"You're still young," Geula repeated, "very young. Perhaps twenty. Perhaps thirty. Young. No girl for you. Too young."

The man replied with a very long and solemn remark in his own language. She laughed nervously, her hands embracing her hips.

"What's the matter with you?" she inquired, laughing still. "Why are you talking to me in Arabic all of a sudden? What do you think I am? What do you want here, anyway?"

Again the nomad replied in his own language. Now a note of terror filled his voice. With soft, silent steps he recoiled and withdrew as though from a dying creature. She was breathing heavily now, panting, trembling. A single wild syllable escaped from the shepherd's mouth: a sign between him and his goats. The goats responded and thronged around him, their feet pattering on the carpet of dead leaves like cloth ripping. The crickets fell silent. The goats huddled in the dark, a terrified, quivering mass, and disappeared into the darkness, the shepherd vanishing in their midst.

Afterward, alone and trembling, she watched an airplane passing in the dark sky above the treetops, rumbling dully, its lights blinking alternately with a rhythm as precise as that of the drums: red, green, red, green, red. The night covered over the traces. There was a smell of bonfires on the air and a smell of dust borne on the breeze. Only a slight breeze among the fruit trees. Then panic struck her and her blood froze. Her mouth opened to scream but she did not scream, she started to run and she ran barefoot with all her strength for home and stumbled and rose and ran as though pursued, but only the sawing of the crickets chased after her.

6

SHE RETURNED to her room and made coffee for all the members of the secretariat, because she remembered her promise to Etkin. Outside the cool of evening had set in, but inside her room the walls were hot and her body was also on fire. Her clothes stuck to her body because she had been running, and her armpits disgusted her. The spots on her face were glowing. She stood and counted the number of times the coffee boiled — seven successive boilings, as she had learned to do it from her brother Ehud before he was killed in a reprisal raid in the desert. With pursed lips she counted as the black liquid rose and subsided, rose and subsided, bubbling fiercely as it reached its climax.

That's enough, now. Take clean clothes for the evening. Go to the showers.

What can that Etkin understand about savages. A great socialist. What does he know about Bedouins. A nomad sniffs out weakness from a distance. Give him a kind word, or a smile, and he pounces on you like a wild beast and tries to rape you. It was just as well I ran away from him.

In the showers the drain was clogged and the bench was greasy. Geula put her clean clothes on the stone ledge. I'm not shivering because the water's cold. I'm shivering with disgust. Those black fingers, and how he went straight for my throat. And his teeth. And the goats. Small and skinny like a child, but so strong. It was only by biting and kicking that I managed to escape. Soap my belly and everything, soap it again and again. Yes, let the boys go right away tonight to their camp and smash their black bones because of what they did to me. Now I must get outside.

7

SHE LEFT the shower and started back toward her room, to pick up the coffee and take it to the secretariat. But on the way she heard crickets and laughter, and she remembered him bent down on all fours, and she was alarmed and stood still in the dark. Suddenly she vomited among the flowering shrubs. And she began to cry. Then her knees gave way. She sat down to rest on the dark earth. She stopped crying. But her teeth continued to chatter, from the cold or from pity. Suddenly she was not in a hurry any more, even the coffee no longer seemed important, and she thought to herself: There's still time. There's still time.

Those planes sweeping the sky tonight were probably on a night-bombing exercise. Repeatedly they roared among the stars, keeping up a constant flashing, red, green, red, green, red. In counterpoint came the singing of the nomads and their drums, a persistent heartbeat in the distance: One, one, two. One, one, two. And silence.

8

FROM EIGHT-THIRTY until nearly nine o'clock we waited for Geula. At five to nine Etkin said that he could not imagine what had happened; he could not recall her ever having missed a meeting or been late before; at all events, we must now begin the meeting and turn to the business on the agenda.

He began with a summary of the facts. He gave details of the damage that had apparently been caused by the Bedouins, although there was no formal proof, and enumerated the steps that had been taken on the committee's initiative. The appeal to good will. Calling in the police. Strengthening the guard around the settlement. Tracking dogs. The meeting with the elder of the tribe. He had to admit, Etkin said, that we had now reached an impasse. Nevertheless, he believed that we had to maintain a sense of balance and not give way to extremism, because hatred always gave rise to further hatred. It was essential to break the vicious circle of hostility. He therefore opposed with all the moral force at his disposal the approach — and particularly the intentions — of certain of the younger members. He wished to remind us, by way of conclusion, that the conflict between herdsmen and tillers of the soil was as old as human civilization, as seemed to be evidenced by the story of Cain, who rose up against Abel, his brother. It was fitting, in view of the social gospel we had adopted, that we should put an end to this ancient feud, too, just as we had put an end to other ugly phenomena. It was up to us, and everything depended on our moral strength.

The room was full of tension, even unpleasantness. Rami twice interrupted Etkin and on one occasion went so far as to use the ugly word "rubbish." Etkin took offense, accused the younger members of planning terrorist activities, and said in conclusion, "We're not going to have that sort of thing here."

Geula had not arrived, and that was why there was no one to cool down the temper of the meeting. And no coffee. A heated exchange broke out between me and Rami. Although in age I belonged with the younger men, I did not agree with their proposals. Like Etkin, I was absolutely opposed to answering the nomads with violence — for two reasons, and when I was given permission to speak I mentioned them both. In the first place, nothing really serious had happened so far. A little stealing perhaps, but even that was not certain: every faucet or pair of pliers that a tractor driver left in a field or lost in the garage or took home with him was immediately blamed on the Bedouins. Secondly, there had been no rape or murder. Hereupon Rami broke in excitedly and asked what I was waiting for. Was I perhaps waiting for some small incident of rape that Geula could write poems about and I could make into a short story? I flushed and cast around in my mind for a telling retort.

But Etkin, upset by our rudeness, immediately deprived us both of the right to speak and began to explain his position all over again. He asked us how it would look if the papers reported that a kibbutz had sent out a lynch mob to settle scores with its Arab neighbors. As Etkin uttered the phrase "lynch mob," Rami made a gesture to his young friends that is commonly used by basketball players. At this signal they rose in a body and walked out in disgust, leaving Etkin to lecture to his heart's content to three elderly women and a long-retired member of Parliament.

After a moment's hesitation I rose and followed them. True, I did not share their views, but I, too, had been deprived of the right to speak in an arbitrary and insulting manner.

9

IF ONLY Geula had come to the meeting and brought her famous coffee with her, it is possible that tempers might have been soothed. Perhaps, too, her understanding might have achieved some sort of compromise between the conflicting points of view. But the coffee was standing, cold by now, on the table in her room. And Geula herself was lying among the bushes behind the Memorial Hall, watching the lights of the planes and listening to the sounds of the night. How she longed to make her peace and to forgive. Not to hate him and wish him dead. Perhaps to get up and go to him, to find him among the wadis and forgive him and never come back. Even to sing to him. The sharp slivers piercing her skin and drawing blood were the fragments of the bottle she had smashed here with a big stone at the beginning of the evening. And the living thing slithering among the slivers of glass among the clods of earth was a snake, perhaps a venomous snake, perhaps a viper. It stuck out a forked tongue, and its triangular head was cold and erect. Its eyes were dark glass. It could never close them, because it had no eyelids. A thorn in her flesh, perhaps a sliver of glass. She was very tired. And the pain was vague, almost pleasant. A distant ringing in her ears. To sleep now. Wearily, through the thickening film, she watched the gang of youngsters crossing the lawn on their way to the fields and the wadi to even the score with the nomads. We were carrying short, thick sticks. Excitement was dilating our pupils. And the blood was drumming in our temples.

Far away in the darkened orchards stood somber, dust-laden cypresses, swaying to and fro with a gentle, religious fervor. She felt tired, and that was why she did not come to see us off. But her fingers caressed the dust, and her face was very calm and almost beautiful.

1963

The Way of the Wind*

1

GIDEON SHENHAV'S LAST DAY began with a brilliant sunrise.

The dawn was gentle, almost autumnal. Faint flashes of light flickered through the wall of cloud that sealed off the eastern horizon. Slyly the new day concealed its purpose, betraying no hint of the heat wave that lay enfolded in its bosom.

Purple glowed on the eastern heights, fanned by the morning breeze. Then the rays pierced through the wall of cloud. It was day. Dark loopholes blinked awake at daylight's touch. Finally the incandescent sphere rose, assaulted the mountains of cloud, and broke their ranks. The eastern horizon was adazzle. And the soft purple yielded and fled before the terrible crimson blaze.

The camp was shaken by reveille a few minutes before sunrise. Gideon rose, padded barefoot out of his hut, and, still asleep, looked at the gathering light. With one thin hand he shaded his eyes, still yearning for sleep, while the other automatically buttoned up his battle dress. He could already hear voices and metallic sounds; a few eager boys were cleaning their guns for morning inspection. But Gideon was slow. The sunrise had stirred a weary restlessness inside him, perhaps a vague longing. The sunrise was

---

* [The Hebrew word *ruah* has multiple meanings: wind, spirit, intellect, ghost, to mention only a few. In this story it also refers to the ideological convictions of the old man. The title is borrowed from Ecclesiastes 11:5. — TRANS.]

over, but still he stood there drowsily, until he was pushed from behind and told to get cracking.

He went back into the hut, straightened his camp bed, cleaned his submachine gun, and picked up his shaving kit. On his way, among whitewashed eucalyptus trees and clustering notices commending tidiness and discipline, he suddenly remembered that today was Independence Day, the Fifth of Iyar. And today the platoon was to mount a celebratory parachute display in the Valley of Jezreel. He entered the washroom and, while he waited for a free mirror, brushed his teeth and thought of pretty girls. In an hour and a half the preparations would be complete and the platoon would be airborne, on its way to its destination. Throngs of excited civilians would be waiting for them to jump, and the girls would be there, too. The drop would take place just outside Nof Harish, the kibbutz that was Gideon's home, where he had been born and brought up until the day he joined the army. The moment his feet touched the ground, the children of the kibbutz would close around him and jump all over him and shout, "Gideon, look, here's our Gideon!"

He pushed in between two much bigger soldiers and began to lather his face and try to shave.

"Hot day," he said.

One of the soldiers answered, "Not yet. But it soon will be."

And another soldier behind him grumbled, "Hurry it up. Don't spend all day jawing."

Gideon did not take offense. On the contrary, the words filled him with a surge of joy for some reason. He dried his face and went out onto the parade ground. The blue light had changed meanwhile to gray-white, the grubby glare of a *khamsin.*

2

SHIMSHON SHEINBAUM had confidently predicted the previous night that a *khamsin* was on its way. As soon as he got up he hurried over to the window and confirmed with calm satisfaction that he had been right yet again. He closed the shutters, to protect the room from the hot wind, then washed his face and his shaggy shoulders and chest, shaved, and prepared his breakfast, coffee with a roll brought last night from the dining hall. Shimshon Sheinbaum loathed wasting time, especially in the productive morning hours: you go out, walk to the dining hall, have a chat, read the paper, discuss the news, and that's half the morning gone. So he always made do with a cup of coffee and a roll, and by ten past six, after the early news summary, Gideon Shenhav's father was sitting at his desk. Summer and winter alike, with no concessions.

He sat at his desk and stared for a few minutes at the map of the country that hung on the opposite wall. He was straining to recapture a nagging dream which had taken hold of him in the early hours, just before he had awakened. But it eluded him. Shimshon decided to get on with his work and not waste another minute. True, today was a holiday, but the best way to celebrate was to work, not to slack off. Before it was time to go out and watch the parachutists — and Gideon, who might actually be among them and not drop out at the last minute — he still had several hours of working time. A man of seventy-five cannot afford to squander his hours, especially if there are many, painfully many, things he must set down in writing. So little time.

The name of Shimshon Sheinbaum needs no introduction. The Hebrew Labor Movement knows how to honor its founding fathers, and for decades now Shimshon Sheinbaum's name has been invested with a halo of enduring fame. For decades he has fought body and soul to realize the vision of his youth. Setbacks and disappointments have not shattered or weakened his faith but, rather, have enriched it with a vein of wise sadness. The better he has come to understand the weakness of others and their ideological deviations, the more ferociously he has fought against his own weaknesses. He has sternly eliminated them, and lived according to his principles, with a ruthless self-discipline and not without a certain secret joy.

At this moment, between six and seven o'clock on this Independence Day morning, Shimshon Sheinbaum is not yet a bereaved father. But his features are extraordinarily well suited to the role. A solemn, sagacious expression, of one who sees all but betrays no reaction, occupies his furrowed face. And his blue eyes express an ironic melancholy.

He sits erect at his desk, his head bent over the pages. His elbows are relaxed. The desk is made of plain wood, like the rest of the furniture, which is all functional and unembellished. More like a monastic cell than a bungalow in a long-established kibbutz.

This morning will not be particularly productive. Time and again his thoughts wander to the dream that flickered and died at the end of the night. He must recapture the dream, and then he will be able to forget it and concentrate on his work. There was a hose, yes, and some sort of goldfish or something. An argument with someone. No connection. Now to work. The Poalei Zion Movement appears to have been built from the start on an ideological contradiction that could never be bridged, and which it only succeeded in disguising by means of verbal acrobatics. But the contradiction is only apparent, and anyone who hopes to exploit it to undermine or attack the movement does not know what he is talking about. And here is the simple proof.

Shimshon Sheinbaum's rich experience of life has taught him how arbitrary, how senseless is the hand that guides the vagaries of our fate, that of the individual and that of the community alike. His sobriety has not robbed him of the straightforwardness which has animated him since his youth. His most remarkable and admirable characteristic is his stubborn innocence, like that of our pure, pious forebears, whose sagacity never injured their faith. Sheinbaum has never allowed his actions to be cut loose from his words. Even though some of the leaders of our movement have drifted into political careers and cut themselves off completely from manual labor, Sheinbaum has never abandoned the kibbutz. He has turned down all outside jobs and assignments, and it was only with extreme reluctance that he accepted nomination to the General Workers' Congress. Until a few years ago his days were divided equally between physical and intellectual work: three days gardening, three days theorizing. The beautiful gardens of Nof Harish are largely his handiwork. We can remember how he used to plant and prune and lop, water and hoe, manure, transplant, weed, and dig up. He did not permit his status as the leading thinker of the movement to exempt him from the duties to which every rank-and-file member is liable: he served as night watchman, took his turn in the kitchens, helped with the harvest. No shadow of a double standard has ever clouded the path of Shimshon Sheinbaum's life; he is a single complex of vision and execution, he has known no slackness or weakness of will — so the secretary of the movement wrote about him in a magazine a few years ago, on the occasion of his seventieth birthday.

True, there have been moments of stabbing despair. There have been moments of deep disgust. But Shimshon Sheinbaum knows how to transform such moments into secret sources of furious energy. Like the words of the marching song he loves, which always inspires him to a frenzy of action: *Up into the mountains we are climbing, Climbing up toward the dawning day; We have left all our yesterdays behind us, But tomorrow is a long long way away.* If only that stupid dream would emerge from the shadows and show itself clearly, he could kick it out of his mind and concentrate at last on his work. Time is slipping by. A rubber hose, a chess gambit, some goldfish, a great argument, but what is the connection?

For many years Shimshon Sheinbaum has lived alone. He has channeled all his vigor into his ideological productions. To this life's work he has sacrificed the warmth of a family home. He has managed, in exchange, to retain into old age a youthful clarity and cordiality. Only when he was fifty-six did he suddenly marry Raya Greenspan and father Gideon, and after that he left her and returned to his ideological work. It would be sanctimonious to pretend, however, that before his marriage Shimshon Sheinbaum maintained a monastic existence. His personality attracted women just as it attracted disciples. He was still young when his thick mop of hair turned white, and his sunbeaten face was etched with an appealing pattern of lines and wrinkles. His square back, his strong shoulders, the timbre of his voice — always warm, skeptical, and rather ruminative — and also his solitude, all attracted women to him like fluttering birds. Gossip attributes to his loins at least one of the urchins of the kibbutz, and elsewhere, too, stories are current. But we shall not dwell on this.

At the age of fifty-six Shimshon Sheinbaum decided that it befitted him to beget a son and heir to bear his stamp and his name into the coming generation. And so he conquered Raya Greenspan, a diminutive girl with a stammer who was thirty-three years his junior. Three months after the wedding, which was solemnized before a restricted company, Gideon was born. And before the kibbutz had recovered from its amazement, Shimshon sent Raya back to her former room and rededicated himself to his ideological work. This episode caused various ripples, and, indeed, it was preceded by painful heart-searchings in Shimshon Sheinbaum himself.

Now let's concentrate and think logically. Yes, it's coming back. She came to my room and called me to go there quickly to put a stop to that scandal. I didn't ask any questions, but hurried after her. Someone had had the nerve to dig a pond in the lawn in front of the dining hall, and I was seething because no one had authorized such an innovation, an ornamental pond in front of the dining hall, like some Polish squire's château. I shouted. Who at, there is no clear picture. There were goldfish in the pond. And a boy was filling it with water from a black rubber hose. So I decided to put a stop to the whole performance there and then, but the boy wouldn't listen to me. I started walking along the hose to find the faucet and cut off the water before anybody managed to establish the pond as a *fait accompli*. I walked and walked until I suddenly discovered that I was walking in a circle, and the hose was not connected to a faucet but simply came back to the pond and sucked up water from it. Stuff and nonsense. That's the end of it. The original platform of the Poalei Zion Movement must be understood without any recourse to dialectics, it must be taken literally, word for word.

3

AFTER HIS separation from Raya Greenspan, Shimshon Sheinbaum did not neglect his duties as his son's mentor, nor did he disclaim responsibility. He lavished on him, from the time the boy was six or seven, the full warmth of his personality. Gideon, however, turned out to be something of a disappointment, not the stuff of which dynasties are founded. As a child he was always sniveling. He was a slow, bewildered child, mopping up blows and insults without retaliating, a strange child, always playing with candy wrappers, dried leaves, silkworms. And from the age of twelve he was constantly having his heart broken by girls of all ages. He was always lovesick, and he published sad poems and cruel parodies in the children's newsletter. A dark, gentle youth, with an almost feminine beauty, who walked the paths of the kibbutz in obstinate silence. He did not shine at work; he did not shine in communal life. He was slow of speech and no doubt also of thought. His poems seemed to Shimshon incorrigibly sentimental, and his parodies venomous, without a trace of inspiration. The nickname Pinocchio suited him, there is no denying it. And the infuriating smiles he was perpetually spreading on his face seemed to Shimshon a depressingly exact replica of the smiles of Raya Greenspan.

And then, eighteen months before, Gideon had amazed his father. He suddenly appeared and asked for his written permission to enlist in the paratroopers — as an only son this required the written consent of both parents. Only when Shimshon Sheinbaum was convinced that this was not one of his son's outrageous jokes did he agree to give his consent. And then he gave it gladly: this was surely an encouraging turn in the boy's development. They'd make a man of him there. Let him go. Why not.

But Raya Greenspan's stubborn opposition raised an unexpected obstacle to Gideon's plan. No, she wouldn't sign the paper. On no account. Never.

Shimshon himself went to her room one evening, pleaded with her, reasoned with her, shouted at her. All in vain. She wouldn't sign. No reason, she just wouldn't. So Shimshon Sheinbaum had to resort to devious means to enable the boy to enlist. He wrote a private letter to Yolek himself, asking a personal favor. He wished his son to be allowed to volunteer. The mother was emotionally unstable. The boy would make a first-rate paratrooper. Shimshon himself accepted full responsibility. And incidentally, he had never before asked a personal favor. And he never would again. This was the one and only time in his whole life. He begged Yolek to see what he could do.

At the end of September, when the first signs of autumn were appearing in the orchards, Gideon Shenhav was enrolled in a parachute unit.

From that time on, Shimshon Sheinbaum immersed himself more deeply than ever in ideological work, which is the only real mark a man can leave on the world. Shimshon Sheinbaum has made a mark on the Hebrew Labor Movement that can never be erased. Old age is still far off. At seventy-five he still has hair as thick as ever, and his muscles are firm and powerful. His eyes are alert, his mind attentive. His strong, dry, slightly cracked voice still works wonders on women of all ages. His bearing is restrained, his manner modest. Needless to say, he is deeply rooted in the soil of Nof Harish. He loathes assemblies and formal ceremonies, not to mention commissions and official appointments. With his pen alone he has inscribed his name on the roll of honor of our movement and our nation.

4

GIDEON SHENHAV's last day began with a brilliant sunrise. He felt he could even see the beads of dew evaporating in the heat. Omens blazed on the mountain peaks far away to the east. This was a day of celebration, a celebration of independence and a celebration of parachuting over the familiar fields of home. All that night he had nestled in a half-dream of dark autumnal forests under northern skies, a rich smell of autumn, huge trees he could not name. All night long pale leaves had been dropping on the huts of the camp. Even after he had awakened in the morning, the northern forest with its nameless trees still continued to whisper in his ears.

Gideon adored the delicious moment of free fall between the jump from the aircraft and the unfolding of the parachute. The void rushes up toward you at lightning speed, fierce drafts of air lick at your body, making you dizzy with pleasure. The speed is drunken, reckless, it whistles and roars and your whole body trembles to it, red-hot needles work at your nerve ends, and your heart pounds. Suddenly, when you are lightning in the wind, the chute opens. The straps check your fall, like a firm, masculine arm bringing you calmly under control. You can feel its supporting strength under your armpits. The reckless thrill gives way to a more sedate pleasure. Slowly your body swings through the air, floats, hesitates, drifts a little way on the slight breeze, you can never guess precisely where your feet will touch ground, on the slope of that hill or next to the orange groves over there, and like an exhausted migrating bird you slowly descend, seeing roofs, roads, cows in the meadow, slowly as if you have a choice, as if the decision is entirely yours.

And then the ground is under your feet, and you launch into the practiced somersault which will soften the impact of landing. Within seconds you must sober up. The coursing blood slows down. Dimensions return to normal. Only a weary pride survives in your heart until you rejoin your commanding officer and your comrades and you're caught up in the rhythm of frenzied reorganization.

This time it is all going to happen over Nof Harish.

The older folk will raise their clammy hands, push back their caps, and try to spot Gideon among the gray dots dangling in the sky. The kids will rush around in the fields, also waiting excitedly for their hero to touch down. Mother will come out of the dining hall and stand peering upward, muttering to herself. Shimshon will leave his desk for a while, perhaps take a chair out onto his little porch and watch the whole performance with pensive pride.

Then the kibbutz will entertain the unit. Pitchers of lemonade glistening with chilly perspiration will be set out in the dining hall, there will be crates of apples, or perhaps cakes baked by the older women, iced with congratulatory phrases.

By six-thirty the sun had grown out of its colorful caprice and risen ruthlessly over the eastern mountain heights. A thick heat weighed heavily on the whole scene. The tin roofs of the camp huts reflected a dazzling glare. The walls began to radiate a dense, oppressive warmth into the huts. On the main road, which passed close to the perimeter fence, a lively procession of buses and trucks was already in motion: the residents of the villages and small towns were streaming to the big city to watch the military parade. Their white shirts could be discerned dimly through the clouds of dust, and snatches of exuberant song could be caught in the distance.

The paratroopers had completed their morning inspection. The orders of the day, signed by the Chief of Staff, had been read out and posted on the bulletin boards. A festive breakfast had been served, including a hard-boiled egg reposing on a lettuce leaf ringed with olives.

Gideon, his dark hair flopping forward onto his forehead, broke into a quiet song. The others joined him. Here and there someone altered the words, making them comical or even obscene. Soon the Hebrew songs gave way to a guttural, almost desperate Arabic wail. The platoon commander, a blond, good-looking officer whose exploits were feted around the campfires at night, stood up and said: That's enough. The paratroopers stopped singing, hastily downed the last of their greasy coffee, and moved toward the runways. Here there was another inspection; the commanding officer spoke a few words of endearment to his men, calling them "the salt of the earth," and then ordered them into the waiting aircraft.

The squadron commanders stood at the doors of the planes and checked each belt and harness. The CO himself circulated among the men, patting a shoulder, joking, predicting, enthusing, for all the world as though they were going into battle and facing real danger. Gideon responded to the pat on his shoulder with a hasty smile. He was lean, almost ascetic-looking, but very suntanned. A sharp eye, that of the legendary blond commander, could spot the blue vein throbbing in his neck.

Then the heat broke into the shady storage sheds, mercilessly flushing out the last strongholds of coolness, roasting everything with a gray glow. The sign was given. The engines gave a throaty roar. Birds fled from the runway. The planes shuddered, moved forward heavily, and began to gather the momentum without which takeoff cannot be achieved.

5

I MUST get out and be there to shake his hand.

Having made up his mind, Sheinbaum closed his notebook. The months of military training have certainly toughened the boy. It is hard to believe, but it certainly looks as though he is beginning to mature at last. He still has to learn how to handle women. He has to free himself once and for all from his shyness and his sentimentality: he should leave such traits to women and cultivate toughness in himself. And how he has improved at chess. Soon he'll be a serious challenge to his old father. May even beat me one of these days. Not just yet, though. As long as he doesn't up and marry the first girl who gives herself to him. He ought to break one or two of them in before he gets spliced. In a few years he'll have to give me some grandchildren. Lots of them. Gideon's children will have two fathers: my son can take care of them, and I'll take care of their ideas. The second generation grew up in the shadow of our achievements; that's why they're so confused. It's a matter of dialectics. But the third generation will be a wonderful synthesis, a successful outcome: they will inherit the spontaneity of their parents and the spirit of their grandparents. It will be a glorious heritage distilled from a twisted pedigree. I'd better jot that phrase down, it will come in handy one of these days. I feel so sad when I think of Gideon and his friends: they exude such an air of shallow despair, of nihilism, of cynical mockery. They can't love wholeheartedly, and they can't hate wholeheartedly, either. No enthusiasm, and no loathing. I'm not one to deprecate despair per se. Despair is the eternal twin of faith, but that's real despair, virile and passionate, not this sentimental, poetic melancholy. Sit still, Gideon, stop scratching yourself, stop biting your nails. I want to read you a marvelous passage from Brenner. All right, make a face. So I won't read. Go outside and grow up to be a Bedouin, if that's what you want. But if you don't get to know Brenner, you'll never understand the first thing about despair or about faith. You won't find any soppy poems here about jackals caught in traps or flowers in the autumn. In Brenner, everything is on fire. Love, and hatred as well. Maybe you yourselves won't see light and darkness face to face, but your children will. A glorious heritage will be distilled from a twisted pedigree. And we won't let the third generation be pampered and corrupted by sentimental verses by decadent poetesses. Here come the planes now. We'll put Brenner back on the shelf and get ready to be proud of you for a change, Gideon Sheinbaum.

6

SHEINBAUM STRODE purposefully across the lawn, stepped up onto the concrete path, and turned toward the plowed field in the southwest corner of the kibbutz, which had been selected for the landing. On his way he paused now and again at a flower bed to pull up a stray weed skulking furtively beneath a flowering shrub. His small blue eyes had always been amazingly skillful at detecting weeds. Admittedly, because of his age he had retired a few years previously from his work in the gardens, but until his dying day he would not cease to scan the flower beds mercilessly in search of undesirable intruders. At such moments he thought of the boy, forty years his junior, who had succeeded him as gardener and who fancied himself as the local water-colorist. He had inherited beautifully tended gardens, and now they were all going to seed before our very eyes.

A gang of excited children ran across his path. They were fiercely absorbed in a detailed argument about the types of aircraft that were circling above the valley. Because they were running, the argument was being carried out in loud shouts and gasps. Shimshon seized one of them by the shirttail, forcibly brought him to a halt, put his face close to the child's, and said:

"You are Zaki."

"Leave me alone," the child replied.

Sheinbaum said: "What's all this shouting? Airplanes, is that all you've got in your heads? And running across the flower beds like that where it says Keep Off, is that right? Do you think you can do whatever you like? Are there no rules any more? Look at me when I'm speaking to you. And give me a proper answer, or . . ."

But Zaki had taken advantage of the flood of words to wriggle out of the man's grasp and tear himself free. He slipped in among the bushes, made a monkey face, and stuck out his tongue.

Sheinbaum pursed his lips. He thought for an instant about old age, but instantly thrust it out of his mind and said to himself: All right. We'll see about that later. Zaki, otherwise Azariah. Rapid calculation showed that he must be at least eleven, perhaps twelve already. A hooligan. A wild beast.

Meanwhile the young trainees had occupied a vantage point high up on top of the water tower, from which they could survey the length and breadth of the valley. The whole scene reminded Sheinbaum of a Russian painting. For a moment he was tempted to climb up and join the youngsters on top of the tower, to watch the display comfortably from a distance. But the thought of the manly handshake to come kept him striding steadily on, till he reached the edge of the field. Here he stood, his legs planted well apart, his arms folded on his chest, his thick white hair falling impressively over his forehead. He craned his neck and followed the two transport planes with steady gray eyes. The mosaic of wrinkles on his face enriched his expression with a rare blend of pride, thoughtfulness, and a trace of well-controlled irony. And his bushy white eyebrows suggested a saint in a Russian icon. Meanwhile the planes had completed their first circuit, and the leading one was approaching the field again.

Shimshon Sheinbaum's lips parted and made way for a low hum. An old Russian tune was throbbing in his chest. The first batch of men emerged from the opening in the plane's side. Small dark shapes were dotted in space, like seeds scattered by a farmer in an old pioneering print.

Then Raya Greenspan stuck her head out of the window of the kitchen and gesticulated with the ladle she was holding as though admonishing the treetops. Her face was hot and flushed. Perspiration stuck her plain dress to her strong, hairy legs. She panted, scratched at her disheveled hair with the fingernails of her free hand, and suddenly turned and shouted to the other women working in the kitchens:

"Quick! Come to the window! It's Gidi up there! Gidi in the sky!"

And just as suddenly she was struck dumb.

While the first soldiers were still floating gently, like a handful of feathers, between heaven and earth, the second plane came in and dropped Gideon Shenhav's group. The men stood pressed close together inside the hatch, chest against back, their bodies fused into a single tense, sweating mass. When Gideon's turn came he gritted his teeth, braced his knees, and leapt out as though from the womb into the bright hot air. A long wild scream of joy burst from his throat as he fell. He could see his childhood haunts rushing up toward him as he fell he could see the roofs and treetops and he smiled a frantic smile of greeting as he fell toward the vineyards and concrete paths and sheds and gleaming pipes with joy in his heart as he fell. Never in his whole life had he known such overwhelming, spine-tingling love. All his muscles were tensed, and gushing thrills burst in his stomach and up his spine to the roots of his hair. He screamed for love like a madman, his fingernails almost drawing blood from his clenched palms. Then the straps drew taut and caught him under the armpits. His waist was clasped in a tight embrace. For a moment he felt as though an invisible hand were pulling him back up toward the plane into the heart of the sky. The delicious falling sensation was replaced by a slow, gentle swaying, like rocking in a cradle or floating in warm water. Suddenly a wild panic hit him. How will they recognize me down there. How will they manage to identify their only son in this forest of white parachutes. How will they be able to fix me and me alone with their anxious, loving gaze. Mother and Dad and the pretty girls and the little kids and everyone. I mustn't just get lost in the crowd. After all, this is me, and I'm the one they love.

That moment an idea flashed through Gideon's mind. He put his hand up to his shoulder and pulled the cord to release the spare chute, the one intended for emergencies. As the second canopy opened overhead he slowed down as though the force of gravity had lost its hold on him. He seemed to be floating alone in the void, like a gull or a lonely cloud. The last of his comrades had landed in

the soft earth and were folding up their parachutes. Gideon Shenhav alone continued to hover as though under a spell with two large
canopies spread out above him. Happy, intoxicated, he drank in the
hundreds of eyes fixed on him. On him alone. In his glorious isola-
tion.

As though to lend further splendor to the spectacle, a strong, almost cool breeze burst from the west, plowing through the hot air,
playing with the spectators' hair, and carrying slightly eastward the
last of the parachutists.

7

FAR AWAY in the big city, the massed crowds waiting for the military parade greeted the sudden sea breeze with a sigh of relief. Perhaps it marked the end of the heat wave. A cool, salty smell caressed
the baking streets. The breeze freshened. It whistled fiercely in the
treetops, bent the stiff spines of the cypresses, ruffled the hair of the
pines, raised eddies of dust, and blurred the scene for the spectators
at the parachute display. Regally, like a huge solitary bird, Gideon
Shenhav was carried eastward toward the main road.

The terrified shout that broke simultaneously from a hundred throats could not reach the boy. Singing aloud in an ecstatic
trance, he continued to sway slowly toward the main electric cables,
stretched between their enormous pylons. The watchers stared in
horror at the suspended soldier and the powerlines that crossed
the valley with unfaltering straightness from west to east. The five
parallel cables, sagging with their own weight between the pylons,
hummed softly in the gusty breeze.

Gideon's two parachutes tangled in the upper cable. A moment
later his feet landed on the lower one. His body hung backward in
a slanting pose. The straps held his waist and shoulders fast, pre-
venting him from falling into the soft plowland. Had he not been
insulated by the thick soles of his boots, the boy would have been
struck dead at the moment of impact. As it was, the cable was al-

ready protesting its unwonted burden by scorching his soles. Tiny sparks flashed and crackled under Gideon's feet. He held tight with both hands to the buckles on the straps. His eyes were open wide and his mouth was agape.

Immediately a short officer, perspiring heavily, leapt out of the petrified crowd and shouted:

"Don't touch the cables, Gidi. Stretch your body backward and keep as clear as you can!"

The whole tightly packed, panic-stricken crowd began to edge slowly in an easterly direction. There were shouts. There was a wail. Sheinbaum silenced them with his metallic voice and ordered everyone to keep calm. He broke into a fast run, his feet pounding on the soft earth, reached the spot, pushed aside the officers and curious bystanders, and instructed his son:

"Quickly, Gideon, release the straps and drop. The ground is soft here. It's perfectly safe. Jump."

"I can't."

"Don't argue. Do as I tell you. Jump."

"I can't, Dad, I can't do it."

"No such thing as can't. Release the straps and jump before you electrocute yourself."

"I can't, the straps are tangled. Tell them to switch off the current quickly, Dad, my boots are burning."

Some of the soldiers were trying to hold back the crowd, discourage well-meaning suggestions, and make more room under the powerlines. They kept repeating, as if it were an incantation, "Don't panic please don't panic."

The youngsters of the kibbutz were rushing all around, adding to the confusion. Reprimands and warnings had no effect. Two angry paratroopers managed to catch Zaki, who was idiotically climbing the nearest pylon, snorting and whistling and making faces to attract the attention of the crowd.

The short officer suddenly shouted: "Your knife. You've got a knife in your belt. Get it out and cut the straps!"

But Gideon either could not or would not hear. He began to sob aloud.

"Get me down, Dad, I'll be electrocuted, tell them to get me down from here, I can't get down on my own."

"Stop sniveling," his father said curtly. "You've been told to use your knife to cut the straps. Now, do as you've been told. And stop sniveling."

The boy obeyed. He was still sobbing audibly, but he groped for the knife, located it, and cut the straps one by one. The silence was total. Only Gideon's sobbing, a strange, piercing sound, was to be heard intermittently. Finally one last strap was left holding him, which he did not dare to cut.

"Cut it," the children shrilled, "cut it and jump. Let's see you do it."

And Shimshon added in a level voice, "Now what are you waiting for?"

"I can't do it," Gideon pleaded.

"Of course you can," said his father.

"The current," the boy wept. "I can feel the current. Get me down quickly."

His father's eyes filled with blood as he roared:

"You coward! You ought to be ashamed of yourself!"

"But I can't do it, I'll break my neck, it's too high."

"You can do it and you must do it. You're a fool, that's what you are, a fool and a coward."

A group of jet planes passed overhead on their way to the aerial display over the city. They were flying in precise formation, thundering westward like a pack of wild dogs. As the planes disappeared, the silence seemed twice as intense. Even the boy had stopped crying. He let the knife fall to the ground. The blade pierced the earth at Shimshon Sheinbaum's feet.

"What did you do that for?" the short officer shouted.

"I didn't mean it," Gideon whined. "It just slipped out of my hand."

Shimshon Sheinbaum bent down, picked up a small stone, straightened up, and threw it furiously at his son's back.

"Pinocchio, you're a wet rag, you're a miserable coward!"

At this point the sea breeze also dropped.

The heat wave returned with renewed vigor to oppress both men and inanimate objects. A red-haired, freckled soldier muttered to himself, "He's scared to jump, the idiot, he'll kill himself if he stays up there." And a skinny, plain-faced girl, hearing this, rushed into the middle of the circle and spread her arms wide:

"Jump into my arms, Gidi, you'll be all right."

"It would be interesting," remarked a veteran pioneer in working clothes, "to know whether anyone has had the sense to phone the electric company to ask them to switch off the current." He turned and started off toward the kibbutz buildings. He was striding quickly, angrily, up the slight slope when he was suddenly alarmed by a prolonged burst of firing close at hand. For a moment he imagined he was being shot at from behind. But at once he realized what was happening: the squadron commander, the good-looking blond hero, was trying to sever the electric cables with his machine gun.

Without success.

Meanwhile, a beaten-up truck arrived from the farmyard. Ladders were unloaded from it, followed by the elderly doctor, and finally a stretcher.

At that moment it was evident that Gideon had been struck by a sudden decision. Kicking out strongly, he pushed himself off the lower cable, which was emitting blue sparks, turned a somersault, and remained suspended by the single strap with his head pointing downward and his scorched boots beating the air a foot or so from the cable.

It was hard to be certain, but it looked as though so far he had not sustained any serious injury. He swung limply upside down in space, like a dead lamb suspended from a butcher's hook.

This spectacle provoked hysterical glee in the watching children. They barked with laughter. Zaki slapped his knees, choking and heaving convulsively. He leapt up and down screeching like a mischievous monkey.

What had Gideon Shenhav seen that made him suddenly stretch his neck and join in the children's laughter? Perhaps his peculiar posture had unbalanced his mind. His face was blood-red, his tongue protruded, his thick hair hung down, and only his feet kicked up at the sky.

8

A SECOND group of jets plowed through the sky overhead. A dozen metallic birds, sculpted with cruel beauty, flashing dazzlingly in the bright sunlight. They flew in a narrow spearhead formation. Their fury shook the earth. On they flew to the west, and a deep silence followed.

Meanwhile, the elderly doctor sat down on the stretcher, lit a cigarette, blinked vaguely at the people, the soldiers, the scampering children, and said to himself: We'll see how things turn out. Whatever has to happen will happen. How hot it is today.

Every now and again Gideon let out another senseless laugh. His legs were flailing, describing clumsy circles in the dusty air. The blood had drained from his inverted limbs and was gathering in his head. His eyes were beginning to bulge. The world was turning dark. Instead of the crimson glow, purple spots were dancing before his eyes. He stuck his tongue out. The children interpreted this as a gesture of derision. "Upside-down Pinocchio," Zaki shrilled, "why don't you stop squinting at us, and try walking on your hands instead?"

Sheinbaum moved to hit the brat, but the blow landed on thin air because the child had leapt aside. The old man beckoned to the blond commander, and they held a brief consultation. The boy was in no immediate danger, because he was not in direct contact with the cable, but he must be rescued soon. This comedy could not go on forever. A ladder would not help much: he was too high up. Perhaps the knife could be got up to him again somehow, and he could be persuaded to cut the last strap and jump into a sheet of canvas. After all, it was a perfectly routine exercise in parachute training. The main thing was to act quickly, because the situation was humiliating. Not to mention the children. So the short officer removed his shirt and wrapped a knife in it. Gideon stretched his hands downward and tried to catch the bundle. It slipped between his outstretched arms and plummeted uselessly to the ground. The children snickered. Only after two more unsuccessful attempts did Gideon manage to grasp the shirt and remove the knife. His fingers were numb and heavy with blood. Suddenly he pressed the blade to his burning cheek, enjoying the cool touch of the steel. It was a delicious moment. He opened his eyes and saw an inverted world. Everything looked comical: the truck, the field, his father, the army, the kids, and even the knife in his hand. He made a twisted face at the gang of children, gave a deep laugh, and waved at them with the knife. He tried to say something. If only they could see themselves from up here, upside down, rushing around like startled ants, they would surely laugh with him. But the laugh turned into a heavy cough; Gideon choked and his eyes filled.

9

GIDEON'S UPSIDE-DOWN antics filled Zaki with demonic glee.

"He's crying," he shouted cruelly, "Gideon's crying, look, you can see the tears. Pinocchio the hero, he's sniveling with fear-o. We can see you, we can."

Once again Shimshon Sheinbaum's fist fell ineffectually on thin air.

"Zaki," Gideon managed to shout in a dull, pain-racked voice, "I'll kill you, I'll choke you, you little bastard." Suddenly he chuckled and stopped.

It was no good. He wouldn't cut the last strap by himself, and the doctor was afraid that if he stayed as he was much longer he was likely to lose consciousness. Some other solution would have to be found. This performance could not be allowed to go on all day.

And so the kibbutz truck rumbled across the plowland and braked at the point indicated by Shimshon Sheinbaum. Two ladders were hastily lashed together to reach the required height, and then supported on the back of the truck by five strong pairs of hands. The legendary blond officer started to climb. But when he reached the place where the two ladders overlapped, there was an ominous creak, and the wood began to bend with the weight and the height. The officer, a largish man, hesitated for a moment. He decided to retreat and fasten the ladders together more securely. He climbed down to the floor of the truck, wiped the sweat from his forehead, and said, "Wait, I'm thinking." Just then, in the twinkling of an eye, before he could be stopped, before he could even be spotted, the child Zaki had climbed high up the ladder, past the join, and leapt like a frantic monkey up onto the topmost rungs; suddenly he was clutching a knife — where on earth had he got it from? He wrestled with the taut strap. The spectators held their breath: he seemed to be defying gravity, not holding on, not caring, hopping on the top rung, nimble, lithe, amazingly efficient.

10

THE HEAT beat down violently on the hanging youth. His eyes were growing dimmer. His breathing had almost stopped. With his last glimmer of lucidity he saw his ugly brother in front of him and felt his breath on his face. He could smell him. He could see the pointed teeth protruding from Zaki's mouth. A terrible fear closed in on him, as though he were looking in a mirror and seeing a monster. The nightmare roused Gideon's last reserves of strength. He kicked into space, flailed, managed to turn over, seized the strap, and pulled himself up. With outstretched arms he threw himself onto the cable and saw the flash. The hot wind continued to tyrannize the whole valley. And a third cluster of jets drowned the scene with its roaring.

11

THE STATUS of a bereaved father invests a man with a saintly aura of suffering. But Sheinbaum gave no thought to this aura. A stunned, silent company escorted him toward the dining hall. He knew, with utter certainty, that his place now was beside Raya.

On the way he saw the child Zaki, glowing, breathless, a hero. Surrounded by other youngsters: he had almost rescued Gideon. Shimshon laid a trembling hand on his child's head, and tried to tell him. His voice abandoned him and his lips quivered. Clumsily he stroked the tousled, dusty mop of hair. It was the first time he had ever stroked the child. A few steps later, everything went dark and the old man collapsed in a flower bed.

As Independence Day drew to a close the *khamsin* abated. A fresh sea breeze soothed the steaming walls. There was a heavy fall of dew on the lawns in the night.

What does the pale ring around the moon portend? Usually it heralds a *khamsin*. Tomorrow, no doubt, the heat will return. It is May, and June will follow. A wind drifts among the cypresses in the night, trying to comfort them between one heat wave and the next. It is the way of the wind to come and to go and to come again. There is nothing new.

1962

Before His Time

1

THE BULL WAS warm and strong on the night of his death.

In the night, Samson the bull was slaughtered. Early in the morning, before the five o'clock milking, a meat trader from Nazareth came and took him away in a gray tender. Portions of his carcass were hung on rusty hooks in the butcher shops of Nazareth. The ringing of the church bells roused droves of flies to attack the bull's flesh, swarming upon it and exacting a green revenge.

Later, at eight o'clock in the morning, an old effendi arrived, carrying a transistor radio. He had come to buy Samson's hide. And all the while Radio Ramallah piped American music into the palm of his hand. It was the wildest of tunes, some unbearably mournful piece of jazz. The church bells accompanied the wailing melody. As the tune came to an end, the transaction was concluded. The bull's hide was sold. What will you do, O Rashid Effendi, with the hide of Samson the mighty bull? I will make ornaments from it, objects of value, souvenirs for rich tourists, pictures in many colors on a screen of hide: here is the alleyway where Jesus lived, here is the carpenter's workshop with Joseph himself inside, here little angels are striking a bell to proclaim the birth of the Saviour, here the kings are coming to bow down before the cradle, and here is the Babe with light on His forehead, parchment work, real bullskin, all handmade with an artist's vision.

Rashid Effendi went to Zaim's cafe to spend the morning at the backgammon table. In his hand the radio with its cheerful music, and at his feet, in a sack, the hide of the dead bull.

And a Nazareth breeze, heavy with smells, plucked at the bells and the treetops, stirring the hooks in the butcher shops, and the flesh of the bull gave out a crimson groan.

2

SAMSON THE bull was at the height of his powers, the pride of the kibbutz herdsman, the finest bull in the valley. Had it not been that his potency failed, Yosh would not have come to him suddenly in the night to slit his throat.

Samson was asleep on his feet, his head bowed. The steam of his breath mingled with the smell of sticky cattle sweat. The beam of the pocket flashlight caressed his chest and lingered on his neck. The bull sensed nothing.

Poisoned bait, thought Yosh. The howl of the jackals rose from the darkness. In late autumn a stray jackal had broken into the cattle shed, rabid or crazed with hunger, and had bitten Samson in the leg. Samson killed him with a kick, but the poison in the bite killed the bull's potency. Thus was sealed the fate of the most ferocious bull in the Valley of Jezreel.

With a gentle, quiet hand Yosh gripped the bull's jaw and raised the dark head. The bull breathed deeply. His eyes quivered, almost winked. Yosh pressed the point of the knife to Samson's gullet. The bull's nostrils flared suddenly and his foreleg kicked at the balls of dung beneath him. Still he did not open his eyes. Nor did he open them for a long while — not until the blade had pierced his hide and flesh and jugular vein.

First to appear were a few thin, tentative drops. The bull let out a muffled groan of unease and swung his head from side to side as if shaking off an obstinate fly, or expressing violent disagreement on a conversational point. Then came a weak, hesitant trickle, as if from a trivial scratch.

"Well," said Yosh.

Samson lashed his muddy hindquarters with his tail and exhaled nervously, warmly.

"Well, get on with it," said Yosh, and he thrust his hand into his pocket. The cigarette that appeared between his lips was moist and somehow unclean. What possessed Yosh to stub out the match on the forehead of the dying bull? The flame died and darkness returned. The bull was groaning in pain now, but his groaning was restrained, and he fell silent, took two clumsy paces backward, raised his head, and stared at the man.

And as he lifted his wonderful head the blood burst out from the wound and streamed down in black torrents, bubbling in the flashlight beam. Yosh felt disgust and impatience.

"Well, really," he said.

The sight of the spurting blood tickled his bladder. Something prevented him from urinating in the presence of the dying bull. But his patience was ready to snap, and he smoked nervously and angrily. Samson was dying very slowly. His blood was warm and sticky. The bull fell on his knees, his forelegs first, then unhurriedly he lay down. His drooping horns tried to butt, searching in vain for a target.

The bull's eyes died first, while his hide still quivered. Then his hide was still, and there was just one foreleg poking at the straw like a blind man's stick. The leg stopped moving, and all was quiet. The tail flicked weakly once, and once again, like a hand waving goodbye. And when his blood had all drained away, Samson curled up as if he chose to die in the fetal position.

"Well, well," said Yosh.

Then the herdsman finished his cigarette and emptied his bladder and turned and went to the little kitchen where Zeshka kept watch at night.

Zeshka, the estranged wife of Dov Sirkin, gave Yosh a drink of warm, sweet milk in an earthenware cup. She was an old, wrinkled woman with sunken eyes like an owl's. The earthenware cup was large and thick. There was something sharp and nervous in Zeshka's movements. Her body was stunted, shriveled. Steam rose from the cup, and a film of grease floated on the surface of the milk.

3

EVERY NIGHT, until daybreak, Zeshka sits in the little kitchen where special food is prepared for the babies and the sick children. Her angular face rests on her knees. Her knees are gripped in her arms, like a closed penknife. Every hour she wraps herself up in a long, rough overcoat and goes out to patrol the nursery buildings. She straightens a blanket here, closes a window there, but she does not like this new breed of children, and she feels that there is now no need for children or parents or anything but total quiet.

In between she sits on her bench, not moving, not thinking, as if in the no man's land on the frontiers of sleep. But she is not asleep. If a child cries in the night or coughs in the distance, she sniffs her way to him and touches him and says:

"Shh. That's enough, now."

Or: "That's enough, now. Quiet."

And to herself she says:

"So be it."

Ever since that day, long ago, when Dov Sirkin left his family and his kibbutz, Zeshka has been growing bitter. She speaks ill of the kibbutz and of certain individuals in particular. We do our best to be patient. When her eldest son, Ehud, was killed in a ferocious reprisal raid, we stood by her and guarded her against the threat of insanity. We would come in turns to sit with her in the evening hours. We sent her to a craft training course. And when it occurred to her to demand without shame that we allow her to serve as a regular night watchman, relieving her of all other duties, we did not insist on our principles but said: All right. By all means. You are a special case, and we have decided to grant your request. But please bear in mind . . . and so on.

If Samson had chosen to die with a wild shriek rather than a groan of resignation, Zeshka would certainly have nodded her head and said, "Right," or "That's it." But Samson chose to die quietly, and Yosh sipped the drink that she prepared for him and left without saying more, without telling one of his stories from the old days. Sometimes he would stay for a while and even tell jokes. Tonight he came, drank, and went out into the darkness.

And then, until the light of morning, the jackals.

Outbursts of weeping, outbursts of laughter, sometimes you would think a child was being burned alive next door. And sometimes it sounds as if lustful men are clinging to a loose woman, pushing her this way and that and scratching and tickling her until she shrieks and laughs and they groan and then even Zeshka smiles and says to herself:

"Yes, that's right."

At five or at five-fifteen, when the sky grows pale and a ghostly luster appears on the mountains in the east, long before sunrise, Zeshka goes to her room to sleep. On the way she pauses in the younger members' quarters, knocks loudly on Geula's door, and shouts:

"Time to get up. It's well after five. Good morning. Get up!"

Geula Sirkin, the surviving child of Zeshka and Dov, wakes up in hatred and rises to wash her face under the cold-water faucet. She runs to the dining hall, and if anyone says, "Good morning, Geula," she may reply wearily, drowsily, "Fine. All right." When she gets to the kitchen she switches on the big urns and makes coffee for the workers. Her nails are cracked, her hands rough and scabby, and there are two bitter creases at the corners of her mouth. Her legs are thin and pale and covered with a down of black hairs. That is why she always wears trousers, never a skirt or a dress. And although she is now more than twenty years old, there are still adolescent pimples on her cheeks. She is also in the habit of reading modern poetry.

Coffee in big urns, thinks Geula, is revolting stuff. You make proper coffee in an Arabic coffeepot. Ehud did not come home on leave often, but every visit had been a delight to the unmarried girls. And sometimes to the married girls as well. He used to prepare coffee like a primeval wizard, with spells and whispered incantations. And he would laugh suddenly as if to say: What do you know, and what could you know, about the terrors of bazooka fire at close range? But he was a man of few words. He just burst out laughing and asked why they were all hanging around him, as if they had no homes to go to, as if they had nothing to do. And long before he died, his eyes were full of death. He did not leave the kibbutz, but he did not live there, either: his army service was extended from year to year, and he became a legendary figure in the army and in the border settlements; he was twenty-three years old and they gave him command of a battalion. He roamed the land in a tattered uniform and sandals, with a submachine gun plundered from the corpse of a Syrian. He took part in all the reprisal raids — he did not miss a single one. Once he set out, while suffering from a severe case of pneumonia, and blew up the police station in Bet Ajar. It was he who caught, singlehanded, in a night expedition to Mount Hebron, Isa Tubasi, the murderer of the Yaniv family from the *moshav* of Bet Hadas. When he returned from his solitary mission to Mount Hebron he said to his sister, Geula, "I killed him and six others as well. I had to."

As the coffee urns begin to steam and Geula smokes her first cigarette of the day on an empty stomach, the jackals of the valley disperse to their hiding places. The smell of Samson's blood has disturbed their night. The jackals of the valley are feeble creatures, dripping saliva, mad-eyed. They have diffident paws and quivering tails. Sometimes one of them goes mad with hunger or jubilation and breaks into the farmyard and starts biting until the watchmen shoot him. And his comrades laugh maliciously amid their bitter whining.

At one time, many years ago, Dov Sirkin would lay poisoned bait for these jackals, also little gin traps that he himself had designed and constructed. He laughs longest who laughs last, Dov Sirkin used to say. Later he got up and left the kibbutz and his family and went out to roam the land. To his wife he said, "A man must try to leave some fingerprints that will remain after he is dead; otherwise there is no point in being born at all."

According to the orders of the general staff, our soldiers are forbidden to withdraw from enemy territory until all the wounded and the dead have been evacuated. How was it that Ehud's corpse was left in no man's land? Two commissions of inquiry had investigated this disgraceful episode and lessons had been learned. For three nights Ehud lay in no man's land. The enemy soldiers tried to retrieve the body so they could display it in one of their cities and thus soften the humiliation of their defeat in this and other battles. Crazed with anger and shame, Ehud's comrades thwarted the enemy's purpose with a heavy, continuous stream of fire from our frontier. The enemy forces also covered the dead man and would not let his comrades retrieve him. Night after night Ehud's comrades risked their lives, crawling into that godforsaken patch of ground, riddled with bushes and mines, but they were driven back again and again. The enemy set up powerful searchlights and scattered the darkness. On the fourth night, and at the cost of six casualties, Ehud's comrades succeeded in recovering him — in spite of all the dangers, and although they had been ordered to abandon the attempt. They brought him to the camp, and from there to his home, and they said to him: Ehud, our friend, you would not have deserted us even to save your life, and we have not deserted you. Rest in peace.

But the jackals had torn his face and ruined his beautiful square chin. Dov Sirkin appeared at his son's funeral looking mortally ill. Zeshka did not talk to him and he did not talk to her. He tried to speak to Geula, but she did not answer.

Jet-black and frothy, the coffee bubbles in the steaming urns. Let it boil seven times, Geula Sirkin decides, a full seven times. Her lips are clenched. Her teeth are clenched. Her mouth is like a curved dagger.

4

AT SIX in the morning the sound of engines is heard from the direction of the tractor sheds, and the kibbutz members start moving down toward the dew-drenched fields. By eight o'clock the sky is already ablaze, its color changing from blue to a dirty white. Tractors, irrigation pipes, farming implements, all metal objects become inflamed. Put out your hand to touch or to take, and the response is white-hot hatred. The rusty faucets gurgle and emit splinters of iron.

At one time, many years ago, Dov Sirkin was in charge of all the orchards. He used to sing happily, ecstatically, as, stripped to the waist, he flitted like a knife among the rows of trees, appearing at one end of the orchard, shouting to scold and encourage the pickers, then disappearing and springing up at the other end. He had powerful shoulders and a chest and trunk like a bear's: dark and dense.

Toward evening on summer days, he would wander around the orchards carrying on his shoulders a fair-haired little boy with slender, finely molded limbs, as pretty as a girl. Dov taught this boy to be ready to be tossed suddenly into the air without any warning, as high as the treetops, and to fall into his strong father's arms without a cry of fear, without a sound.

"A man needs to be strong and self-assured," he used to say, although he knew that these words were as yet beyond the child's understanding. "To murder an innocent victim is the most repulsive crime in the world. To be the innocent victim yourself is almost as bad. And you, Ehud, you're going to be a terribly strong man. So strong that nobody will be able to harm you, and you won't need to harm other people, because they won't dare start a fight. Now it's getting dark and we're going home. No, not together. You're going on your own through the wadi and I'm going a different way. You must learn not to be afraid of the dark. Yes, there are all kinds of creatures in the wadi, but they will be afraid of you if you're not afraid of them. Off you go."

The orchard is laid out in blocks, each variety divided from the next by a neat furrow. Alexander the Great apples, coarse and lacking flavor. Gallia apples. Juicy Golden Delicious. Then come the peach trees, whose fruit is furry and smells intoxicating. And dark plums, and melancholy guavas, and then another block of apple trees of the variety called Incomparable. It was Dov Sirkin who laid out the plots and planted the saplings in the early days. This orchard would never have existed had it not been for Dov Sirkin and his persistence. He argued and threatened and bullied the founders of the kibbutz into accepting his schemes, and on two occasions he made mistakes and they told him he was mad, he should give up, and twice he uprooted and replanted. Twenty years ago he left his orchard and his family and the kibbutz and went out to roam the land. He did not even take the trouble to leave a letter behind.

Generations of jackals have passed away since then, but the young ones follow the lead of their fathers, and nothing is changed. In every generation the gray open spaces are filled night after night with sounds of wailing and jubilation, with cries of impiety, malice, and despair.

After the departure of Dov Sirkin the kibbutz was filled with noisy indignation: in those days, anybody who left the kibbutz was sure to be one of the weaklings, not a central pillar. And if one of the central pillars left, before going he would address a meeting and beat the table with his fist and call a spade a spade and expose once and for all the corruption that lay hidden behind the façade, and then sit back and listen to the speeches of reply in which they told him once and for all exactly what they thought of him and his motives. But Dov slipped away without any argument, without accusations or excuses: he disappeared early one morning and did not return in the evening, or the following day. Gone.

As time passed our anger subsided. There was perplexity. There was a shrugging of shoulders: He's gone, let him go. We've known him a long time. We always knew.

Later a rumor sprung up concerning a girl from Mexico, an itinerant artist, and everything became clear. The kibbutz assumed responsibility for Zeshka and her children. It was Ehud who, at the age of fourteen and a half, constructed with his own hands the revolving milking-drum that transformed our dairy. When he was sixteen years old, he left school and began wandering about the mountains, and at that time he may already have been in the habit of slipping across the cease-fire line and returning unscathed. He made love behind the barn to girls from the Training Corps who were four or five years older than he. When he was drafted into the army he became more settled. At the age of twenty-three he was a major, and his name was known throughout the land. Only Geula caused us concern. Zeshka, too.

Dov went first to Haifa, where he worked on the docks to save a little money — he had sixty-two piasters in his pocket when he left the kibbutz. From Haifa he went to the Novomeisky mineral works on the shores of the Dead Sea. And from there he traveled to places both in Israel and abroad, and we lost track of him. In recent years — and this we know from a first-hand source — Dov Sirkin has settled in Jerusalem and become a geography teacher in the lower classes of a secondary school. His first heart attack forced him to slow down. After the second he gave up teaching and stayed at home. His face has turned very gray.

5

DOV SIRKIN was sitting in his home. It was night. He sat in his chair motionless and erect, not blinking, not yawning. He sketched with firm lines.

Two o'clock in the morning. An unshaded yellow electric light burned overhead. A flake of plaster drifted down from the ceiling and landed on an old wooden chair. Dov's room was meticulously tidy. Every object lay in the exact spot where Dov had decided to place it, two years before the Declaration of Independence. Despite its precise order, the room seemed to be filled with a strident and unruly herd of piebald furniture. There was chaos in the combination of incongruous objects: the contrast between light, transparent curtains and an antique chest of drawers, an oval table dating from the years of Jerusalem's Sephardic aristocracy and a dark wardrobe with legs carved in the shape of weird prehistoric creatures. In the middle of all this was a garish, flowery bedspread, colored red and blue and made of lingerie silk. A heavy chandelier hovered above the chaos. In the corner of the room a large flowerpot sent out twisted snakes of cactus in all directions, and in the center, at an ornate desk with gold and silver fittings, Dov Sirkin sat and sketched.

He laid down the compass and picked up a ruler. He put the ruler back in its place and began sharpening his pencil. He pressed too hard, breaking the point twice. Dov decided some compromise was necessary. From a heap of colored pencils he picked out a red and a black.

Many years before Dov had been a laborer in the port of Haifa, then a factory foreman, a trooper in His Majesty's Bedouin Cavalry, an arms dealer in Latin America on behalf of the Jewish un-

derground, a staff officer in the War of Independence, a development consultant in the Negev, and finally a teacher of geography,
which in those days still retained its literal meaning of "drawing the
Earth."

He sat leaning forward with bowed head. His face cold, as if spar-
ingly made, each detail for a purpose. There was a parsimonious
look on his features, a pure, concentrated parsimony, without any
element of avarice or enjoyment. Only his eyebrows were on a lav-
ish scale, as if mocking the square forehead in whose folds they
grew. His pencil squeaked on a page torn from a mathematics notebook.

And silence, the silence of a desolate suburb of Jerusalem at a
desolate hour of the early morning, roaming the streets outside and
plucking needles from the tops of the pine trees in the gardens. The
plucked needles rustled softly, the sound penetrating the sealed
shutters, penetrating bones. Cats bristled with fear on the balcony
rails in the darkness. Dov turned his head to look at the door:

All right. Closed. Locked.

Then a faraway jackal let out a short bark, like the leader of an
orchestra who is the first to tune his strings. Many years had passed
since Ehud's one and only visit to this place: there was some youth
congress in Jerusalem, or it may have been a camp for archeology
enthusiasts, and the young man found out the address for himself
and came and stayed for two days. That is, he appeared after midnight with a girl, smiled at his father wearily, and said that he would
explain everything in the morning; then they both immediately fell
asleep in their clothes. When Dov woke up at six o'clock the next
morning, they had gone, and there was just a note saying, "Thanks
a lot. Be seeing you. P.S.: everything's OK." The next night he arrived with two girls. He also brought some ancient pieces of pot-
tery. Until three o'clock in the morning he worked at repairing a
leaking hot-water pipe in the bathroom, and then he went out to

join the girls, who were in their sleeping bags on the balcony. In the morning he was gone, leaving no trace besides the pipe that he had repaired.

Four years later they met briefly and by chance in Beersheba, and Ehud half-promised to come again to visit him. "Some night in the summer," he said. "I'm taking these miserable clods out for training in the Adullam hills, trying to turn alley cats into tigers. And I'm sure you'll be surprised if I turn up some time in the middle of the night to visit you and take a shower." Dov did not believe this promise and hardly expected to hear footsteps at night during the next summer. At the end of that summer Dov Sirkin received a personal letter of condolence from the commander of the paratroopers, and among other expressions of eulogy appeared the words "Happy is the father." He shook his head and decided to concentrate on his drawing and dispel these random thoughts. He was tired, but steeped in self-discipline. The churches behind the walls of the Old City, across the border in the Kingdom of Jordan, began to converse, in the language of bells, with the churches of Bethlehem, also on the alien side of the truce line. The bells of Bethlehem chimed in reply: Yes, here, yes, here He was born. And the bells of East Jerusalem sang: And here He died and here He arose.

6

DOV PUT down the black and red pencils. With the aid of his compass he drew a neat semicircle. Then he picked up the blue pencil and sketched for about a quarter of an hour without a break.

On the paper a gigantic port took shape. Its blue water flowed from his gray eyes to his fingers and through them to the pencil, which swallowed up the squares on the paper until almost the whole of the page was covered with blue. The jetties of Dov's harbor were broader than the broadest jetties, the piers longer than any ever built by human hands, and the cranes more massive than the greatest cranes in the world. And the warehouses were as tall as the silence poking its dark fingers through the cracks in Dov Sirkin's shutters. A complex of highways, connecting roads, bridges, tunnels, and approach routes writhed like a nest of snakes. Yellow machines spewed out giant sparks. Steel platforms and rubber conveyor belts were sketched in, capable of unloading whole mountains of merchandise from colossal ships. All in meticulous architectural perspective, in matching scale, lunatic fire trapped in the amber crystals of mathematics. If the greatest ship in the world were enticed to lay anchor between Dov's quays in his harbor of the Jerusalem night, this ship would look like a beetle crawling on an elephant's tusk.

The blue pencil shaded in the whole of the bay and then delicately scattered water into a network of canals. A stranger's footsteps sounded on the stairs outside. Somebody leaned heavily on the banister. There was a creak. And silence.

Dov leapt up from his seat, rushed to the window, and checked the bolts of the shutters. They were screwed down. In the cracks the empty street appeared. Beam upon beam of desolate starlight stretched across the street, from rooftops to balcony rails, from garbage cans to the crowns of cypress trees, from the Municipal Information Bureau to the telephone booth, from the top of the stone steps to the cracks in the sidewalk. A silent crust covered the earth, and a blue vapor came down. Or dew.

Another fragment of plaster fell from the ceiling, larger than the first. Tiny flakes of whitewash were scattered over the bedspread that resembled the intimate clothing of a loose woman. The footsteps on the staircase ceased. Perhaps the stranger was now on the first floor. There was silence, no sound of a key turning in a lock, or of a bell ringing. He must be standing motionless, examining the peeling doors and perhaps taking in the names of the residents on the mailboxes. Dov clenched his teeth. His jaws tensed like a fist. He stood up, hid his plan of the port of Jerusalem in the antique

chest of drawers, and returned to the writing desk. He ripped out a
fresh sheet of graph paper, sat down, and started to draw a picture-
map of a mountainous land.

7

HE WAS a gray man: gray eyes, face, and hair. But he almost invariably chose to wear a blue shirt of the kind favored by young ath-
letes, and sandals of biblical style. Hidden beneath his shirt was a
strong and hairy torso, crisscrossed with sinews. At first sight he
seemed still in his prime, and he had the build of a stevedore. Only
his heart was weak, but this was not evident to the eye. In the autumn he would be sixty years old.

He sketched the map of a mountainous land. A green police patrol car raced down the street, ripping the silence apart, and then silence returned and sewed up the breach with a cool, dreamy hand.
The patrol car receded southward, toward the steep alleyways at
the approaches to the railway station. On three sides the truce line
encircled the city of Jerusalem. To the north and east of this line a
different Jerusalem brooded. And to the south lay Bethlehem and,
farther still, the godforsaken hills of Hebron, and at their feet, forever, the desert.

Dov drew a land of black basalt hills. To these hills he gave sharp
snow-capped peaks tall enough to pierce the embroidered-silk
screen of the stars. He drew monsters of rock, sharp daggers of
stone, summits like drawn swords. And wild ravines cleaving the
vaulted ranges. Here and there were ominous overhangs, threatening at any moment to hurl primeval cataracts of smashed rock
down into the abyss. Canyons and gorges carved out in drunken-
ness. Brooding labyrinths and volcanic caves, the menace of a different silence.

At last he stopped drawing and stared at the page. His jaws were gray. He took a red crayon and began to write in the altitudes of his peaks. The foothills of these mountains could have laughed the summits of the Alps to scorn.

8

DRIVEN BY hunger and cold, perhaps by regret, one of the jackals of Bethlehem began to weep bitterly. At once he was answered by jackal packs from the heights of Bet Zafafa, from Zur Bahar, from the hill of Mar Elias, in an outburst of perverted laughter and malice. The wind stopped blowing, as if listening with rapt attention.

The stairs creaked again. A thrill passed through his body. His fingers turned pale. Heavily the stranger climbed another step, then another, and a third, coughed, and then paused. And again the stillness of death descended on the house, on the street, and on the city. This time Dov ran into the kitchen. Close the window. Seal the lattice. Keep the light on.

Until a few years before he had been teaching geography to a junior class of the national secondary school. Hundreds of pupils had passed through his hands over the years. They used to respect his grayness and obey his gray voice. Rumors proliferated among them and passed from generation to generation, rumors concerning the elderly schoolmaster who was once a leading figure in the underground and one of the founding fathers of the kibbutz movement. As they gripped the chalk his fingers looked strong and decisive. With one firm sweep of his hand he was capable of drawing a thin, straight line that no ruler in the world could have improved upon. Sometimes he would try to entertain his class: his jokes were thin, gray. Occasionally he would suddenly become animated by a sort of restrained pathos, and something would come alive in his eyes. This would be interpreted by his pupils as anger; it would fade and disappear as suddenly as it had arisen.

Two or three times a year he used to put on khaki clothes, take a bundle of maps and a smart army knapsack that always aroused envy in the hearts of his pupils, and lead a party of schoolchildren on a hiking tour. He cut a strange and almost eccentric figure in his hiking gear: tattered windbreaker with many pockets and buckles, tall walking boots, a rather antiquated firearm that he called a Tommy gun. With his pupils from the intermediate classes he would often climb to the heights of the hills of Naphtali, and with his senior students he used to cross over Little Crater to the Scorpion's Path and beyond, to the Meshar.

Once, during one of these trips, Dov's party was held up in Beersheba. A representative of the Military Authority told them to change their route and not to pass through the Desert of Paran. For security reasons. In a general sense; he did not go into details. The officer was thin and tall, curly-haired, barefoot and taciturn, his uniform disgracefully casual. It was four years since Dov had seen this young man. Four years before the young man had come to Jerusalem for some congress or other and had spent two nights in Dov's apartment. The first night he arrived with a girl whom he did not even bother to introduce to his father, and the second night there were two girls with him. Dov remembered the beauty of these girls, the softness of their voices, the muffled laughter from the sleeping bags in the early morning. Now he did not know what words he could use, or if the proper words even existed. His pupils pressed around him and the thin officer, and he found nothing to say.

"Anyway," said Ehud casually, drawling as if too lethargic to move his lips and speak intelligibly, "anyway, as far as I'm concerned the best thing you can do is turn around and go home. We've got enough problems as it is. We don't need schoolkids and teachers here. Still, seeing as you've got this far, you may as well go on a little farther. Head straight for Eilat, sing your "Southward Ho!" songs there, and go home. Don't waste any time on the way."

The teacher let his shoulders droop. He was taller and more

powerfully built than the arrogant officer. In the days of the War of Independence he had been a staff officer in the Negev, with the rank of lieutenant colonel. But at that moment he could not speak of these things to his pupils or to the drowsy youth who stood before him chewing something, perhaps gum, perhaps his tongue.

"I know," he murmured, "you don't need to tell me. I know." The Beersheba sun drew sweat from every pore of his body. "I know this terrain much better than you do. I was fighting here in the Negev when you were so high."

"OK," said the curly-haired officer, "fine, OK, just don't start giving me your memoirs now. If you know the terrain, you can stop wasting my time. I've got too many tourists making nuisances of themselves. Good-bye."

"Just a moment," said Dov angrily, "one moment, please. Listen. In my day they would have cleared the area of terrorists within twenty-four hours. What's the matter with you people? You let infiltrators stroll around the Negev as if it were the Baghdad bazaar. What have you got to be so arrogant about? Why don't you do something, instead of chasing girls?"

The schoolchildren were stunned. Even Ehud was taken aback. He turned. The ghost of a smile passed over his lips and disappeared.

"Pardon?"

"It's just . . . what I meant was, perhaps we could talk about this, just the two of us. Not now. Why don't you drop in some time? Why not, really?"

"Why not? Some night in the summer," he said. "I'm taking these miserable clods of mine out for some training in the Adullam hills. Making tigers out of alley cats. That would be a real shock for you, wouldn't it, if I turned up some time in the middle of the night to take a shower at your place and sleep for a couple of hours."

Later, when the summer was over, Dov's request was granted, and he was allowed to take a last look at the lean and tousled officer.

Something about him had changed. The pride of those casual lips had disappeared. Little night predators had eaten half his face.

In the course of every one of these trips Dov Sirkin would raise his voice — only slightly — and give a brief and fluent lecture on terrace cultivation in Galilee, or on the export of minerals and merchandise to Africa and Asia through the Red Sea Straits. His eyes were as sharp as the needle of a compass. At times he would suddenly halt the bored and weary party, point to a silent ruin, and tell a story. Or he would show the hikers an innocent-looking mound and say: There is a mystery hidden here. Sometimes in the desert he would sniff out the skeleton of a camel, a hyena, or a jackal. Or a spring that an inexperienced traveler would be unable to find even if he was dying of thirst twenty paces from it.

After such trips Dov Sirkin used to ask the Hebrew teacher to lend him the notebooks in which the pupils had described their expedition — a thousand versions of a thousand trifling details. Even in the most mundane account Dov would find something of interest. Sometimes he even took the trouble to copy items from his pupils' essays into his own journal, before returning the notebooks to the Hebrew teacher and the journal to the bottom drawer of the brown Berlin-style chest of drawers.

Geula used to come once a year, on the eve of Independence Day. After the festival she would always return to the kibbutz. Throughout the night and the morning after, she would sit by herself on Dov's little balcony, watching with trembling lips the fireworks erupting in the Jerusalem sky and in the sky above the mountains and the desert, listening to the loudspeakers blasting out their message far away in the main thoroughfares of the city, chain-smoking as she watched the young people singing their festive songs. She called her father Dov. She never talked to him about herself, or about her mother and brother. She spoke sometimes about Ben-Gurion, about the politics of moderation and restraint as opposed to the politics of revenge and summary retaliation. Altermann she considered a very Polish poet, incorrigibly in love with the tools of power, in love with death. Dov tried hard to engage her in conversation, to understand, to influence, but Geula asked him not to disturb her as she listened to the dance music from Terra Sancta Square and imagined the distant revelry. At the funeral Dov said to her, "You must, you must believe me when I say that I had no idea. How could I have known?"

She did not answer but moved away from him. Her eyes were dry. Her teeth were clenched. And her mouth was like a curved Arabian sword.

After that she stopped visiting him and never again appeared in Dov's apartment in Jerusalem.

9

DOV COMPLETED his sketch of the mountainous country and began to draw a raging river unlike any other river on the face of the earth. He carved out a huge canal, added a series of tributary waterways, and laid out a complicated network of gradients, slopes, dams, reservoirs, and lakes, complete with measurements. He also drew up an intricate scheme for calculating angles of incline, tolerance of road surfaces, pressure of water against the stress capacity of the dam, strength of rock, stability of the subsoil beneath lakewater, pressure of currents and winds, accumulations of eroded sand. About an hour earlier the sound of footsteps on the staircase had stopped. Now it returned. Somebody was treading the stairs, slowly, very heavily, leaning on the creaking old banister. The heart attack had come near the end of the school year. Between the first attack and the second there had been solid months of extreme discomfort and horrific nightmares: he was alone in the desert, alone on a raft in the middle of the ocean, alone in an airplane without any idea of how to handle the controls or how to land or avoid crashing into the mountains that drew closer by the second. Dov decided to give in. He retired from teaching and shut himself away in his room. There was nobody to interfere with his daily and nightly routine: light meals, a slow and pensive walk, the evening paper, music, working at his desk until daybreak, morning sleep, and at midday, yogurt, bread, and a cup of lemon tea.

He lived on a pension. In addition to this, he sometimes took original and perhaps artistic landscape photographs, which he would send to one of the weekly magazines. But these pictures were almost invariably printed on inferior paper and appeared at the bottom of page sixteen, between the recipes and crossword solutions. All that was left of their beauty was a smudgelike stain and a caption such as, "Monastery in the village of Ein-Kerem at evening, photographed by Sirkin."

All these photographs find their way eventually into Zeshka's massive old album. Week by week, one by one, she cuts the smudged pictures out of the magazine, sticking them with thick homemade paste to the black pages of her album. As she works her eyes sparkle with a kind of delight. And wrinkles of cold cunning converge around her sunken eyes. Behind her back we call her by the unkind nickname Owl.

Every morning, after finishing his night's work and before going to bed, Dov Sirkin would stand at the window and gaze out eastward, watching the sun climb up from beyond the mountains of Moab, casting white flames on the surface of the Dead Sea, thrusting its rays like spears into the flanks of the bare mountains, striking down without mercy on the walls of shaded monasteries, heavy with bells. The day would begin.

At midday, after waking up, after tea, bread, yogurt, and olives, he would sit on his little balcony among potted cacti and dead houseplants, watching the street. The street was curved, with stone walls, gardens, rusty iron latticework at every window. And a long line of garbage cans along the sidewalk. Toward evening he used to go out for a walk, and in the course of his stroll he would sometimes photograph some unexpected scene. The charm of the approaching night, the distant cries of children, a radio blaring in a neighboring house, all of these contributed to a sense of peace. He ate supper at a small cooperative cafe: eggplant salad, fried egg with pickled cucumber, yogurt, and cafe au lait.

At night he sketched. All the drawers of his cupboard were crammed with drawings and photographs, plaster models, detailed arithmetical calculations regarding the properties of raw materials, development costs, building techniques, mechanical equipment, manpower, synchronized schedules for construction and communication projects, integrated systems, geometrical and architectonic principles expressed numerically and in diagrams. There were also timetables for trains faster than the fastest trains in existence, winding railways plunging into giant tunnels, carved out of the bedrock of imaginary lands. Avenues of a thousand fountains bathed in dazzling light, crossroads of dream cities that never were and could never be. Exquisite spires of tall cities rising beyond the line of the mountain peaks and looking down on the bays of the sea, blue rollers breaking on the threshold of silence.

10

AT FOUR o'clock in the morning the wind began to walk the streets. It plucked the lid from a rusty garbage can and tossed it against the asphalt road and the stone steps.

Light, brisk footsteps approached the door of the apartment. For two hours the stranger had been loitering between the ground floor and Dov's apartment. Now he suddenly began to hurry. He was running, racing up the stairs two at a time. He had no time to spare. What's the matter, where's the fire, Dov grumbled.

He stood up and stumbled to the door, his shoulders drooping.

Many years before, Dov used to seal the shutters of his little room on the edge of the kibbutz, closing the window and the curtain, shutting the stillness into the room and the night with its darkness outside. He would sit on the carpet and build a tower of bricks for his children: raising it higher and higher, laughing, making jokes, laying brick upon brick until it reached his waist, reached his shoulders, with the children watching in disbelief and starting to gasp and giggle in anticipation, and sure enough, in the end there was always an avalanche. From the sofa came the sound of Zeshka's knitting needles, calmly going about their business. And the smell of coffee and the smell of children washed spotlessly clean. Outside, beyond the walls, the shutters and the curtain, the jackals were crying piteously. Geula laughed and Ehud laughed and Dov, too, would smile a neat smile to himself as if saying: Good.

The jackals are pathetic creatures, dripping saliva and mad-eyed. Their footsteps are soft and their tails quiver. Their eyes shoot out sparks of cunning or despair, their ears prick up, their mouths hang open and their white teeth flash, spittle and foam drip from their jaws.

The jackals circle on tiptoe. Their snouts are soft and moist. They dare not approach the lights of the perimeter fence. Around and around they shuffle, mustering as if in readiness for some obscure ritual. A ring of jackals prowls every night about the circle of shadows that encloses the island of light. Till daybreak they fill the darkness with their weeping, and their hunger breaks in waves against the illuminated island and its fences. But sometimes one of them goes insane and with bared teeth invades the enemy's fortress, snatching up chickens, biting horses or cattle, until the watchmen kill him with an accurate volley from medium range. Then his brothers break into mourning, a howl of terror and impotence and rage and anticipation of the coming day.

Day will come. Or night.

Slowly, like black-robed priests in a ceremony of mourning, they will approach the young man's corpse in no man's land. With agile steps, as if caressing, not treading, the dust of the earth. With dripping muzzles. First they will form a circle, at a distance, and sniff softly. Then one of them will approach the body and bend down, probing with the tip of his snout. A lick, or a final sniff. Another will advance and rip open the tunic with razor-sharp teeth. A third and a fourth and a fifth will come to lap his blood. Then the first will give a low chuckle. The oldest jackal will cut himself a portion with his gleaming curved teeth. And then the whole pack will roar with laughter.

An everlasting curse stands between house dwellers and those who live in mountains and ravines. It happens sometimes in the middle of the night that a plump house-dog hears the voice of his accursed brother. It is not from the dark fields that this voice comes; the dog's detested foe dwells in his own heart. "Ehud," said Dov, and he gripped the doorknob.

First there was a light cough. Then a shudder. Great weariness. A shivering fit. A shuffling of feet. Sit down. Lie down. Fall. The pain was sharp and persistent, like a Latin monk repeating and repeating a thousand times the same obscure verse. The jackal pack of the Bethlehem hills gave a laugh. Their laughter ran through the empty streets of the night, Ramat Rachel, Talpiot, Bakah, the German Colony and the Greek Colony, Talbiah, and like a monkey the laughter climbed the gutters of the house and penetrated inward in a thousand jagged splinters. When the kibbutz was founded we believed that we really could turn over a new leaf, but there are things that cannot be set right and should be left as they have been since the beginning of time. I said, There are things that man can do if he wants them with all his heart. But I did not know that there is no point in leaving a fingerprint on the face of the water. I am the last, my child, and I am not laughing.

11

THE FIRST cracks appeared in the east, above the Mount of Olives and between the two towers. A light-shunning bird let out a shriek of hatred. Stealthily some pale-red force arrived and slipped through the chinks in the eastern shutter. Flocks of birds began frantically ripping the silence.

And then it was day. Kerosene sellers began to sing. Children with satchels appeared on their way to school. Yellow smells arose from vegetable stands. Newspaper vendors proclaimed the great tidings. A minister's car appeared in the street, its tires squealing on the asphalt. Shop after shop opened up, folding iron shutters like winking eyes.

Around a stall laden with antiques stood a crowd of rosy-cheeked tourists. There was excitement. Among the knickknacks on the stall were sacred pictures on parchment screens, all of fine craftsmanship, genuine leather, strong and ancient, declared Rashid Effendi.

How sublime are the distant bells of the monasteries. How contemptible, how savage and irreverent are these jackals, answering the pure message of the bells with their twisted laughter. Malice inspires them, incorrigible malice, malice and sacrilege.

1962

The Trappist Monastery

1

IN THE AUTUMN the provocations intensified. There was no longer any reason for restraint. Our unit was ordered to cross the border at night and raid Dar an-Nashef.

"Tonight a nest of murderers will be wiped off the face of the earth," our commander declared in his deep, calm voice, "and the whole Coastal Plain can breathe freely." The men replied with a great cheer. Itcheh shouted loudest of all.

The whitewashed huts of the base camp looked clean and cheerful. Already the busy supply men were grappling with the steel doors of the armory. Mortars and heavy machine guns were brought out from the darkness into the light and laid in neat rectangles on the edge of the parade ground.

The last rays of the sun were fading in the west. Soon there was no dividing line between the peaks of the mountains to the east and the cloud banks that stooped over them. A small group of staff officers, wrapped in windbreakers, were conferring around a map that was spread out on the ground and held down by a stone at each corner. They were studying the map by the light of a pocket flashlight, and their voices were muffled. One man suddenly left the group and went bounding off toward the operations room: Rosenthal, thin and always immaculate; rumor had it that he was the son of a well-known candy manufacturer. Then a voice was heard calling out in the darkness, "Itamar, come on, it's getting late." And another voice replied, "Go to hell. Leave me alone."

The battalion paraded in readiness for the sortie. On the edge of the square, facing the combatants who meandered sleepily into position in ragged ranks of three, stood a noisy group of general-duty men. They did not look sleepy; on the contrary, they were feverishly excited, talking in whispers, pointing with their fingers, giggling in shame or malice. Among them was a medical orderly named Nahum Hirsch who was forever scratching his cheeks; he had shaved in a hurry and his skin smarted with irritating little wounds. He took off his glasses and, staring at the combat troops, made a joke that was lost on his fellow orderlies. Nahum Hirsch rephrased the joke. They still did not find it funny, perhaps it was too subtle for them to understand. They told him to shut up. So he kept quiet. But the night would not keep quiet; it began to resound with all kinds of different noises. From a distant orchard we heard the sound of an irrigation pump, throbbing as if dividing time itself into equal symmetrical squares. Next the generator began its dull persistent hum, and along the perimeter fences of the camp the searchlights were switched on. The parade ground, too, was suddenly floodlit, so that the soldiers and their weapons suddenly appeared pure white.

Far away, on the foothills of the eastern mountains, rose the beam of the enemy searchlight. It began wandering nervously, aimlessly, across the sky. Once or twice the trails of falling stars were caught in this beam and their light was swallowed by its glare. The combat troops huddled over their final cigarettes. Some had already taken a last deep gulp of smoke and were stubbing out the butts on the rubber soles of their heavy boots. Others tried hard to smoke slowly. A convoy of trucks with dimmed lights moved to the edge of the square and stopped there, engines still running. The commander said: "Tonight we shall obliterate Dar an-Nashef and bring a bit of peace to the Coastal Plain. We shall operate in two columns and with two rear-guard parties. We shall try to cause a minimum of civilian casualties, but we won't leave a stone standing in that nest of murderers. Every man is to act precisely in accordance with his instructions. In the event of any unforeseen development, or if any man gets cut off from the rest, then use the brains that God gave you and I've sharpened for you. That is all. Take care. And I don't want anyone drinking cold water when he's sweating. I promised your mothers I'd take care of you. Now, let's get going."

The squad answered him with a clicking of buckles on shoulder straps. Without any further signal, all began jumping lightly up and down in place, listening for any tinkling of metal or splashing of water in a canteen that had not been properly filled. Then a group of general-duty men walked between the lines, carrying tin pots full of soot. They passed from soldier to soldier, and each dipped his finger in the soot and smeared it on his cheeks, forehead, and chin: if the light of the enemy's searchlights should catch their faces as they crawled on their stomachs toward the objective, the soot would prevent their sweating skin from giving them away. To Nahum Hirsch, the medical orderly, the procedure looked like some primeval initiation ritual, and the men carrying soot were like priests.

The battalion began trudging toward the trucks. The girls swooped upon them: clerks, typists, and nurses, all handing out candy and chewing gum. Itcheh flung his bear-like arms around the waist of Bruria, the adjutant, swung her through the air in a wide circle, and roared, "Make sure our cognac's ready, girls, or you won't get any pretty souvenirs!"

There was laughter. And silence again.

Nahum Hirsch wanted to boil over with anger or disgust, but laughter got the better of him and he laughed with the rest of them and he was still laughing to himself as the soldiers began climbing aboard the trucks that waited for them with lights dimmed.

2

AND THEN the enemy threw up into the sky three nervous flares, red, green, and purple. Dar an-Nashef crouched there at the foot of the eastern mountains, chewing its fingernails in fear. All its lights were extinguished. The darkness of guilt or of terror brooded over its cottages. Only the beam of the searchlight rose from it, probing the sky as if the danger lay there. At that very moment our reconnaissance party was making its way through the dense orchards toward the crossroads that were to be blocked against enemy reinforcements.

The general-duty men, those who never took part in any raid and for that reason were dubbed by Itcheh Les Misérables, began crowding around the trucks, staring awkwardly at the combat troops. They tried to cheer them up with jokes. Nahum Hirsch put his arm around little Yonich, then clapped him twice on the shoulder and whispered, "A sheep in wolf's clothing, eh?" It was supposed to sound ironical, but his voice betrayed him, and the words rang with venom.

Yonich was not one of the combat troops but a general-duty man. He was a refugee from Yugoslavia, a gloomy little survivor who served the men of our unit from behind the canteen counter. Sometimes they called him the Biscuit Brigadier. His face was deformed, set in a permanent grimace. The right side of his mouth was always smiling as if he found everything endlessly funny; the left was as grim as death. Some said that the Germans had twisted his face once and for all in some labor camp or in the selection process. Or perhaps it was the Yugoslav partisans who had broken his chin or his jaw with a punch, telling him to stop getting on their nerves with his Jewish misery.

Why had they decided this time to put little Yonich, of all people, into the task force, and authorize him to join in the raid against Dar an-Nashef? Perhaps they saw him as a sort of mascot. His little body looked ludicrous, almost pathetic, in the straps of the tattered harness. Evidently one of the officers had seen some kind of subtle humor in putting Yonich in the task force. He was to serve as personal runner to the unit commander, keeping close to him throughout the progress of the battle and ready to leap up when necessary and run to the commanders of the back-up troops, keeping communications going. He had been told: "You're going to have to run like hell, pal. Imagine that the biscuits are here and the customer's over there, and at the same time there's somebody waiting for soda and somebody else who wants cigarettes and matches."

Nahum Hirsch said: "Yonich, you're going into battle like Samson's little brother, and you don't understand that they're just treating you as a joke. Lucky that the Arabs can't see who's coming to beat the shit out of them."

Yonich turned around, and Nahum saw the twisted half-smile and then the front teeth protruding from the cleft lips. And he stepped back.

At that moment the tank engines suddenly started up beside the pine grove, and the earth shook. These tanks would not participate directly in the raid against Dar an-Nashef but were to be deployed in the mountain passes to anticipate any possible development, however remote. The roar of the mighty engines set all hearts pounding. The signal was given and the convoy set out toward the mouth of the wadi. There the troops would be ordered down from the transports and would set out on foot to cross the dense orchards, then march over the frontier and to the outskirts of Dar an-Nashef from the northwest and the southwest. The girls waved their hands, bidding them good-bye and good luck.

Nahum left the parade ground. He sat down at the foot of a whitewashed eucalyptus tree. Little fragments of whitewash fell from the tree trunk, and some of them stung his sweating brow. As always, his thoughts turned to men and women, and not to the other creatures of which the night is full. The sounds of the night came and dispersed his thoughts.

3

OUR UNIT could boast of a distinguished commander and many daring officers, but Itcheh was our pride. He was a king. It was not only Bruria who loved him and bore everything in silence. We all did. He loved to pinch everybody, the soldiers, the girls, Bruria herself. She would say, "You're disgusting, stop that," but these words always came from her lips warm and moist, as if she were really saying, "More, more!" And he loved to insult her and even to humiliate her in the presence of the entire battalion, from our commanding officer to the last of the general-duty men, Yonich or Nahum Hirsch or somebody of that sort. He used to scold Bruria, telling her to leave him alone, stop running after him all day, and come to him only at night, stop clinging to him as if she were his mother or he were her father: he'd had enough, he was sick of her.

When his insults were more than she could bear, she would sometimes go to the operations room to seek consolation from Rosenthal, the operations officer. Let them tell Itcheh, let him be jealous, she didn't care, he deserved it. Rosenthal did not treat her as Itcheh did. He was not the type to fling up her skirt or thrust his hand inside her blouse when there were drivers and supply men standing around. His courting manners were like something out of a film, and he often tried to impress her by speaking English with a slight American accent. He was slim and athletic, he dressed immaculately, and his compliments were as deft as his tennis shots. Often, when he sat with Bruria in the operations room, he would translate for her into Hebrew the contents of the pornographic magazines that his brother had brought from Europe. But he did not dare touch her, or perhaps he did not want to; if ever he did touch her, it was gently and courteously. In the end she always came back to Itcheh, chastened, moaning and servile, almost begging for punishment, and everything was as before. The whole battalion was waiting for the day when Itcheh's jealousy would explode and there would be a showdown with the soft-spoken operations officer. In fact, Itcheh surprised us and showed not the slightest hint of jealousy; he only laughed and told Bruria to go to blazes, to leave him alone, he was sick of her and he was sick of them all and why did she hang around him all day.

After every reprisal operation Itcheh's name was heard in high military circles. Twice he was seen in newsreels, and once his picture appeared on the cover of the army magazine. It was he who discovered the Viper's Path, leading from the south of Jerusalem across the desert of Judea and through enemy territory to Ein Gedi on the shores of the Dead Sea in one night's march. It was he who settled a longstanding account with the Bedouins of the tribe of Arab al-Attata. The Divisional Commander himself once described him as the spiritual brother of the warriors of King David in Adullam or of the Gideonites and Jephthahites. In the course of one raid he leapt, alone, into a cave where dozens of enemy soldiers were entrenched. He so terrified them with his ferocious, blood-curdling yells that they melted away before him as he darted among the murky rifle pits throwing in hand grenades. Petrified by astonishment or horror, the enemy troops gave themselves up, as if mesmerized, to the bursts of fire from his machine gun. Alone he entered the cave and alone he emerged from it, panting and disheveled, roaring and waving his gun above his head.

Itcheh let his beard grow wild. The hair on his head was thick and matted and seemed always to be full of dust. His beard began at his temples and almost met his thick eyebrows, flowing down over his cheeks and neck and merging without a break into the bear's fur that covered his chest and arms and perhaps the whole of his body.

Sometimes Itcheh surprised Nahum Hirsch in the tin shower hut. The medical orderly would dry himself in a hurry and leave without bothering about the soap bubbles left in his armpits. For it was well known that Itcheh always made a point of humiliating the supply men and the drivers and the orderlies, his greatest admirers, those whom he called Les Misérables. Yet he would sometimes astonish them with an act of unexpected generosity. He would give one of them a pistol taken from a dead Syrian officer, or he would take one of the supply men aside and talk to him as an equal, chatting about politics and girls and striking the poor fellow dumb with his frankness.

Between the men's and the women's shower there was a thin partition of patched tin. The general-duty men had punched peepholes here and there, and they used to spend hours in the shower hut, especially on weekends. Itcheh loved to press his huge naked body against the partition until the tin began to creak and groan. On the other side of the partition the girls responded with squeals of fright or anticipation. Then Itcheh would roar with laughter and all those present on both sides of the wall would join in his laughter. Once it happened that Itcheh sprained his ankle on the camp soccer field. He limped to the clinic and surprised Nahum Hirsch as the young man was cutting nude pictures out of a foreign magazine. Nahum probed the twisted ankle to make quite sure that it was a sprain and not a fracture. Itcheh was his usual carefree self. Even when the young man's fingers groped higher up the leg and his whole body shook, still Itcheh continued to joke and he noticed nothing. Then Nahum fitted an elastic bandage on the ankle joint and stretched it mercilessly. Itcheh let out a low moan of pain but still he seemed not to suspect anything. Finally Itcheh smiled, thanked the orderly for the treatment, and held out his hand. Nahum put his fingers into the huge hand. Itcheh began to squeeze his fingers with fearful pressure. Wave upon wave of pain, pride, and pleasure flowed around the base of the young orderly's spine. Itcheh intensified his grip still further. Nahum abandoned himself to the sweet ripples of pain, but on his face there was only a polite smile as if to say: I only bandaged your ankle because it was my duty. Then Itcheh relaxed his hold and released Nahum's hand. He said, "Perhaps we'll decide to take you on the next raid. The time has come to make you a combat orderly. Eh?"

The sweet smell of chewing gum was wafted over Nahum's face, and he found nothing to say.

Of course Itcheh had forgotten this promise, and perhaps he was in the habit of throwing similar promises around among the general-duty men. They had chosen little Yonich, of all people. Now, at this very moment, he was running around bent double in the clinging darkness, or perhaps crawling on the ground, half of his face grinning foolishly and the other half like a stone carving. Still complete silence, not a sound to be heard. Only crickets and jackals and faint music from a radio in the living quarters. There is still time.

4

A DENSE night breeze came and stirred the treetops. The shower of whitewash fragments grew. Nahum was overcome by the kind of weariness that follows despair. Suddenly he noticed that unconsciously he had been snapping small twigs between his fingers.

The enemy searchlight was still raking the sky. Even the conquered earth kept sending out waves of clinging warmth, heavy with fragrance.

Light footsteps approached. Nahum knew those footsteps. He stood up and pressed himself against the trunk of the eucalyptus. He lay in wait in the darkness, allowing a crazy hallucination to take control of him. When she passed in front of him, he leapt out from his hiding place and blocked her path. She let out a low cry of fear. But at the same moment she recognized him.

"Hey," said the orderly in a low voice.

"Out of my way, cut it out," she said. "Don't be childish."

"He's going to be wounded," said Nahum sadly and patiently.

"Idiot," said Bruria.

"He's going to be wounded tonight. Seriously wounded."

"Let me pass. I don't want to see you or listen to you. You're mad."

"He's going to be wounded seriously, but he won't die. I promise you that he won't die."

"Go away. Go to hell."

"Are you angry? I'm going to save him myself; you shouldn't be angry with me — this very night I'm going to save his life."

"You're a joke. Stop running after me. Don't say things like that to me. I didn't tell you to follow me. Get out. I didn't give you permission to enter this room. Get out, go away, or I'll call the sergeant major. Get out of here or you'll be in trouble."

Nahum followed her movements with a look of longing. She switched on the light, nervous and distracted, began sorting out some papers that were scattered on the chair and the table, pushed something away under the cupboard, and sat down on the unmade camp bed, her face to the wall and her back to him.

"Are you still here? What do you want from me? Tell me, what have I done that makes people like you come here and cause trouble? Get out. Leave me alone. You men make me sick."

"You've insulted me twice in less than ten minutes," said Nahum Hirsch, "but I won't hold that against you, not tonight. I'm going to save his life."

Bruria said: "Any minute now, Jacqueline will be back. If she comes in and finds you here you'll regret it. I don't even know who you are. You're Nahum the orderly. OK, Nahum the orderly, get out of here, now."

Suddenly Nahum ripped off all the buttons of his khaki shirt with a wild, hysterical movement, and the girl pressed herself against the wall, her hand over her mouth, her eyes wide open and terrified. She was speechless. Nahum pointed to his thin, bare chest.

"Now watch carefully," he whispered frantically, "look. This is where the bullet has entered. He's taken the bullet full in the throat. It goes in here and out there. On the way, it cuts his windpipe. The veins are severed as well. And blood starts to flow here, down, inside, straight into his lungs."

His pale fingers sketched the course of the wound on his chest, and the feverish lecture raced on.

"And from the windpipe, here, all the blood pours into the lungs. A hemorrhage like this nearly always causes suffocation and death."

"That's enough. Shut up. Please, stop it."

"They suffocate, simply because there's no room for air if the lungs are full of blood. Now they are bringing him in from the field straight to me, in the clinic. His face is blue, he's choking, vomiting blood, spitting blood, his clothes are full of blood, his beard is full of blood, his eyes have rolled up and you can only see the whites. But I don't panic. I take a knife, a rubber tube, and a pocket light, and I cut his windpipe. Like a butcher, except that I'm doing it to save his life at the last moment. I'm not looking for decorations or prizes. I save his life because we are all brothers-in-arms. Very low down I cut his windpipe — look here, watch — farther down — here. And I insert the rubber tube through the severed windpipe right into his lung. Like this."

Bruria sat upright, her neck taut, as if mesmerized, under a spell, watching the pale, nimble fingers running over the thin chest like sewing needles, as if searching for some invisible opening. She was silent. Nahum went on without a pause, his voice choking and feverish.

"Now I'm gripping the end of the tube in my mouth. I start sucking the blood out of his lungs to give him a chance to breathe, so he won't die of suffocation. Watch, sucking and spitting, sucking and spitting, not pausing for a moment, devotedly, lovingly. And watch, now I'm breathing into his lungs, like this, in-out, in-out, like saving a drowned man."

Gradually, without her realizing it, Bruria's breathing changed as well. She began to follow the rhythm of the orderly's breathing. There was a short silence.

"He's recovering now," Nahum shouted suddenly. "I can see his eyes moving. And his knees. He's showing signs of life now."

Bruria opened her mouth as if to weep or to cry out, yet she neither wept nor cried out, but went on breathing deeply.

"Now he's already breathing by himself — not through his nose or his mouth, but through the tube that I inserted in his lung. Look. Spitting blood. That's good for him. Choking. That's a good sign, too. He won't die on us now. He's going to live. Here, open his blurred eye for a moment. Look. This one. The left. Close it. Pale. Now you can go down on your knees beside the stretcher and take his hand in yours and try to talk to him. He won't be able to answer you, but perhaps he can hear you. I'm going now. Yes. Don't try to stop me, I don't need any thanks. I've done my duty. I'm going, the ambulance is honking outside and the doctor has arrived. An unknown orderly has taken it upon himself to carry out a difficult operation under field conditions and has saved the life of a national hero. Itcheh and I will embrace on the front page of the newspaper. You don't owe me anything. Far from it. You'll get married, live happily ever after. I've only done my duty. And I shall continue to love you both from a distance. Good-bye, good-bye, I'm off, I'm going, good-bye."

Nahum said good-bye, but he did not go. Instead he sank down, exhausted, on the camp bed at Bruria's feet. He began weeping softly. She placed a comforting hand on his shoulder. The room was filled with a pale, sickly light from the unshaded yellow bulb. A sheaf of blank forms lay on the top of a steel filing cabinet in the corner of the room. Here and there pieces of women's clothing were scattered; perhaps underwear, too; Nahum did not dare to look, just buried his head in Bruria's lap and rubbed his burning cheek. She stroked his hair, staring into space and saying over and over again, "That's enough, enough, enough."

The first sounds came unexpectedly, as if prematurely. Bruria had anticipated a thundering salvo, but the battle opened with tentative, stammering shots, cautious and very soft.

"The orchestra is tuning up. Soon it will start," said Nahum.

"Relax," said Bruria, "relax, little baby. You may put your head in my lap as long as you're quiet and don't talk and don't cry any more. You baby. You don't understand anything, anything at all. And what you say is all nonsense. They won't bring Itcheh back to this camp at all. They'll take him straight to the hospital, you won't have a chance. The best surgeons are standing by at the hospital tonight. No sucking blood out of lungs through a rubber tube. They have an operating room, proper instruments, and they will save Itcheh a thousand times quicker and better than you could. You're just a little boy. You don't stand a chance. Stop making me laugh. Just your head, I said, keep still, you're tickling me. Relax. Like that. Good boy. Quiet. Hush. And don't touch me. Let me see your hand. You little fledgling. Maybe Itcheh will take you along on a mission some time, and you can save each other to your hearts' content, because I've had enough now, I've had enough of all of you and I don't care what happens, I just want the time to pass. Put your glasses on the table. Yes. Now I can touch you. Relax. I'll sing you a lullaby. I can persuade Itcheh to take you on the next mission. He'll even make a combat orderly out of you. When Itcheh recovers from the wound in his throat I'll tell him that you were a good boy and you didn't want him to die and you even wanted to save his life. I shall tell him that you didn't say anything and you just lay quietly. Yes. Like this."

The big damp stains on the ceiling were like shadowy monsters. At intervals a little mouse scuttled across the room, hid between the cracks in the tiles, and then appeared again from an unexpected corner. Bruria took off her sandal and threw it at the mouse; she missed. At that moment the ominous distant sounds were renewed. Long bursts of machine-gun fire split the silence. A mortar broke into a thick, angry cough. Sounds like thunder rolled in the darkness outside.

Nahum said: "I can breathe into his lungs quickly and violently, blow him up, burst him. I can pull out the rubber tube and he'll turn blue again and suffocate. But I won't do either of those things. I'll save him if you'll just stop insulting me. And don't sing me to sleep, I mustn't sleep now, I must be ready at any moment to run to the clinic and carry out the operation and save him for you. And don't push me; I'm stronger than you. It will be a gift, and I've earned my reward by saving his life and bringing him back to you alive."

Now the long-range artillery was heard. The enemy batteries on the mountain slopes started shelling the settlements close to the border and lighting up the sky with tracer shells. The demolition squads obliterated Dar an-Nashef house by house, while the spearhead units were still burning out obstinate pockets of resistance. The thunder of the guns tore apart Nahum's pleading. "You'll be the death of me," said Bruria. She groaned and gave in. The young man streamed with sweat and his eyes rolled up. She stretched out her hands to her sides as if awaiting crucifixion and said, "At least get it over with quickly." As it turned out, these words were not necessary.

The frantic sound of automatic fire was scattered in all directions. Dim, faraway salvos echoed in the background. A violent explosion drowned the bursts of machine-gun fire. Gradually the sounds of the battle settled into some secret rhythm; wave upon wave of humble, diffident queries, and thick, hoarse crashes in reply. The strident wail of strings swallowed by the dizzy boom of percussion. At last this rhythm was broken, too. A glittering cataract of blazing sound rose up and roared to the dark horizons. Then the final spasmodic bursts, until they, too, died away. Silence came and pieced together the fragments with gentle, merciful patience. The orderly left the room without another word and hurried to the clinic to prepare the operating instruments that were kept in a sterile pack for use in emergency. The stillness of the night descended on the plain. Soon the crickets and the jackal packs returned to their evil ways.

5

OUR COMMANDER said: "That was sharp and to the point. Just like in the training manuals. No problems. No obstacles. Neat as a Bach fugue. Run along now, girls, and open up a bottle of arak for the maestro."

Parched, dirty, and overflowing with husky elation, Itcheh began shooting off joyful bursts of gunfire into the sky.

"Got it!" he roared. "Got mutton, potatoes, arak, everything we need, and no more Dar-bloody-Nashef! There's not a cat left there! No cat, not even a dog! Not one son-of-a-bitch is left! Where's that whore Bruria, where is she! And all the p-r-r-retty girls, where are they!"

He suddenly stopped roaring when the orderlies dragged the corpse of Yonich off the tailboard of the truck and carried it to the lighted clinic. The body was wrapped in a dirty blanket, but Nahum turned it up for a moment and saw that the eyes were wide open in hurt surprise as if they had made a fool of him again. Even his strange smile seemed to have softened. The smiling half of his face had not relaxed, but the other half had conformed to it. Nahum turned to Itcheh.

"What have you done to Yonich?"

"Why are you looking at me, why me?" cried Itcheh self-righteously. "His name was written on the first bullet. He was killed before things even got started. A volley missed me by a couple of yards, and he was standing in the way." As he spoke, Itcheh began stripping off his belt and weapons and equipment, pulled off his crumpled shirt, and asked quietly, "Where is she, where is she hiding?"

"How should I know?" said Nahum.

"Then go and find her for me and bring her here. You've got five minutes," commanded Itcheh hoarsely and wearily. "And before you do that, get me a drink of water."

Nahum obeyed.

He poured a cup of water, handed it to Itcheh, waited till it was empty, refilled it, waited again, then rinsed the cup in the sink and ran off to look for Bruria.

Almost without hesitation he went to the place where the shadows were darkest, behind the storehouses on the hillside. There he saw Bruria, leaning against the wall. The buttons of her blouse were open, one breast protruded from her brassiere, and Rosenthal, the operations officer, was holding the nipple between two fingers and whispering playfully. But she was not laughing or moving. She stood there as if asleep on her feet or as if all was lost and there was no purpose left. This sight filled Nahum with a silent, heartrending anguish. He did not know why; he knew only that it was all a mistake, all of it, from beginning to end. He turned and went back to Itcheh.

"She isn't here at all," he lied. "She's gone away. The two of them were seen going off in a jeep before you got back. She isn't here."

"OK," said Itcheh very slowly. "I see. He's taken her with him to Jerusalem. She could at least have waited to see if I'd been killed or not."

Nahum trembled and said nothing.

"Come on, pal," Itcheh went on, "come on. Let's find ourselves a jeep. Have you got a cigarette you can spare? No? Never mind. We'll go after them. How long ago were they seen going out? An hour? Half an hour? We'll catch them this side of the Hartuv turn. One crisis after another tonight. Come on, get in, let's go. Pity it's so late. Rosenthal can start hanging a white flag on his jeep. What did you say? I thought you said something. Come on, let's get after them. No time for coffee. Pity about that little guy. He just went out there and got himself killed. Pointless. Next time I'm not taking anyone who isn't essential. The man who makes jokes about death is a bastard, the man who doesn't is a bigger bastard. Say something. Well? Nothing to say? Talk. Say something. At least tell me what your name is. I've forgotten your name. I know you work in the store, but just now I've forgotten your name. I'm tired. Hey, look how fast we're going. A hundred and twenty, a hundred and thirty, at least. And we're not even at top speed yet."

The night road was deserted and cheerless. Far away, on the slopes of the eastern mountains, the night sky reflected the dying flames of the ruined enemy village. And in the irrigation channels of the orchards the black water flowed noiselessly and was swallowed up in the soil of the plain.

6

NAHUM LEANED back in the worn seat of the jeep and turned to look at Itcheh. He saw only a mane of hair and a thick beard. For a moment he was reminded of his Bible classes and the prophet Elijah, wild and jealous, slaughtering the prophets of Baal on the slopes of Carmel. He, too, figured in Nahum's imagination, as a faceless giant, all beard and mane. Itcheh controlled the vehicle with sleepy violence, one hand on the wheel and the other resting wearily on his knee. His heavy body leaned forward, like that of a rider clutching at his horse's neck. Is it really possible that he secretly suffers from bad eyesight? The jeep tore up the road, zigzagging, screeching, and whining. Stormy gusts of wind slapped their faces with blasts of intoxicating scents from the orchards.

One after another the lights of the villages along the Coastal Plain slipped away and were hidden, hastily fleeing behind the backs of the travelers. Here and there were civilians who had left their beds and gathered beneath a lamp in the main street of their sleepy settlements, exchanging speculations and waiting for the light of the approaching day and the early-morning news broadcast, to discover the meaning of the noises in the night and of the fire reflected in the sky. Itcheh and Nahum did not pause to give explanations, nor did they slacken their speed. Once, at a dark road junction, Itcheh braked sharply at the sight of a suspicious figure standing at the roadside, wrapped in an overcoat or a blanket, as if lying in wait. Itcheh picked up the submachine gun that lay at Nahum's feet and swung the muzzle toward the figure. "What's up?" he demanded. The headlamps picked out a young man, a rabbinical student, dressed all in black. Only his face and his socks were white. The student wore spectacles and looked helpless. He gabbled something in Yiddish, and Nahum was surprised to hear Itcheh answer him in Yiddish, patiently and quietly. Then the man blessed them and they went on their way. The jeep sprang into motion, raced across the curve of the road and onward, to the edge of the incline, toward the hills of Jerusalem.

They met no one else that night.

Itcheh did not speak, and Nahum asked no questions. Quiet joy and secret longing filled his heart. He knew the truth and Itcheh did not. Itcheh was driving the jeep like a madman and he was driving Itcheh. The road began to twist. The willing jeep attacked the curves furiously, with squeals of burning hatred. Nahum asked softly:

"What kind of a man are you, Itcheh, what are you really made of?"

The sharp wind swallowed his words. Itcheh must have heard something else, for he answered a quite different question:

"From Rumania. I was born in a place very near Bucharest. You could even say it was a suburb of Bucharest. In the war we escaped to Russia and got split up there. Some died, some disappeared, and a few went back afterward to Rumania. My little sister and I traveled across Poland and Austria to northern Italy, and then Youth Aliya came and took us from there to Israel, to the young people's training farm run by the religious movement. We grew up there. There are still one or two of the family living somewhere in Russia, but I've no idea where. Not that it matters to me now."

"I suppose you'll be a professional soldier," said Nahum. "In ten years you'll be a colonel at least. And then a great general."

Itcheh glanced at the orderly in surprise.

"Not likely! In another year or so I shall be discharged. I'm saving up to buy a share in the bus cooperative, and I've got a good chance of playing center-forward for Petah-Tikva. Not now. Some time. I've still got a lot to learn. It may be there'll be professional soccer in this country one day, and then I'll be in the pink. I'll marry off my sister and live like a human being at last."

"And you haven't lived like a human being up to now?"

"Like a dog," said Itcheh with weary anger.

"Tell me, what were you saying in Yiddish to that guy?"

"I asked him what the matter was. He said he'd heard shots and was scared. I told him the Arabs should be scared, these days it isn't the Jews who need to be scared of gunfire at night. And I took half a pack of cigarettes off him in exchange for my sermon. Do you want one? No? We'll catch them this side of Castel and take care of that Rosenthal once and for all. We'll take Bruria with us to Jerusalem. Do you know Jerusalem? Will we find a cafe open before morning?"

"It's a dead city," said Nahum. "Everything's dead in Jerusalem at night. In the daytime, too, for that matter. Anyway, we won't catch them at Castel or anywhere else if we don't go faster. A lot faster. Rosenthal will take her to his house and straight into his bed, and we'll be standing like a pair of idiots in the dark in the middle of Jerusalem, not knowing which way to go. We'll look like Laurel and Hardy! So step on it, Itcheh, faster, fast as you can, step on it!"

Itcheh hit the accelerator furiously. The engine gathered up its last reserves of strength. The speed intensified, sullen, brooding, whining, roaring. And Nahum was filled with dread and longing. He knew where Bruria was now, and where the bastard Rosenthal was, and Itcheh did not know. He was making the mighty Itcheh race along the road in the night on a fool's errand, and Itcheh did not know. Even now he was savoring the scent of her skin, the scent of strong plain soap, and the taste of her fingers on his neck, and Itcheh did not know. He put his hand into the pocket of his shirt and fingered the instruments, the sterilized lancet, the bandages, the vial of morphine, the rubber tube, all that would be necessary for an emergency operation when the jeep plunged into a crevice at the side of the mountain road. This, too, was something Itcheh did not know and could not know. Here at his right hand sat the man who would save his life in a little while. A grim and demanding assignment, which Nahum would fulfill, to perfection. An unknown orderly has performed an operation at night by flashlight and has saved the life of a national hero. Resourcefulness. Dedication. Cool nerves. Comradeship. Expertise. Also — in a whisper, a movement of the lips without sound — love, too.

Then one of the headlights suddenly went out: it flickered a few times, hesitated, gave in, and went dark. Still the jeep galloped eastward by the light of one blazing Cyclops' eye that stunned the shadows in the hills. Like a phantom the jeep raced on, spurred to ever greater efforts at Itcheh's hands; he was hunched over the wheel, biting his lips and ramming the accelerator down to the floor hard. He will be seriously injured, Bruria, critically injured, but I won't let him die. I'll operate and I'll bandage him with devotion, and I'll disregard my own injuries. You will owe his life to me, and I shall go away humbly. Itcheh is just an ignorant, overgrown bear cub: he knows nothing, understands nothing. Listen: he's started humming to himself; he has no idea what's going to happen to him in a moment.

Perhaps Itcheh remembered the pale student whom they had met on the way up from the plain and his Yiddish entreaties. Perhaps he remembered other places and other times. He was intoning a melancholy song to himself:

> *"Our Father, our King, have mercy and hear us,*
> *For we can do no-o-thing.*
> *Show us ki-indness and grace,*
> *And sa-ave u-us . . ."*

"Amen," whispered Nahum Hirsch fervently. And his eyes filled with tears.

Near the Shaar-Hagay junction, where the Jerusalem road touches enemy territory in the Latrun salient, the travelers were struck by a blast of cold air: the air of Jerusalem, chilling and full of the fragrance of pine. The engine began to groan, coughed hoarsely a few times, spluttered, and fell silent, silent as the lifeless things of which the night is full.

7

ITCHEH ROSE from his seat, heavy and weary, and opened the hood. Nahum took out the pocket light that was to have been used for the emergency operation and trained it on the interior of the engine. He watched Itcheh grappling with the sparkplugs, blindly pulling and pushing, angrily thumping the metal panels with his fist, tightening a screw with strong fingernails, tugging at wires mercilessly, perhaps aimlessly. This only added to the insolence of the engine. Suddenly, without warning, the other headlight gave out, and the machine went dead. Itcheh snatched the torch from Nahum and hurled it with a wild gesture into the rocks at the side of the road.

"Screw everything," he said.

Nahum nodded his head as if to say: Yes, of course, absolutely. But now total darkness had descended on them, and Itcheh could not have seen this movement. Nahum used up match after flickering match. With the last match they both lit cigarettes from the pack that Itcheh had taken from the student on the way.

First Itcheh cursed the engine, then Nahum, Bruria, women in general, heaven and earth. Most of the curses were Russian and ruthless, some were Arabic. Itcheh cursed the Arabs, too, long and hard, Finally he cursed himself. Then he fell silent. His voice was hoarse from all the shouting he had done before the raid, during the battle, and after the return to camp. Now all he could manage was a pathetic, desperate croak. He settled himself on the hood of the dead jeep like a hairy mountain. And he lay there without sound or movement.

Then, when the eyes of both men had begun to adjust a little to the clinging darkness, Itcheh picked out a dark, brooding mass across the border near Latrun: the dim, straggling profile of the Trappist monastery, beyond the ceasefire line, on enemy soil.

"That's a building," Itcheh croaked faintly.

"It's a monastery," explained Nahum brightly. A burning desire to teach suddenly filled his heart. He was wide awake, far from all weariness, feverish. "It's the Trappist monastery. The monks have taken a vow to be silent forever. Till the day they die."

"Why is that?" asked Itcheh in a whisper.

"Because words are the root of sin. Without words there are no lies. It's simple, isn't it. They live there cheek by jowl and never exchange a word among themselves. Imagine what a divine silence that must be. Whoever wishes to join must take a vow. It's like an army. You swear an oath of silence."

"I can't understand it," croaked Itcheh.

"Of course you can't understand. All you can do is destroy a village without knowing anything about its people or its history, without wanting to know. Just like that. Like a mad bull. Of course you don't understand. What do you understand? Fucking and killing, that's what you understand. And soccer. And shares in the bus cooperative. You're a wild animal, not a human being. A wild, stupid animal. They're deceiving you all the time. Rosenthal fucks Bruria, so do the officers, the MPs, even someone like me. Do you think she's in Rosenthal's jeep on the way to Jerusalem? Is that what you think? Because you're a wild animal, not a human being, that's why you think they're all exactly like you. They aren't all like you. They don't all trample and kill everything that moves. The opposite. They're all laughing at you. Rosenthal is fucking Bruria for you, and he's fucking you, too. I fucked her, and now I've fucked you, too. Why did you run like a madman, tell me? Why did you grab a jeep and a submachine gun and me, and start running like a bull on the rampage? I'll tell you why. Because you're not a human being, that's why. Because you're a stupid wild animal. That's why."

Itcheh said with what was left of his voice, "Tell me more about the monastery."

Nahum Hirsch, the thin and bespectacled medical orderly, lifted his knee and rested the sole of his boot on the wheel of the jeep. He smoked and felt power throbbing in his veins like wine.

"'The dust of dead words has clung to you. Purify your soul with silence.' Rabindranath Tagore wrote that, the Indian poet and philosopher. Now, of course, I shall have to start at the beginning and explain to you what a poet is and what a philosopher is and what an Indian is. But who's got the time and patience to make a human being out of you? It's a waste of words. Anyway, it won't help you. Very well, then. Latrun takes its name from a fortress that stood here in the Middle Ages. The Crusaders built a fortress here to control the most convenient route from the Coastal Plain to Jerusalem — the Bet Horon road, that is. Latrun is a corruption of the name of that fortress: Le Touron des Chevaliers — The Tower of the Knights. *Touron* means tower. Like tour. La Tour Eiffel. There's a tower in chess, too. We call it *tora*. Are you asleep yet? Is that too much for one lesson? No? There are some scholars who claim another source, an even older one, for the name Latrun: Castellum Boni Latronis, meaning the castle of the good thief who was crucified with Jesus of Nazareth. Have you ever heard of the Crucifixion, of Jesus, the good thief? Have you ever read a book in your life? Answer me. What's the matter with you? Don't you feel well? Answer me!"

Itcheh said nothing.

The lights of faraway settlements twinkled in the darkness. The enemy outposts in Latrun, where news of the destruction of Dar an-Nashef must have arrived by now, pointed spasmodic searchlight beams at the thick woods that grew on the slopes of the Judean hills. A single shot, derisory almost, rolled between the hills and set up a long echo.

"Hey, isn't it a bit dangerous to stay here like this all night?" asked Nahum, suddenly afraid.

Itcheh said nothing.

"Tell me, isn't this too dangerous? Should we start walking? Maybe there's a settlement or a kibbutz somewhere around here."

Itcheh turned his bearded face for a moment, glanced at Nahum Hirsch, and looked away. He did not speak. Nahum urinated behind the jeep. Suddenly he was scared, afraid of being separated from Itcheh in the dark. He said in a clear voice, grinding his teeth, "What a lump of shit I am! What a miserable bastard!"

Itcheh said nothing.

Then came the first signs of the approaching day, softening the dark masses and sharpening the edges. There was a glimmer of light in the east, like a halo, like a dream of grace. If there are such things as mercy or grace, thought Nahum, that is their color. Bruria will go to the shower to wash away the sweat and the tears, and then she'll sleep. They will bury Yonich — or, as they like to say — they'll lay him to rest. If only there were a little rest for someone like me. If only there were rest for Itcheh; he's tired to death now. After all, everybody needs rest. If only a little. I can't take any more of this. I need silence.

Suddenly the voices of the jackals rose in triumph on every side. From enemy territory the voices came, piercing the steep wadis and spreading over the plains of the beleaguered land. The enemy searchlights moved back and forth haphazardly, sullenly. Now the light swept down the road and passed the dead jeep and the two lost soldiers, now it stopped and retraced its steps to search among the thorns and bushes. A little night predator was caught in the shaft of light. He froze, stunned, his hide bristling. His mangy fur quivered with mortal terror. A moment later he darted off and fled into the depths of the darkness.

But soon the darkness betrayed those who had made it their refuge, fading gradually from the peaks of the eastern hills, the lands of the enemy.

1962

Strange Fire

Night spread his wings over the peoples of the world. Nature spun her yarn and breathed with every turn of the wheel. Creation has ears, but in her the sense of hearing and that which she hears are one thing, not two. The beasts of the forest stir and search for prey and the beasts of the farm stand at the manger. Man returns home from his labor. But as soon as man leaves his work, love and sin are digging his grave. God swore to create a world and to fill the world. And flesh shall draw near to flesh . . .

— *Berdichevski,* Hiding in the Thunder

1

AT FIRST THE two old men walked without exchanging words.

On leaving the brightly lit and overheated clubroom they helped each other on with their overcoats. Yosef Yarden maintained a dogged silence, while Dr. Kleinberger let out a long series of throaty coughs and finally sneezed. The speaker's words had left them both in a state of depression: All this leads nowhere. Nothing ever comes out of these discussions. Nothing practical.

An air of weariness and futility hung over the sparsely attended meetings of the moderate Center Party, of which the two friends had both been members for many years. Nothing will ever come of these meetings. Precipitate action is dragging the whole of the nation into an orgy of arrogant affluence. The voice of reason, the voice of moderation, the voice of common sense, is not heard and cannot be heard in the midst of this jubilation. What are they to do, the few men of sense, no longer young, the advocates of moderate and sober statesmanship, who have seen before in their lifetime the fruits of political euphoria in all its various forms? A handful of men of education and good sense cannot hope to put a stop to the intoxication of the masses and their jubilant, lightheaded leaders, all of them skipping with yells of triumph toward the abyss.

After some thirty paces, at the point where the side street opened into one of the majestic and tranquil boulevards of the suburb of Rehavia, Yosef Yarden stopped, thus causing Dr. Kleinberger to stop as well without knowing why. Yosef Yarden fumbled for a cigarette and, after some difficulty, found one. Dr. Kleinberger hastened to offer his friend a light. Still they had not exchanged a single word. With delicate fingers they shielded the little flame from the wind. Autumn winds in Jerusalem blow strongly, ferociously. Yosef thanked his companion with a nod of his head and inhaled smoke. But three paces farther on, the cigarette went out, for it had not been properly lit. Angrily he threw it down on the sidewalk and crushed it with the heel of his shoe. Then he thought better of it, picked up the crumpled cigarette, and tossed it into a trash can that the municipality of Jerusalem had placed on the iron pole of a bus stop.

"Degeneracy," he said.

"Well, really, I ask you," replied Dr. Kleinberger, "is that not a simplistic, almost vulgar definition for a reality that is by definition complex?"

"Degeneracy and arrogance, too," insisted Yosef Yarden.

"You know as well as anyone, my dear Yosef, that a simplistic definition is a form of surrender."

"I'm sick of this," said Yosef Yarden, adjusting his scarf and the collar of his coat against the freezing daggers of the wind. "I'm sick of all this. From now on I shall not mince words. Disease is disease, and degeneracy is degeneracy."

Dr. Kleinberger passed his tongue over lips that were always cracked in winter; his eyes closed like the embrasures of a tank as he commented:

"Degeneracy is a complex phenomenon, Yosef. Without degeneracy there is no meaning to the word 'purity.' There is a cycle at work here, some kind of eternal wheel, and this was well understood by our Sages when they spoke of the evil side of human nature, and also, on the other hand, by the Fathers of the Christian Church: apparently degeneracy and purity are absolute opposites, whereas in fact one draws the other out, one makes the other possible and makes it flourish, and this is what we must hope for and trust in in this decadent age."

An arrogant wind, sharp and chilly, blew in the streets of Rehavia. The street lamps gave out an intermittent yellowish light. Some of them had been smashed by vandals and hung blind on top of their posts. Birds of the night had nested in these ruined lamps.

The founders of the Rehavia quarter planted trees and laid out gardens and avenues, for it was their intention to create amid the sun-bleached rocks of Jerusalem a pleasant and shady suburb where the piano might be heard all day and the violin or the cello at nightfall. The whole neighborhood basks beneath a cluster of treetops. All day the little houses stand sleepily on the bed of a lake of shadow. But at night dim creatures roost in the foliage and flap their wings in the darkness, uttering despairing cries. They are not so easy to hit as the street lamps; the stones miss their mark and are lost in the gloom, and the treetops whisper in secret derision.

And surely even these opposites are not simple but complex; in fact, one draws the other out and one cannot exist without the other, et cetera, et cetera. Dr. Elhanan Kleinberger, a bachelor, is an Egyptologist with a modest reputation, particularly in the European state from which he escaped by the skin of his teeth some thirty years ago. Both his life and his views bear the mark of a brilliant stoicism. Yosef Yarden, an expert in the deciphering of ancient Hebrew manuscripts, is a widower who is shortly to marry off his eldest son, Yair, to a girl named Dinah Dannenberg, the daughter of an old friend. As for the birds of the night, they roost in the heart of the suburb, but the first fingers of light drive them away every morning to their hiding places in the rocks and woods outside the city.

The two elderly men continued their stroll without finding anything further to add to the harsh words they had heard and spoken before. They passed by the Prime Minister's office on the corner of Ibn Gabirol Street and Keren Kayemet Street, passed the buildings of the secondary school, and paused at the corner of Ussishkin Street. This crossroads is open to the west and exposed to the blasts of cold wind blowing in from the stony fields. Here Yosef Yarden took out another cigarette, and again Dr. Kleinberger gave him a light and shielded it with both his hands like a sailor: this time it would not go out.

"Well, next month we shall all be dancing at the wedding," said the doctor playfully.

"I'm on my way now to see Lily Dannenberg. We have to sit down and draw up a list of guests," said Yosef Yarden. "It will be a short list. His mother, may she rest in peace, always wanted our son to be married quietly, without a great show, and so it will be. Just a modest family ceremony. You will be there, of course, but, then, to us you are like a member of the family. There's no question about that."

Dr. Kleinberger took off his glasses, breathed on them, wiped them with a handkerchief, and slowly replaced them.

"Yes. Of course. But the Dannenberg woman will not agree to that. Better not deceive yourself. She's certain to want her daughter's wedding to be a spectacular event, and the whole of Jerusalem will be invited to bow down and wonder. You will have to give in and do as she wishes."

"It isn't that easy to make me change my mind," replied Yosef Yarden. "Especially in a case where the wishes of my late wife are involved. Mrs. Dannenberg is a sensitive lady, and she is certainly aware of personal considerations."

As Yosef Yarden said that it would not be easy to make him change his mind, he began inadvertently to squeeze the cigarette between his fingers. Bent and crushed, the cigarette still did not go out but continued to flicker. Dr. Kleinberger concluded:

"You're mistaken, my friend. The Dannenberg woman will not do without the big spectacle. Certainly she's a sensitive lady, as you so admirably express it, but she's also an obstinate lady. There is no contradiction between these two qualities. And you had better prepare yourself for a very tough argument. A vulgar argument."

A mutual acquaintance, or perhaps one whose silhouette reminded the two friends of a mutual acquaintance, passed by the street corner. Both put their hands to their hats, and the stranger did the same but pressed on without stopping, hurrying, head bowed, against the wind. And he vanished in the darkness. Then a hooligan roared past on a motorcycle, shattering the peace of Rehavia.

"It's outrageous!" fumed Yosef Yarden. "That dirty gangster deliberately opened up his throttle, just to disturb the peace of ten thousand citizens. And why? Simply because he's not quite sure that he's real, that he exists, and this buffoonery gives him an inflated sense of importance: everybody can hear him. The professors. The President and the Prime Minister. The artists. The girls. This madness must be stopped before it's too late. Stopped forcibly."

Dr. Kleinberger was in no hurry to reply. He pondered these words, turning them this way and that during a long moment of silence. Finally he commented:

"First, it's already too late."

"I don't hold with such resignation. And second?"

"Second — yes, there is a second point, and please pardon my frankness — second, you're exaggerating. As always."

"I'm not exaggerating," said Yosef Yarden, teeth clenched in suppressed hatred. "I'm not exaggerating. I'm just calling the child by his name. That's all. I've got the cigarettes and you've got the matches, so we're tied to each other. A light, please. Thank you. A child should always be called by his name."

"But really, Yosef, my very dear friend, but really," drawled Dr. Kleinberger with forced didactic patience, "you know as well as I do that usually every child has more than one name. Now it's time to part. You must go to your son's future mother-in-law, and don't you be late or she'll scold you. She's a sensitive lady, no doubt about that, but she's hard as well. Call me tomorrow evening. We can finish that chess game that we left off in the middle. Good night. Take the matches with you. Yes. Don't mention it."

As the two elderly men began to go their separate ways, the children's shouts rose from the Valley of the Cross. Evidently the boys of the Youth Movement had gathered there to play games of hide-and-seek in the dark. Old olive trees make good hiding places. Sounds and scents rise from the valley and penetrate to the heart of the affluent suburb. From the olive trees some hidden current passes to the barren trees, which were planted by the landscape gardeners of Rehavia. The night birds are responsible for this current. The weight of responsibility infuses them with a sense of deadly seriousness, and they save their shrieking for a moment of danger or a moment of truth. In contrast, the olive trees are doomed to grow in perpetual silence.

2

MRS. LILY Dannenberg's house lies in one of the quiet side streets between the suburb of Rehavia and her younger and taller sister, the suburb of Kiryat Shemuel. The hooligan who shattered the peace of the entire city with his motorcycle did not disturb the peace of Mrs. Dannenberg, because she had no peace. She paced around the house, arranging and adjusting, then changing her mind and putting everything back in its original place. As if she really intended to sit at home and quietly wait for her guest. At nine-thirty Yosef means to come over to discuss with her the list of wedding invitations. This whole business can bear postponement; there is no need for haste. The visit, the wedding, and the list of guests, too. What's the hurry? In any case, he will arrive at nine-thirty precisely — you can count on him not to be a second late — but the door will be closed, the house empty and in darkness. Life is full of surprises. It's nice to imagine the look on his face — surprised, offended, shocked as well. And nice to guess what will be written on the note that he will certainly leave on my door. There are some people, and Yosef is one of them, who when they are surprised, offended, and shocked become almost likable. It's a sort of spiritual alchemy. He's a decent man, and he always anticipates what is good and fears what is not.

These thoughts were whispered in German. Lily Dannenberg switched on the reading lamp, her face cold and calm. She sat in an armchair and filed her fingernails. At two minutes to nine her manicure was complete. Without leaving her chair she switched on the radio. The day's reading from the Bible had already finished, and the news broadcast had not yet begun. Some sentimental, nauseatingly trite piece of music was repeated four or five times without variation. Lily turned the tuning knob and passed hurriedly over the guttural voices of the Near East, skipped over Athens without stopping, and reached Radio Vienna in time for the evening news summary in German. Then there was a broadcast of Beethoven's *Eroica*. She turned the radio off and went to the kitchen to make coffee.

What do I care if he's offended or shocked? Why should I care what happens to that man and his son? There are some emotions that the Hebrew language isn't sufficiently developed to express. If I say that to Yosef or his friend Kleinberger, the pair of them will attack me, and there'll be a terrific argument about the merits of the Hebrew language, with all kinds of unpleasant digressions. Even the word "digression" does not exist in Hebrew. I must drink this coffee without a single grain of sugar. Bitter, of course it's bitter, but it keeps me awake. Am I allowed one biscuit? No, I'm not allowed to eat biscuits, and there's no room for compromise. And it's already a quarter past nine. Let's go, before he appears. The stove. The light. The key. Let's go.

Lily Dannenberg is a forty-two-year-old divorcee. She could easily claim to be seven or eight years younger, but that would be contrary to her moral principles, so she does not disguise her true age. Her body is tall and thin, her hair naturally blond, not a rich tint but deep and dense. Her nose is straight and strong. On her lips there is a permanent and fascinating unease, and her eyes are bright blue. A single, modest ring seems to accentuate the lonely and pensive quality of her long fingers.

Dinah won't be back from Tel Aviv before twelve. I've left her a little coffee in the pot for tomorrow morning. There's salad in the fridge and fresh bread in the basket. If the girl decides to have a bath at midnight, the water will still be hot. So everything is in order. And if everything's in order, why am I uneasy, as if I've left something burning or open? But nothing is burning and nothing's open and already I'm two streets away heading west, so that man Yosef isn't likely to meet me by chance on his way to the house. That would spoil everything. Most young Levantines are very attractive at first glance. But only a few of them stand up to a second look. A great spirit is always struggling and tormented, and this distorts the body from within and corrodes the face like a rainstorm eating limestone. That is why people of spiritual greatness have something written on their faces, sometimes in letters that re-

semble scars, and usually they find it hard to keep their bodies upright. By contrast, the handsome Levantines do not know the taste
of suffering, and that is why their faces are symmetrical, their bodies strong and well proportioned. Twenty-two minutes after nine.
An owl just said something complicated and raucous. That bird is
called *Eule* in German, and in Hebrew, I think, *yanshuf.* Anyway,
what difference does it make? In exactly seven minutes, Yosef will
ring the doorbell of my house. His punctuality is beyond doubt. At
that precise moment I shall ring the doorbell of his house on Alfasi
Street. Shut up, *Eule,* I've heard everything you have to say more
than once. And Yair will open the door to me.

3

A PERSON who comes from a broken home is likely to destroy the
stability of other people's homes. There is nothing fortuitous about
this, although there is no way of formulating a rule. Yosef Yarden is
a widower. Lily Dannenberg is a divorcee whose ex-husband died
of a broken heart, or jaundice, less than three months after the di-
vorce. Even Dr. Kleinberger, Egyptologist and stoic, a marginal figure, is an aging bachelor. Needless to say, he has no children. That
leaves Yair Yarden and Dinah Dannenberg. Dinah has gone to Tel
Aviv to pass the good news along to her relatives and to make a few
purchases and arrangements, and she will not be back before midnight. As for Yair, he is sitting with his brother, a grammar-school
student, in the pleasant living room of the Yarden household on
Alfasi Street. He has decided to spend the evening grappling with
a backlog of university work: three exercises, a tedious project, a
whole mountain of bibliographical chores. Studying political economy may be important and profitable, but it can also be wearisome
and depressing. If he had been able to choose, he might have chosen to study the Far East, China, Japan, mysterious Tibet, or perhaps Latin America. Rio. The Incas. Or black Africa. But what

could a young man do with studies such as these? Build himself an igloo, marry a geisha? The trouble is that political economy is full of functions and calculations, words and figures that seem to disintegrate when you stare at them. Dinah is in Tel Aviv. When she comes back, perhaps she'll forget that unnecessary quarrel that we had yesterday. Those things I said to her face. On the other hand, she started it. Dad has gone to see her mother, and he won't be back before eleven. If only there was some way of persuading Uri to stop sitting there picking his nose. How disgusting. There's a mystery program on the radio at a quarter past nine called *Treasure Hunt,* broadcast live. That's the solution for an uncomfortable evening like this. We'll listen to the program and then finish the third exercise. That should be enough.

The brothers switched on the radio.

The antics of the night birds do not abate until a quarter past nine. Even before the twilight is over, the owls and the other birds of darkness begin to move from the suburbs to the heart of the city. With their glassy dead eyes they stare at the birds of light, who rejoice with carefree song at the onset of the day's last radiance. To the ears of the night birds, this sounds like utter madness, a festival of fools. On the edge of the suburb of Rehavia, where the farthest houses clutch at the rocks of the western slope, the rising birds meet the descending birds. In the light that is neither day nor night the two camps move past each other in opposite directions. No compromise ever lasts long in Jerusalem, and so the evening twilight flickers and fades rapidly, too. Darkness comes. The sun has fled, and the rear-guard forces are already in retreat.

At nine-thirty, Lily had meant to ring the doorbell of the Yardens' house. But at the corner of Radak Street she saw a cat standing on a stone wall. His tail was swishing, and he was whining with lust. Lily decided to waste a few moments observing the feverish cat. Meanwhile the brothers were listening to the start of the mystery program. The first clue was given to the studio panel and the listeners by a jovial fellow; the beginning of the thread was contained in a song by Bialik:

> *Not by day and not by night*
> *Quietly I set out and walk;*
> *Not on the hill or in the vale,*
> *Where stands an old acacia tree...*

And at once Yair and Uri were on fire with detective zeal. An old acacia tree, that's the vital point. Not on the hill or in the vale, that's where it starts getting complicated. Yair had a bright idea: Maybe we should look the poem up in the big book of Bialik's poetry and find the context, then we'll know which way to turn. He pounced on the bookcase, rummaged around, found the book, and within three minutes had located the very poem. However, the lines that followed did not solve the puzzle, but only tantalized the hunters still further:

> *The acacia solves mysteries*
> *And tells what lies ahead...*

Yes. I see. But if the acacia itself is the mystery, how can it be expected to solve mysteries and even tell the future? How does it go on? The next stanza is irrelevant. The whole poem's irrelevant. Bialik's no use. We must try a different approach. Let's think, now. I've got it: the Hebrew word *shita* isn't only the name of a tree. It also means "method." *Shita* is a system. These inquiries would do credit to that buffoon Kleinberger. Well, then, let's think some more. Shut up, Uri, I'm trying to think. Well, my dear Watson, tell me what you make of the first words. I mean "Not by day and not by night." Don't you understand anything? Of course you don't. Think for a while. Incidentally, I don't understand it yet, either. But give me a moment, and you'll see.

The doorbell rang.

An unexpected guest stood in the doorway. Her face was set, her lips nervous. She was a weird and beautiful woman.

An alley cat is a fickle creature; he will abandon anything for the caress of a human hand. Even at the height of rutting fever he will not turn away from the caress of a human hand. When Lily touched him, he began to shudder. With her left hand she stroked his back firmly, while the fingers of her right hand gently tickled the fur of his neck. Her combination of tenderness and strength filled the animal with pleasure. The cat turned over on his back and offered his stomach to the gentle fingers, purring loudly and contentedly. Lily tickled him as she spoke.

"You're happy. Now you're happy. Don't deny it, you're happy," she said in German. The cat narrowed his eyes until two slits were all that was left, and continued purring.

"Relax," she said, "you don't need to do anything. Just enjoy yourself."

The fur was soft and warm. Thin vibrations passed through it and ceased. Lily rubbed her ring against the cat's ear.

"And what's more, you're stupid as well."

Suddenly the cat shuddered and stirred uneasily. Perhaps he guessed or half-sensed what was coming. A yellow slit opened in his face, the wink of an eye, a fleeting glimmer. Then her fist rose, made a wide sweep in the air, and struck a violent blow at the belly of the cat. The creature took fright and leapt away into the darkness, collided with the trunk of a pine tree, and dug in his claws. From the murky height he hissed at her like a snake. All his fur stood on end. Lily turned and walked to the Yardens' house.

"Good evening, Yair. It seems you're free. And on your own."

"Uri is here and we . . . but isn't Dad on his way to see you?"

"Uri here, too. I'd forgotten about Uri. Good evening, Uri. How you've grown! I'm sure all the girls must be chasing you. No, you needn't invite me inside. I just came to get something straight with you, Yair. I didn't mean to intrude."

"But Mrs. . . . but Lily, how can you say that. You're always welcome. Come in. I was so sure that just now you'd be at your house drinking coffee with Dad, and suddenly . . ."

"Suddenly your dad will find the door locked and the windows dark, and he won't understand what's become of me. He's disappointed and worried—which makes him look almost agreeable. Pity I'm not there among the trees in the garden, secretly watching him, enjoying the expression on his face. It doesn't matter. I'll explain everything. Come on, Yair, let's go out, let's go for a little walk outside, there's something I need to straighten out with you. Yes. This very evening. Be patient."

"What . . . Has something happened? Didn't Dinah go to Tel Aviv, or . . ."

"She went like a good little girl, and she'll come back like a good little girl. But not until later. Come on, Yair. You won't need your coat. It isn't cold outside. It's pleasant outside. You'll have to excuse us, Uri. How you've grown! Good night."

In the yard, near the pepper tree, she spoke to Yair again: "Don't look so puzzled. Nothing serious has happened."

But Yair already knew that he had made a mistake. He should have brought his coat, in spite of what Lily had said. The evening was cold. And later it would be very cold. He could still excuse himself, go back, and fetch his coat. Lily herself was wearing a coat that was stylish, almost daring. But to go back to the house for a coat seemed to him somehow dishonorable, perhaps even cowardly. He put the thought aside and said:

"Yes. It's really pleasant out here."

Since she was in no hurry to reply, Yair had time to wonder if there really were acacia trees in Jerusalem, and if so, where, and if not, perhaps *shita* should be taken as a clue to the verb *leshatot*—"to jest." Who knows, maybe the treasure's hidden in one of the wadis to the west or the south of Rehavia. Pity about the program. Now I'll never know the solution.

4

AFTER A brief moment of astonishment and confusion and a few indecisive speculations, Yosef Yarden made up his mind to go to Dr. Kleinberger's house. If he found him at home he would go in, apologize for the lateness of the hour and the unexpected visit, and tell his friend about this strange incident. Who would have thought it? And just imagine the look she would have given me if I had been a few minutes late. And there I was, standing and waiting, ten o'clock already, two and a half minutes past. If something had happened to her, she would have phoned me. There's no way of understanding or explaining this.

"And for the time being you have avoided a vulgar and possibly painful argument," said Elhanan Kleinberger, smiling. "She wouldn't have given in to you over the guest list. She'll send invitations all over the city, all over the university. To the President of the State and the Mayor of Jerusalem. And really, Yosef, why should you expect her to give up what she wants in deference to what you want? Why shouldn't she invite the Pope and his wife to the wedding of her only daughter? What's the matter, Yosef?"

His guest began to explain, patiently:

"Times are not easy. In general, I mean. And remember, all these years we have been preaching, both in speech and in writing, the need to 'walk humbly.' Yair's mother wanted an intimate wedding, a small circle of relatives, and that is a kind of imperative, at least from the ethical point of view. And ... then there's the cost. I mean, who wants to go into debt for the sake of a society wedding?"

Dr. Kleinberger felt that he had lost the thread. He made coffee, set out milk and sugar. And at this point he also took the opportunity to add something to his previous remarks concerning the interplay of opposite extremes. The conversation soon diversified. They discussed Egyptology, they discussed Hebrew literature, they conducted a scathing inquiry into the workings of the municipality of Jerusalem. Elhanan Kleinberger has a great flair for linking together Egyptology, his professional field, and Hebrew literature, which is his heart's love, as he puts it, and of which he is a passionate lover, as he also puts it. In general, Yosef is used to having his views overruled by those of his friend, although he tends on most occasions to reject the particular wording adopted by Elhanan Kleinberger. So their arguments end with the last word going to Yosef Yarden and not to his old friend.

Were it not for the cold, the two friends would have gone out together to stand on the balcony and gaze at the starlight on the hills, as was their habit in summer. The Valley of the Cross lies opposite. There old olive trees grow in bitter tranquillity.

In passionate, almost violent hunger, the olive trees send out their tendrils into the blackness of the heavy earth. There the roots pierce the rocky subsoil, cleaving the hidden stones and sucking up the dark moisture. They are like sharpened claws. But above them the green and silver treetops are caressed by the wind: theirs is the peace and the glory.

And you cannot kill the olive. Olive trees burned in fire sprout and flourish again. A vulgar growth, quite shameless, Elhanan Kleinberger would say. Even olives struck by lightning are reborn and in time clothe themselves with new foliage. And they grow on the hills of Jerusalem, and on the modest heights on the fringes of the Coastal Plain, and they hide away in the cloisters of monasteries enclosed within walls of stone. There the olives thicken their knotted trunks generation after generation and lasciviously entwine their stout branches. They have a savage vitality like that of birds of prey.

To the north of Rehavia lie sprawling suburbs, poor neighborhoods with charming streets. In one of these winding alleyways stands an old olive tree. One hundred and seven years ago an iron gate was erected here and the lintel was supported by the tree. Over the years the tree leaned against the iron, and the iron bit deep into the trunk like a roasting spit.

Patiently the olive began to enfold the iron wedge. In the course of time it closed around it and set tight. The iron was crushed in the tree's embrace. The tree's wounds healed over, and the vigorous foliage of its upper branches was in no way impaired.

5

YAIR YARDEN is a young man of handsome appearance. He is not tall, but his shoulders are powerful and his torso is trim, well proportioned, and athletic. His chin is firm and angular, with a deep dimple. Girls secretly long to touch this dimple with their fingertips, and some of them even blush or turn pale when they feel the impulse. They say, "And what's more, he thinks he knows a thing or two. He's about as brainy as a tailor's dummy."

His arms are strong and covered in black hair. It would be wrong to say that Yair Yarden is clumsy, but there is a certain heaviness, a kind of slow solidity, perceptible in all his movements. Lily Dannenberg would have called this "massivity" and returned to her theme of the inadequacy of the Hebrew language, with its dearth of nuances. Of course, Elhanan Kleinberger is capable of refuting such barbed comments and of suggesting in the twinkling of an eye a suitable Hebrew adjective, or even two. And at the same time he will come up with a Hebrew expression to fit the word "nuance."

It may be that this fascinating "massivity" with which Yair Yarden is endowed will change within a few years into the patriarchal corpulence for which his father is noted. A sharp eye may detect the first signs. But at present — Lily has no intention of disguising the truth — at present, Yair is a handsome, captivating youth. The mustache gives a special force to his appearance. It is blond, droopy, sometimes flecked with shreds of tobacco. Yair is studying economics and business management at the university; his whole future lies before him. Romantic follies, kibbutzim, and life in border settlements hold no attraction for him. His political views are temperate; he has learned them from his father. To be precise, Yosef Yarden sees in the political situation a wasteland of degeneracy and arrogance, whereas Yair sees a wide-open prospect before him.

"Will you offer me a cigarette, please," said Lily.

"Of course. Here you are. Please take one, Lily."

"Oh, thank you. I left mine at home, I was in such a hurry."

"A light, Lily?"

"Thank you. Dinah Yarden — a name almost as musical as Dinah Dannenberg. Perhaps a little simpler. When you have a child you can call him Dan. Dan Yarden: like something out of a ballad about camels and bells. How much time are you going to give me, how long will it be, before you make me a grandmother? A year? A bit less? You needn't answer. It was a rhetorical question. Yair, how do you say 'rhetorical question' in Hebrew?"

"I don't know," said Yair.

"I wasn't asking you. It was a rhetorical question."

Yair began scratching the lobe of his ear uneasily. What's the matter with her? What's she up to? There's something about her that I don't like at all. She isn't being sincere. It's very hard to tell.

"Now you're searching for something to say and not finding it. It doesn't matter. Your manners are perfect, and for heaven's sake, you're not in front of a board of examiners."

"I wasn't thinking of you as a board of examiners, Lily. Not at all. I mean, I . . ."

"You're a very spontaneous boy. And quick and witty replies don't matter to me. What interests me is, rather, your . . . how shall I put it, your *esprit*." And she smiled in the dark.

Chance led them to the upper part of the suburb. They reached the center of Rehavia and turned north. A passerby, thin and bespectacled, definitely a student of extreme views and crossed in love, passed in front of them with a transistor radio in his hand.

Yair paused for a moment and turned his head, straining to catch a fragment of the fascinating program that Lily had interrupted. *Not on the hill or in the vale, where stands an old acacia tree.* Thanks to her he had gone out of the house without a coat, and now he was cold. He did not feel comfortable, either. And he had missed the climax of the program. Time to get to the point, and get it over with.

"Right," said Yair. "OK, Lily. Are you going to tell me what the problem is?"

"Problem?" She seemed surprised. "There's no problem. You and I are going for a stroll on a pleasant evening because Dinah has gone away and your father isn't at home. We are talking, exchanging views, getting to know each other. There are so many things to talk about. So many things that I don't know about you, and there may even be things that you would like to know about me."

"You said before" — Yair scratched his ear — "you said there was something that you —"

"Yes. It's just a formality and really quite unimportant. But I would like you to sort it out as soon as possible. Let's say tomorrow or the day after, at the latest by the beginning of next week."

She put out her cigarette and refused the offer of another.

Many years ago a famous architect sketched the plan of Rehavia. He wanted to give it the character of a quiet garden suburb. Narrow shady lanes like Alharizi Street, a well-tended boulevard called Ben-Maimon Avenue, squares like Magnes Square, full of the pensive murmur of cypresses even at the height of summer. An enclave of security, a sort of rest home for fugitives who have suffered in their lives. The names of great medieval Jewish scholars were given to the streets, to enrich them with a sense of antiquity and an air of wisdom and learning.

But over the years, New Jerusalem has spread and encircled Rehavia with a noose of ugly developments. The narrow streets have become choked with motor traffic. And when the western highway was opened and the heights of Sheikh-Badar and Naveh Shaanan became the heart of the city and the state, Rehavia ceased to be a garden suburb. Demented buildings sprouted on every rock. Small villas were demolished and tenements built in their place. The original intentions were swept away by the exuberance of the new age and the advance of technology.

The nights give back to Rehavia something of its plundered dreams. The trees that have survived draw a new dignity from the night and sometimes even act like a forest. Weary, slow-moving residents leave their homes to stroll at dusk. From the Valley of the Cross a different air arises, and with it a scent of bitter cypresses and night birds. It is as if the olive groves rise up and come into the lanes and the courtyards of houses. By electric light, book-laden shelves appear through the windows. And there are women who play the piano. Perhaps their hearts are heavy with longing or desire.

"That man on the other side of the street, the one feeling the sidewalk with his stick," said Lily, "that's Professor Shatski. He's getting old now. I don't suppose you knew Professor Shatski was still alive. I dare say you thought he was something out of the last century. Perhaps you'd have been right. He was an elegant and venomous man who believed in mercy, and in his writings he demanded mercilessly that all men show mercy to all men. Even the victim should show mercy to his killer. Now he's blind."

"I've never heard of him," said Yair. "He isn't exactly in my field, as they say."

"And now, if I may just ask for one more cigarette, let's talk about your field, as they say."

"By all means. Take one. I'm curious to know about the formality that you started talking about before."

She narrowed her eyes. Tried hard to concentrate. Remembered moments of pain that she had lived through long before this clumsy cavalier was born. She felt a momentary nausea and almost changed her mind. But after a while she said:

"It has to do with an examination. I want you to have a medical examination as soon as possible, certainly before we announce the wedding officially."

"I don't understand," said Yair, and his hand stopped halfway to his ear. "I don't understand. I'm a hundred percent fit. Why do I need an examination?"

"Just a screening examination. Your mother died of a hereditary disease. Incidentally, if she had been examined in time, she might have lived a few years longer."

"I had a physical two years ago, when I started at the university. They said I was as healthy as an ox. I know very little about my mother. I was young then."

"Now, Yair, don't go making a big fuss over a little examination, OK? There's a good boy. Just for my peace of mind, as they say. If you knew any German, I'd make you a present of all the economics books that Erich Dannenberg left me. He's someone else that I'm sure you don't remember. A new leaf, as they say. I shall have to think of some other present for you."

Yair said nothing.

As they walked up Ibn Ezra Street, they were confronted by an elegantly dressed old woman.

"There is a personal link that joins all creation. God is angry and man does not see it. One meaning to all deeds, fine deeds and ugly deeds. They that walk in the darkness shall see a great light. Not tomorrow — yesterday. The throat is warm and the knife is sharp. To all of creation there is one meaning."

Yair moved away from the madwoman and quickened his pace. Lily paused for a moment without speaking, then caught up with him. A poisonous, twisted sort of expression spread over her face like a disease. And then passed. In Jerusalem they called the elegant woman "One Meaning." She had a startlingly deep voice and a German accent. From a distance the madwoman of Rehavia blessed the two who were walking by:

"The blessing of the sky above, and the blessing of the water beneath, from Düsseldorf to Jerusalem, one meaning to all deeds, to those that build and those that destroy. Peace and success and full redemption to you and to all refugees and sufferers. Peace, peace, to near and far."

"Peace," replied Lily in a whisper. From there until they reached the Rothschild School, not a word was said. Yair was humming or murmuring to himself, "Not by day and not by night . . ." and then he stopped.

Lily said, "Let's not quarrel over this examination, even though it may sound to you like a whim. Your mother died only because of negligence, and as a result your father was left alone again and you became an orphan."

Yair said, "All right, all right, why make an issue of it?" Then, with a slow realization, he began to see the significance of something she had said. He put his tongue to the edge of his mustache, caught a fragment of tobacco, and said:

"Again? Did you say that my father was left alone again?"

Now Lily's voice had a cold and authoritative sound to it, like that of a clerk at an information counter:

"Yes. Your father's second wife died of cancer when you were six. Your father's first wife did not die of cancer; she left him. She was divorced. Soon you will be a married man yourself, and it's time your father stopped hiding elementary facts from you as if you were still a child."

"I don't understand," said Yair, hurt. "I don't understand — you say my father was married before?"

In his puzzlement he raised his voice beyond what was appropriate to the time and place. Lily was anxious to restore things to their proper level.

"Your father was married for four months," she said, "to the woman who later married Erich Dannenberg."

"That's impossible," said Yair.

He stopped. He took out a cigarette and put it between his lips but forgot to light it. Then for a moment he forgot his companion and forgot to offer her a cigarette. He stared into the darkness, deep in thought. At last he managed to say:

"So what? What has that got to do with us?"

"Be a dear," Lily said, smiling, "and give me another cigarette. I left mine at home. You're right. I myself find it hard to believe that there ever was, or could have been, such a marriage. I myself can hardly believe what I've just told you. But you should know, and you must learn what there is to be learned from that episode. Now, please light the cigarettes, mine and yours. Or give me the matches and I'll light them. Don't let it upset you. It happened in the past. A long time ago. And it lasted less than four absurd months. It was just an episode. Come on, let's walk a little farther. Jerusalem is wonderful at this time of night. Come on."

Yair began to follow her northward, lost in thought. And she was filled with a savage joy. A car honked and she ignored it. A night bird spoke to her and she did not answer. She watched her shoes and his on the sidewalk. And she took the lighter from his distracted fingers and lit both the cigarettes.

"And I was never told anything about it," said Yair.

"Well, you've been told now. That's enough. Relax. Don't get yourself all worked up," said Lily warmly, as if to console him.

"But it's . . . it's so strange. And not very nice, somehow."

She touched the back of his neck. Caressed the roots of his hair. Her hand felt warm and comforting to the boy. They walked on, out of Rehavia and into the neighboring quarter. The winding streets became sharp-angled alleyways. And there in front of them was the olive tree, embracing and crushing the iron gatepost.

6

ELHANAN KLEINBERGER and Yosef Yarden were engrossed in their game of chess. A lamp styled in the shape of an old Bavarian street lamp shed a dim light on the table. On the bindings of the scholarly books danced gold letters which gave back a light still dimmer than the one they took from the lamp. All around stood Dr. Kleinberger's bookshelves, set out along the length and height of the walls of the room, from floor to ceiling. One special shelf was devoted to the Egyptologist's stamp albums. Another was reserved for Hebrew literature, Elhanan Kleinberger's secret love. In the few spaces among the rows of books there were African miniatures, vases, primitive statuettes of a crudely erotic style. But these statuettes also served as vases, holding colored paper flowers that never wilted.

"No, Yosef, you can't do that," said Dr. Kleinberger. "In any case, you have no choice now but to exchange your knight for my rook."

"Just a moment, Elhanan, give me a chance to think. I still have a small advantage in this game."

"A temporary advantage, my friend, a temporary advantage," replied Dr. Kleinberger playfully. "But think, by all means. The more you think, the better you will appreciate just how temporary your advantage is. Temporary and irrelevant." He leaned back comfortably in his armchair.

Yosef Yarden thought hard: Now I must concentrate. What he says about the weakness of my position is just tactics in a war of nerves. I must concentrate. The next move will decide the game.

"The next move will decide the game," said Dr. Kleinberger. "Should we call a ten-minute break and have a cup of tea?"

"A Machiavellian suggestion, Elhanan, and I don't hesitate to call the child by his name. A diabolical suggestion designed to upset my concentration, and you have succeeded in doing that already. Anyway, the answer is: no, thank you."

"Did we not say before that every child has more than one name, Yosef? We were talking about that only two or three hours ago. It seems that you have already forgotten our conversation. Pity."

"I have already forgotten what I was intending to do to you. To your rook, I mean. You've succeeded in distracting me, Elhanan.

Please, let me concentrate. Look, so. Yes. I am here and you are there. What do you say to that, my dear doctor?"

"For the time being I don't say anything. All that I will say is: let's break off for a moment and listen to the news. But after the news I shall say 'check,' Yosef, and then I shall say 'checkmate.'"

It was nearly midnight when the two men parted. Yosef bore his defeat with dignity. He consoled himself with the glass of brandy that his host offered him, and said:

"At the end of the week we shall meet at my house. On my territory you will be the loser. You have my word on it."

"And this," said Dr. Kleinberger, laughing, "this is the man who wrote that eloquent article 'Against the Politics of Revenge' in *The Social Democrat.* Sleep well, Yosef."

Outside were the night and the wind. An ill-mannered owl urged Yosef to hurry up. I forgot to phone her to ask what happened. Better wait until tomorrow. She will phone and apologize and I won't accept her excuses. At least, not right away.

7

THE ACACIA solves mysteries/And tells what lies ahead,/I shall ask the acacia tree/Oh, who is my bride to be?

The insistent tune takes no account of circumstances and will not leave Yair alone. Already he has whistled it, hummed it, and sung it, and still the song gives him no peace.

Lily has questioned Yair about his professors, about his studies, about the girl students who were sure to be mad with grief at the thought of his forthcoming marriage.

Yair was thinking: That's enough. Let's go home. What she's told me isn't necessarily true. And even if it is true, so what? What does she want? What's the matter with her? Time to put a stop to all this and go home. Besides, I'm cold.

"Perhaps," he said cautiously, "perhaps we should start heading back home. It's late, and there's a dampness in the air. It's cold as well. I don't want it to be my fault if you catch a chill."

He gripped her arm, just above the elbow, and began gently drawing her toward a street corner lit by a lamp.

"Do you know, my dear child," she said, "the amount of patience that is required of a man and a woman to prevent their marriage from turning into a tragedy after a few months?"

"But I think . . . Let's talk about that on the way home. Or some other time altogether."

"For the first few months there is sex and sex is all that matters. Sex in the morning, at midday, and at night, before and after meals, instead of meals. But after a few months you suddenly begin to have a lot of time to sit and think — and you think all kinds of thoughts. Infuriating habits come to the surface, on both sides. And this is when subtlety is required."

"It'll be all right. Don't worry. Dinah and I . . ."

"Who said anything about you and Dinah? I'm talking in general terms. Now I can also tell you something from my personal experience. Put your arm around my shoulders. I'm cold. Yes. Don't be so shy. Be a nice boy. Like this. I'm going to tell you something about Dinah and something about you, too."

"But I already know."

"No, my child, you don't know everything. I think you should know, for example, that Dinah is in love with your outward appearance and not with you. She doesn't think about you. She's still a child. And so are you. I don't suppose you have ever once been depressed. Don't answer me now. No, I'm not saying that you're a crude boy. Far from it. I just mean you're strong. You're straightforward and strong, as our young people should be. Here, give me your hand. Yes. Don't ask so many questions. I asked for your hand. Yes. Like this. Now, squeeze my hand, please. Because I'm asking you, isn't that reason enough? Squeeze. Not gently. Hard. Harder. Harder still. Don't be afraid. You're afraid of me. There, that's good. You're very strong. Have you noticed that your hand is cold and mine is warm? Soon you'll understand why. But stop whining and trying to persuade me to go home all the time, or I'll begin to think I came out for a walk with a spoiled toddler who just wants to go home and sleep. Look, child, look at the moon peeping out from behind the clouds. Do you see? Yes. Just relax completely for a few moments. Don't say anything. Hush."

The dim wailing of jackals is heard from far away. Words flee from him. Something other than words now strives to assert itself but finds no outlet. A sharp and mischievous wind rises from the desolation on the fringes of the town and comes to play in the stone-flagged side streets. Windows are shut. Shutters closed. Drains with iron gratings. A long procession of trash cans frozen on the sidewalk. Cats prowl on the mounds of Jerusalem stone. Lily Dannenberg is sure that the things that she has said to Yair Yarden are "educational." She tries hard to keep to the rhythm of events, lest everything be wasted. But the blood is pounding in her temples, and some inner agitation urges her to go racing on without drawing breath. Here among the houses there is no acacia solving riddles. The two walkers emerge from the side streets and pass through the market of Mahaneh Yehuda toward Jaffa Road. Here Lily leads the young man to a cheap cafe that caters to the all-night taxi drivers.

Beneath the electric light the moths are singeing their wings in token of their love for the yellow bulb. Mrs. Dannenberg orders black coffee without sugar or saccharine. Yair asks for a cheese sandwich. He hesitates and asks for a small glass of brandy as well. She lays her hand on his broad brown hand and carefully counts his fingers. In a state of mild dizziness he responds with a smile. She takes his hand in hers and raises the fingers to her lips.

8

IN THIS taxi drivers' cafe in the Mahaneh Yehuda district there was a certain driver, a giant named Abbu. All day he sleeps. At midnight, like a bear, he wakes up and goes out to prowl Jaffa Road, his kingdom. All the taxi drivers willingly defer to him, for he is strong and goodhearted, but a hard man, too. Now he was sitting at one of the tables with three or four of the younger members of the flock, showing them how to load the dice in the game of backgammon. When Yair and Lily came into the café, Abbu said to his young cronies:

"Here come the Queen of Sheba and King Solomon."

And when Yair said nothing and Lily smiled, he added:

"Never mind. Health is what matters. Hey, lady, are you letting the kid drink brandy?"

His fellow drivers turned to look. The cafe proprietor, a tubercular and melancholic man, also turned to watch the approaching scene.

"And as for you, little boy, I'm damned if I understand what you're playing at. What is this, is it Grandma's Day today? Giving your grandma a treat? What are you doing going around at night with a vintage model like that?"

Yair leapt to his feet, his ears reddening, willing and ready to fight for his honor. But Lily motioned him back to his seat, and when she spoke her voice was warm and happy.

"There are some models that a man of experience and taste would sell his soul for — and not just his soul, but any number of these newfangled toys of today, all tin and glass."

"Touché!" said Abbu, laughing. "So why not come over to my place and get a good hand on your wheel, an experienced hand with clever fingers, how about it? Why go around with that slip of a boy?"

Yair sprang up, his mustache bristling. But once again she got in first and snuffed out the quarrel before it began. A new light danced in her eyes.

"What's the matter with you, Yair? This gentleman doesn't mean to insult me but to make me happy. He and I think exactly the same thoughts. So don't lose your temper, but sit down and learn how to make me happy. Now I am happy." And in her happiness the divorcee pulled Yair toward her and kissed the dimple in the middle of his chin. Abbu said slowly, as if about to faint at the sweetness of the sight:

"Lord God of Hosts, where, oh, where have you been all this time, lady, and where have I been?"

Lily said:

"Today is Grandson's Day. But maybe tomorrow or the day after, Grandma will need a taxi, and maybe Grandpa will be around, or he will discover where the Queen of Sheba is enthroned and bring her tribute of monkeys and parrots. Come on, Yair, let's go. Good night, sir. It's been a great pleasure meeting you."

As the couple passed the drivers' table on their way to the door, Abbu murmured in a tone of reverent awe:

"Go home, young man, go home and sleep. By God, you're not fit to touch the tip of her little finger."

Lily smiled.

And outside Yair said angrily:

"They're a gang of thugs. And savages."

9

THE TIPS of her little fingers were pressed in the flesh of his arm.

"Now I'm cold, too," she said, "and I want you to hold me. If you know by now how you should hold me."

Yair embraced her around the shoulders in anger and shame, emotions that breathed violence into his movements.

Lily said, "Yes. Like that."

"But . . . I think, anyway, it's time we turned around and headed back. It's late," he said, unconsciously gripping the lobe of his ear between thumb and forefinger. What does she want from me? What's the matter with her?

"It's too late now to go home," she whispered, "and the house is empty. What is there at home? There's nothing at home. Arm-

chairs. Disgusting armchairs. Erich Dannenberg's chairs. Dr. Kleinberger's. Your father's. All the miserable people. There is nothing
for us there at home. Here outside you can meet anything and feel
anything. Owls are bewitching the moon. You're not going to leave
me now, outside in the night with those wild thugs of drivers and
all the owls. You must stay and protect me. No, I'm not raving, I'm
perfectly rational and I'm almost frozen to death; don't leave me
and don't say a word, Hebrew is such a rhetorical language, nothing but Bible and commentaries. Don't say another word to me in
Hebrew, don't say anything at all. Just hold me. To you. Close. Like
this. Please, not politely, please, not gently, hold me as if I'm trying
to get away from you, biting and scratching, and you're not letting
me go. Hush. And that wretched *Eule* can shut up as well, because I
shall hear and see nothing more because you have covered my head
and my ears and gagged my mouth and tied my hands behind my
back because you are much stronger because I am a woman and you
are a man."

10

AS SHE spoke, they walked through the Makor Baruch quarter toward the Schneller Barracks, approaching the last of the dirt paths
and the zoo in North Jerusalem, which lies on the frontier between
the city and enemy territory.

The treasure hunt had come to nothing. Nobody had interpreted correctly the clue of the old acacia tree, and the treasure was
not found. Uri was asleep curled up in the armchair when Yosef
Yarden returned from his visit to Dr. Kleinberger. The house was
in chaos. In the middle of the table lay an open volume of Bialik's
poetry. All the lights were on. Yair was not at home. Yosef Yarden
roused his younger son and sent him off to bed with a scolding.
Yair must have gone to the station to meet his fiancee. Tomorrow I
will let Lily apologize for not being home tonight. She will have to

apologize profusely before I agree to accept her excuses and forgive her. The most disagreeable thing was the quarrel with Kleinberger. Naturally I had the last word in the argument, but I have to admit that I was beaten, just as I was in the chess game. I must be honest. I don't believe that our wretched party will ever succeed in shaking off its apathy and depression. Weakness of heart and weakness of will have eroded all the good intentions. All is lost. Now it's time to sleep, so that tomorrow I won't be sleepwalking like the majority of people. But if I get to sleep now, Yair will come home and make a lot of noise. Then I won't be able to sleep until morning, which means another dreadful night. Who's that shouting out there? Nobody's shouting. A bird, perhaps.

Dr. Elhanan Kleinberger had also put out the light in his room. He stood at one end of the room, with his face to the wall and his back to the door. The radio was playing late-night music. The scholar's lips moved silently. He was trying, in a whisper, to find the right word for a lyric poem. Unbeknownst to anyone, he was composing poetry. In German. He, the passionate lover of Hebrew literature and the defender of the language's honor, whispered his poetry in German. Perhaps it was for this reason that he concealed what he was doing from even his closest friend. He himself felt that he was committing a sin and was guilty of hypocrisy as well.

With his lips he strove to put ideas into words. A wandering light flickered among the dark shelves. For a moment this light danced on the lenses of his spectacles, creating a flash as of madness or of utter despair. Outside, a bird screeched with malicious joy. Slowly, and very painfully, things became clearer. But still there were things for which no words existed. His frail shoulders began to shake in choking desire. The right words would not come; they only slipped by and eluded him like transparent veils, like fragrances, like longings that the fingers cannot grasp. He felt that there was no hope for him.

Then he switched on the lamp again. Suddenly he felt a vicious hatred for the African ornaments and the erotic vases. And for words.

He stretched out his hand and casually selected a scientific volume from one of the bookshelves. The title shone in gold letters on the leather binding: *Demons and Ghosts in Ancient Chaldee Ritual* All words are whores, forever betraying you and slipping away into the darkness while your soul yearns for them.

11

THE LAST wood. In its center stands the Jerusalem Biblical Zoo, and its northern flank marks the frontier between Jerusalem and the enemy villages across the cease-fire line. Lily had been married to Yosef Yarden for less than four months, and he was a delightful youth, full of dreams and ideals. All this happened many years ago, and still there is no peace. It is the way of flesh to hold its grudges, and it is the way of the moon to hover with calm and cold insolence in the night sky.

Within the zoo is a nervous silence.

All the predators are asleep, but their slumber is not deep. They are never totally free from smells and voices borne on the breeze. The night never ceases to penetrate their sleep, sometimes drawing from their lungs a low growl. Their hide bristles in the frozen wind. A tense vibration, a ripple of fear or of nightmare, comes and goes. A moist, suspicious nose probes the night air and takes in the unfamiliar scents. Everywhere there is dew. The rustling cypresses breathe a sigh of quiet sorrow. The pine needles whisper as they search in the darkness, thirsty for the black dew.

From the wolves' cage comes a sound. A pair of wolves in heat, lusting for each other in the darkness. The bitch bites her mate but his fury is only redoubled. In the height of their fever they hear the cries of the birds and the vicious growl of the wildcat.

A blue-tinted vapor rises from the valleys. Strange lights twinkle across the border. The moon sheds her light upon all and shrinks, enchanted, in the whiteness of the rocks: cancers of shining venom in beams of sickly, primeval light.

Moon-struck jackals roam the valleys. From the murky groves they call to their brothers in the cages. These are the lands of nightmare, and perhaps beyond them lie those gardens that no eye has seen, and only the heart reaches out to them as if wailing: Homeward.

Out of the depths of your terror lift up your eyes. See the tops of the pine trees. A halo of pale-gray light enfolds the treetops like a gift of grace. Only the rocks are as dry as death. Give them a sign.

1964

A Hollow Stone

1

THE NEXT DAY we went out to assess the damage. The storm had ruined the crops. The tender shoots of winter corn had been wiped off the fields as if by a gigantic duster. Saplings were uprooted. Old trees lay writhing, kissed by the terrible east wind. Slender cypresses hung limply with broken spines. The fine avenue of palm trees planted to the north of our kibbutz thirty years earlier by the founders when they first came to these barren hills had lost their crowns to the storm: even their dumb submission had not been able to save them from its fury. The corrugated iron roofs of the sheds and barns had been carried far away. Some old shacks had been wrenched from their foundations. Shutters, which all night long had beaten out desperate pleas for help, had been broken off by the wind. The night had been filled with howls and shrieks and groans; with the dawn had come silence. We went out to assess the damage, stumbling over broken objects.

"It isn't natural," said Felix. "After all, it's spring."

"A typhoon. Here. A real tornado," added Zeiger with mingled awe and pride.

And Weissman concluded:

"The loss will come to six figures."

We decided on the spot to turn to the government and the movement for help. We agreed to advertise for volunteer specialists to work with us for a few days. And we resolved not to lose heart, but to make a start on the work right away. We would face this challenge as we had faced others in the past, and we would refuse to be disheartened — this is the substance of what Felix was to write in the kibbutz newsletter that weekend — and above all we must keep a clear head.

As regards clarity, we had only to contemplate the polished brilliance of the sky that morning. It was a long time since we had seen such a clear sky as on that morning when we went out to assess the damage, stumbling over broken objects.

2

A LIMPID crystal calm had descended on the hills. Spring sunlight on the mountains to the east, benign and innocent, and excited choruses of birds. No breeze, not a sign of dust. We inspected each part of the farm methodically, discussing, taking notes, making decisions, issuing immediate instructions. Not wasting a word. Speaking quietly and almost solemnly.

Casualties: Old Nevidomsky the night watchman, slightly injured by a falling beam. Shoulder dislocated, but no bones broken, according to the doctor at the district hospital. *Electricity:* Cables severed at various points. First priority, to switch off the current before letting the children come out to play, and to inspect the damage. *Water:* Flooding in the farmyard and no water in the nursery. *Provisions:* For today, a cold meal and lemonade. *Transport:* One jeep crushed; several tractors buried in wreckage. Condition impossible to ascertain at present. *Communications:* Both telephones dead. Take the van into town to find out what has happened in other places and how much the outside world knows of our plight.

Felix saw to the dispatch of the van and proceeded to the nursery. From there he went on to the cowsheds and chicken coops. Then to the schoolhouse, where he gave instructions for lessons to be resumed not later than ten o'clock "without fail."

Felix was animated by a passionate energy, which made his small, sturdy frame throb. He stowed his glasses away in his shirt pocket. His face took on a new look: a general, rather than a philosopher.

The farmyard was full of hens, unconcernedly scrabbling hither and thither, just like old-fashioned chickens in an old-fashioned village, as if oblivious that they had been born and bred in cages and batteries.

The livestock showed slight signs of shock: the cows kept raising their foolish heads to look for the roof, which had been carried off by the wind. Occasionally they uttered a long, unhappy groan, as if to warn of worse things still to come. The big telegraph pole had fallen on Batya Pinski's house and broken some roof tiles. By five past eight, the electricians had already trampled all over her flower beds rigging up a temporary line. First priority in restoring the electricity supply was given to the nurseries, the incubators for the chicks, and the steam boilers so there would be hot meals. Felix asked to have a transistor radio brought to him, so that he could follow developments elsewhere. Perhaps someone should look in on Batya Pinski and one or two invalids and elderly people, to reassure them and find out how they had weathered the terrors of the night. But social obligations could wait a little longer, until the more essential emergency arrangements had been made. For instance, the kitchens reported a gas leak whose source could not be traced. Anyway, one could not simply drop in on people like Batya Pinski for a brief chat: they would start talking, they would have complaints, criticisms, reminiscences, and this morning was the least suitable time possible for such psychological indulgence.

The radio news informed us that this had been no typhoon or tornado, but merely a local phenomenon. Even the nearby settlements had hardly been touched. Two conflicting winds had met here on our hills, and the resulting turbulence had caused some local damage. Meanwhile the first volunteers began to appear, followed by a mixed multitude of spectators, reporters, and broadcasters. Felix delegated three boys and a fluent veteran teacher to stem the tide of interlopers at the main gate of the kibbutz, and on no account to let them in to get under our feet. Only those on official business were to be admitted. The fallen telegraph pole was already temporarily secured by steel cables. The power supply would soon be restored to the most essential buildings. Felix demonstrated the qualities of theorist and man of action combined. Of course, he did not do everything himself. Each of us played his part to the best of his ability. And we would keep working until everything was in order.

3

CONDENSATION ON the windows and the hiss of the kerosene stove.

Batya Pinski was catching flies. Her agility belied her years. If Abrasha had lived to grow old along with her, his mockery would surely have turned to astonishment and even to gentleness: over the years he would have learned to understand and appreciate her. But Abrasha had fallen many years before, in the Spanish Civil War, having volunteered to join the few and fight for the cause of justice. We could still remember the eulogy that Felix had composed in memory of his childhood friend and comrade; it was a sober, moving document, free from rhetorical hyperbole, burning with agony and conviction, full of love and vision. His widow squashed the flies she caught between her thumb and forefinger. But her mind was not on the job, and some of the flies continued to wriggle even after they were dropped into the enamel mug. The room was perfectly still. You could hear the flies being squashed between her fingers.

Abrasha Pinski's old writings were the issue of the moment. Thanks to Felix's energetic efforts, the kibbutz-movement publishing house had recognized the need to bring out a collected volume of the articles he had written in the thirties. These writings had not lost their freshness. On the contrary, the further we went from the values that had motivated us in those days, the more pressing became the need to combat oblivion. And there was also a certain nostalgia at this time for the atmosphere of the thirties, which promised a reasonable market for the book. Not to mention the vogue for memories of the Spanish Civil War. Felix would contribute an introduction. The volume would also contain nine letters written by Abrasha from the siege of Madrid to the committed socialist community in Palestine.

Batya Pinski sliced the dead flies at the bottom of the mug with a penknife. The blade scraped the enamel, producing a grating yellow sound.

At last the old woman removed the glass cover and poured the mess of crushed flies into the aquarium. The quick, colorful fish crowded to the front of the tank, their tails waving, their mouths opening and closing greedily. At the sight of their agile movements and magical colors, the widow's face lit up, and her imagination ran riot.

Fascinating creatures, fish: they are both cold and alive. A striking paradox. This, surely, is the longed-for bliss: to be cold and alive.

Over the years Batya Pinski had developed an amazing ability. She was capable of counting the fish in her aquarium, up to forty or fifty, despite their perpetual motion. At times she could even guess in advance what course an individual fish or a shoal would take. Circles, spirals, zigzags, sudden totally capricious swerves, swoops, and plunges, fluid lines that drew delicate, complicated arabesques in the water of the tank.

The water in the tank was clear. Even clearer were the bodies of the fish. Transparency within transparency. The movement of fins was the slightest movement possible, hardly a movement at all. The quivering of the gills was unbelievably fine. There were black fish and striped fish, blood-red fish and fish purple like the plague, pale-green fish like stagnant water in fresh water. All of them free. None of them subject to the law of gravity. Theirs was a different law, which Batya did not know. Abrasha would have been able to discern it over the years, but he had chosen instead to lay down his life on a faraway battlefield.

4

THE ILLUSION of depth is produced by aquatic plants and scattered stones. The green silence of the underwater jungle. Fragments of rock on the bottom. Columns of coral up which plants twine. And on top of a hill of sand at the back of the tank is a stone with a hole.

Unlike the fish, the plants and stones in the aquarium are subject to the law of gravity. The fish continually swoop down on the stones and shrubs, now and then rubbing themselves against them or pecking at them. According to Batya Pinski, this is a display of malicious gloating.

As a procession of blood-red fish approaches the hollow stone, Batya Pinski rests her burning forehead against the cool glass. The passage of the live fish through the dead stone stirs a vague power deep inside her, and she trembles. That is when she has to fight back the tears. She feels for the letter in the pocket of her old dressing gown. The letter is crumpled and almost faded, but the words are still full of tenderness and compassion.

"I feel," writes Abramek Bart, one of the directors of the kibbutz-movement publishing house, "that if we have been unfair to the beloved memory of Abrasha, we have been even more unfair to the minds of our children. The younger generation needs, and deserves, to discover the pearls of wisdom contained in the essays and letters of our dear Abrasha. I shall come and see you one of these days to rummage, in quotation marks of course, through your old papers. I am certain that you can be of great assistance to us in sorting through his literary remains and in preparing the work for publication. With fraternal good wishes, yours," signed by some Ruth Bardor for Abramek Bart.

The old woman held the envelope to her nose. She sniffed it for a moment with her eyes closed. Her mouth hung open, revealing gaps in her teeth. A small drop hung between her nose and upper lip, where a slight mustache had begun to grow during these bad years. Then she put the letter back in the envelope, and the envelope in her pocket. Now she was exhausted and must rest in the armchair. She did not need to rest for long. It was enough for her to doze for a minute or two. A stray surviving fly began to buzz, and already she was up and ready for the chase.

Years before, Abrasha would come and bite. Love and hate. He would burst and collapse on her, and at once he would be distracted, not here, not with her.

For months before his departure the tune was always on his lips, sung in a Russian bass, shamelessly out of tune. She recalled the tune, the anthem of the Spanish freedom-fighters, full of longing, wildness, and revolt. It had swept their bare room up into the maelstrom of teeming forces as he enumerated the bleeding Spanish towns that had fallen to the enemies of mankind, counting them off one by one on his fingers. Their outlandish names conveyed to Batya a resonance of unbridled lechery. In her heart of hearts she disliked Spain and wished it no good; after all, that was where our ancestors had been burned at the stake and banished. But she held her peace. Abrasha enlarged on the implications of the struggle, expounding its dialectical significance and its place in the final battle that was being engaged all over Europe. He considered all wars as a snare and a delusion; civil wars were the only ones worth dying in. She liked to listen to all this, even though she could not and did not want to understand. It was only when he reached the climax of his speech — describing the iron laws of history and averring that the collapse of reaction would come like a thunderbolt from the blue — that she suddenly grasped what he was talking about, because she could see the thunderbolt itself in his eyes.

And suddenly he was tired of her. Perhaps he had seen the tortured look on her face, perhaps he had had a momentary glimpse of her own desires. Then he would sit down at the table, propping up his large square head with his massive elbows, and immerse himself in the newspaper, abstractedly eating one olive after another and arranging the pits in a neat pile.

5

THE KETTLE whistles fiercely as it passes boiling point. Batya Pinski gets up and makes herself some tea. Since the storm died down, at about four o'clock in the morning, she has been drinking glass after glass of tea. She has still not been out to inspect the damage. She has not even tried to open the shutters. She sits behind her drawn curtains and imagines the damage in all its details. What is there to see? It is all there before her eyes: shattered roofs, trampled flower beds, torn trees, dead cows, Felix, plumbers, electricians, experts, and talkers. All boring. Today will be devoted to the fish, until the premonition is confirmed and Abramek Bart arrives. She always relies unhesitatingly on her premonitions. One can always know things in advance, if only one really and truly tries and is not afraid of what may emerge. Abramek will come today to see the havoc. He will come because he won't be able to contain his curiosity. But he won't want to come just like that, like the other good-for-nothings who collect wherever there's been a disaster. He will find some excuse. And then he'll suddenly remember his promise to Batya, to come and rummage in and sort through Abrasha's papers. It's half past eight now. He will be here by two or three. There is still time. Still plenty of time to get dressed, do my hair, and get the room tidy. And to make something nice to serve him. Plenty of time now to sit down in the armchair and drink my tea quietly.

She sat down in the armchair opposite the sideboard, under the chandelier. On the floor was a thick Persian carpet, and by her side an ebony card table. All these beautiful objects would shock Abrasha if he were to come back. On the other hand, if he had come back twenty years before, he would have risen high up the ladder of the party and the movement; he would have left all those Felixes and Abrameks behind, and by now he'd be an ambassador or a minister, and she would be surrounded by even nicer furnishings. But he made up his mind to go and die for the Spaniards, and the furnishings were bought for her by Martin Zlotkin, her son-in-law. After he married Ditza he brought all the presents, then took his young bride away with him to Zurich, where he now managed a division of his father's bank, with branches on three continents. Ditza ran a Zen study group, and every month she sent a letter with a mimeographed leaflet in German preaching humility and peace of mind. Grandchildren were out of the question, because Martin hated children and Ditza herself called him "our big baby." Once a year they came to visit and contributed handsomely to various charities. Here in the kibbutz they had donated a library of books on socialist theory in memory of Abrasha Pinski. Martin himself, however, regarded socialism the same way he regarded horse-drawn carriages: very pretty and diverting, but out of place in this day and age, when there were other, more urgent problems.

6

ON THE eve of Abrasha's departure Ditza was taken ill with pneumonia. She was two at the time; blonde, temperamental, and sickly. Her illness distracted Batya from Abrasha's departure. She spent the whole day arguing with the nurses and pedagogues and by evening they had given in and allowed the sick child to be transferred in her cot from the nursery to her parents' room in one of the shabby huts. The doctor arrived from the neighboring settlement in a mule cart, prescribed various medicines, and instructed her to keep the temperature of the room high. Meanwhile Abrasha packed some khaki shirts, a pair of shoes, some underwear, and a few Russian and Hebrew books into a knapsack and added some cans of sardines. In the evening, fired with the spirit, he stood by his daughter's cot and sang her two songs, his voice trembling with emotional fervor. He even showed Batya the latest lines dividing the workers from their oppressors on a wall map of Spain. He enumerated the towns: Barcelona, Madrid, Malaga, Granada, Valencia, Valladolid, Seville. Batya half-heard him; she wanted to shout, What's the matter with you, madman, don't go away, stay, live; and she also wanted to shout, I hope you die. But she said nothing. She pursed her lips like an old witch. And she had never since lost that expression. She recalled that last evening as if it had been re-enacted every night for twenty-three years. Sometimes the fish moved across the picture, but they did not obscure it: their paths wound in and out of its lines, bestowing upon it an air of strange, desolate enchantment, as though the widow were confronted not by things that had happened a long time previously, but by things that were about to happen but could still be prevented. She must concentrate hard and not make a single mistake. This very day Abramek Bart will step into this room, all unawares, and then I shall have him in my power.

The cheap alarm clock started ringing at three o'clock. He got out of bed and lit the kerosene lamp. She followed him, slender and barefoot, and said, "It's not morning yet." Abrasha put his finger to his lips and whispered, "Sssh. The child." Secretly she prayed that the child would wake up and scream its head off. He discovered a cobweb in the corner of the shack and stood on tiptoe to wipe it away. The spider managed to escape and hide between the boards of the low ceiling. Abrasha whispered to her: "In a month or two, when we've won, I'll come back and bring you a souvenir from Spain. I'll bring something for Ditza, too. Now, don't make me late; the van's leaving for Haifa at half past three."

He went out to wash in the icy water of the faucet that stood twenty yards downhill from the shack. An alarmed night watchman hurried over to see what was going on. "Don't worry, Felix," Abrasha said. "It's only the revolution leaving you for a while." They exchanged some more banter in earnest tones, and then, in a more lighthearted voice, some serious remarks. At a quarter past, Abrasha went back to the shack, and Batya, who had followed him out in her nightdress, went inside with him again. Standing there shivering, she saw by the light of the kerosene lamp how carelessly he had shaved in his haste and the dark: he had cut himself in some places and left dark bristles in others. She stroked his cheeks and tried to wipe away the blood and dew. He was a big, warm boy, and when he began to hum the proud, sad song of the Spanish freedom-fighters deep in his chest, it suddenly occurred to Batya that he was very dear and that she must not stand in his way, because he knew where he was going and she knew nothing at all. Felix said, "Be seeing you," and added in Yiddish, "Be well, Abrasha." Then he vanished. She kissed Abrasha on his chest and neck, and he drew her to him and said, "There, there." Then the child woke up and started to cry in a voice that was almost effaced by the illness. Batya picked her up, and Abrasha touched them both with his large hands and said, "There, there, what's the trouble."

The van honked, and Abrasha said cheerfully, "Here goes. I'm off."

From the doorway he added, "Don't worry about me. Goodbye."

She soothed the child and put her back in the cot. Then she put out the lamp and stood alone at the window, watching the night paling and the mountaintops beginning to show in the east. Suddenly she was glad that Abrasha had cleared the cobweb from the corner of the shack but had not managed to kill the spider. She went back to bed and lay trembling, because she knew that Abrasha would never come back, and that the forces of reaction would win the war.

7

THE FISH in the aquarium had eaten all the flies and were floating in the clear space. Perhaps they were hankering after more tidbits. They explored the dense weeds and pecked at the arch of the hollow stone, darting suspiciously toward one another to see if one of them had managed to snatch a morsel and if there was anything left of it.

Only when the last crumbs were finished did the fish begin to sink toward the bottom of the tank. Slowly, with deliberate unconcern, they rubbed their silver bellies on the sand, raising tiny mushroom clouds. Fish are not subject to the laws of contradiction: they are cold and alive. Their movements are dreamy, like drowsy savagery.

Just before midnight, when the storm had begun to blow up, the widow had awakened and shuffled to the bathroom in her worn bedroom slippers. Then she made herself some tea and said in a loud, cracked voice, "I told you not to be crazy." Clutching the glass of tea, she wandered around the room and finally settled in the armchair facing the aquarium, after switching on the light in the water. Then, as the storm gathered strength and battered the shutters and the trees, she watched the fish waking up.

As usual, the silverfish were the first to respond to the light. They rose gently from their haunts in the thick weeds and propelled themselves up toward the surface with short sharp thrusts of their fins. A single black molly made the rounds of its shoal, as if rousing them all for a journey. In no time at all the whole army was drawn up in formation and setting out.

At one o'clock an old shack next to the cobbler's hut collapsed.

The storm banged the tin roof against the walls, and the air howled and whistled. At the same moment the red swordfish woke up and ranged themselves behind their leader, a giant with a sharp black sword. It was not the collapse of the shack that had awakened the swordfish. Their cousins the green swordfish had weighed anchor and gently set sail into the forest, as if bent on capturing the clearing abandoned by the silverfish. Only the solitary fighting-fish, the lord of the tank, still slept in his home among the corals. He had responded to the sudden light with a shudder of disgust. The zebra fish played a childish game of tag around the sleeping monarch.

The last to come back to life were the guppies, the dregs of the aquarium, an inflamed rabble roaming restlessly hither and thither in search of crumbs. Slow snails crawled on the plants and on the glass walls of the tank, helping to keep them clean. The widow sat all night watching the aquarium, holding the empty glass, conjuring the fish to move from place to place, calling them after the Spanish towns: Malaga, Valencia, Barcelona, Madrid, Cordova. While outside the clashing winds sliced the crowns off the stately palm trees and broke the spines of the cypresses.

She put her feet up on the ebony card table, a present from Martin and Ditza Zlotkin. She thought about Zen Buddhism, humility, civil war, the final battle where there would be nothing to lose, a thunderbolt from the blue. She fought back exhaustion and despair and rehearsed the unanswerable arguments she would use when the time came. All the while her eyes strayed to another world, and her lips whispered: There, there, quiet now.

Toward dawn, when the wind had died away and we were going out to assess the damage, the old woman fell into a half-sleep full of curses and aching joints. Then she got up, made a fresh glass of tea, and began to chase flies all over the room with an agility that belied her years. In her heart she knew that Abramek Bart would definitely come today, and that he would use his promise as an excuse. She saw the plaster fall from the ceiling as the pole fell and broke some of the roof tiles. The real movement was completely noiseless. Without a sound the monarch arose and began to steer himself toward the hollow stone. As he reached the arched tunnel he stopped and froze. He took on a total stillness. The stillness of the water. The immobility of the light. The silence of the hollow stone.

8

HAD IT not been for Ditza, Batya Pinski would have married Felix in the early nineteen-forties.

It was about two years after the awful news had come from Madrid. Once again a final war was being waged in Europe, and on the wall of the dining hall there hung a map covered with arrows, and a collection of heartening slogans and news clippings. Ditza must have been four or five. Batya had got over the disaster and had taken on a new bloom, which was having a disturbing effect on certain people's emotions. She always dressed in black, like a Spanish widow. And when she spoke to men, their nostrils flared as if they had caught a whiff of wine. Every morning, on her way to the sewing room, she walked, erect and slender, past the men working in the farmyard. Occasionally one of those tunes came back to her, and she would sing with a bitter sadness that made the other sewing women exchange glances and whisper, "Uh-huh, there she goes again."

Felix was biding his time. He helped Batya over her minor difficulties and even concerned himself with the development of Ditza's personality. Later, when he had submitted to the desires of the party and exchanged the cowsheds for political office, he made a habit of bringing Ditza little surprises from the big city. He also treated the widow with extreme respect, as if she were suffering from an incurable illness and it was his task to ease somewhat her last days. He would let himself into her room in the middle of the morning and wash the floor, secreting chocolates in unlikely places for her to discover later. Or put up metal coat hooks, bought out of his expense allowance, to replace the broken wooden ones. And he would supply her with carefully selected books: pleasant books, with never a hint of loss or loneliness, Russian novels about the development of Siberia, the five-year plan, change of heart achieved through education.

"You're spoiling the child," Batya would sometimes say. And Felix would word his answer thoughtfully and with tact:

"Under certain circumstances it is necessary to pamper a child, to prevent it from being deprived."

"You're a sweet man, Felix," Batya would say, and occasionally she would add, "You're always thinking of others. Why don't you think about yourself for a change, Felix?"

Felix would read a hint of sympathy or personal interest into those remarks; he would stifle his excitement and reply: "It doesn't matter. Never mind. In times like these one can't be thinking of oneself all the time. And I'm not the one who's making the real sacrifice."

"You're very patient, Felix," Batya would say, with pursed lips.

And Felix, whether shrewdly or innocently, would conclude, "Yes, I'm very patient."

Indeed, after a few months or perhaps a year or two, the widow began to soften. She permitted Felix to accompany her from the dining hall or the recreation hall to the door of her room, or from the sewing room to the children's house, and occasionally she would stand and listen to him for half an hour or so by one of the benches on the lawn. He knew that the time was not yet ripe for him to try to touch her, but he also knew that time was on his side. She still insisted on wearing black, she did not temper her arrogance, but she, too, knew that time was on Felix's side; he was closing in on her from all sides, so that soon she would have no alternative.

It was little Ditza who changed everything.

She wet her bed, she ran away from the children's house at night, she escaped to the sewing room in the morning and clutched her mother, she kicked and scratched the other children and even animals, and as for Felix, she nicknamed him "Croakie." Neither his gifts and attentions nor his sweets and rebukes did any good. Once, when Felix and Batya had begun to eat together openly in the dining hall, the child came in and climbed on his knee. He was touched, convinced that a reconciliation was coming. But he had just started to stroke her hair and call her "my little girl" when suddenly she wet his trousers and ran away. Felix got up and ran after her in a frenzy of rage and reformist zeal. He pushed his way among the tables trying to catch the child. Batya sat stiffly where she was and did not interfere. Finally Felix snatched up an enamel mug, threw it at the elusive child, missed, tripped, picked himself up, and tried to wipe the pee and yogurt off his khaki trousers. There were smiling faces all around him. By now Felix was acting secretary general of the Workers' Party, and here he was, flushed and hoarse, with a murderous gleam showing through his glasses. Zeiger slapped his belly, sighing, "What a sight," until laughter got the better of him. Weissmann, too, roared aloud. Even Batya could not suppress a smile as the child crawled under the tables and came to sit at her feet with the expression of a persecuted saint. The nursery teachers exclaimed indignantly, "I ask you, is that a way to carry on, a grown-up man, a public figure, throwing mugs at little children in the middle of the dining hall, isn't that going too far?"

Three weeks later it came out that Felix was having an affair with Zeiger's wife, Zetka. Zeiger divorced her, and early in that spring she married Felix. In May Felix and Zetka were sent to Switzerland to organize escape routes for the survivors of the death camps. In the party Felix was regarded as the model of the young leadership that had risen from the ranks. And Batya Pinski started to go downhill.

9

WHEN ABRAMEK comes, I'll make him a glass of tea, I'll show him all the old papers, we'll discuss the layout and the cover, and eventually we'll have to settle the problem of the dedication, so that there won't be any misunderstanding.

She picked up the last photograph of Abrasha, taken in Madrid by a German Communist fighter. He looked thin and unshaven, his clothes were crumpled, and there was a pigeon on his shoulder. His mouth hung open slackly and his eyes were dull. He looked more as if he had been making love than fighting for the cause. On the back was an affectionate greeting, in rhyme.

Over the years Batya Pinski had got into the habit of talking to herself. At first she had done it under her breath. Later, when Ditza married Martin Zlotkin and went away with him, she started talking out loud, in a croaking voice that made the children of the kibbutz call her Baba Yaga, after the witch in the stories they had heard from their Russian nurses.

Look here, Abramek, there's just one more point. It's a slightly delicate matter, a bit complicated, but I'm sure that we can sort it out, you and I, with a bit of forethought. It's like this. If Abrasha were still alive, he would of course want to bring his own book out. Right? Right. Of course. But Abrasha isn't alive and he can't supervise the publication of the book himself. I mean the color, the jacket, the preface, that sort of thing, and also the dedication. Naturally he would want to dedicate the book to his wife. Just like anybody else. Now that Abrasha isn't with us any more, and you are collecting his articles and his letters and bringing out his book, there isn't a dedication. What will people say? Just think, Abramek, work it out for yourself: what will people make of it? It's simply an incitement to the meanest kind of gossip: poor fellow, he ran away to Spain to get away from his wife. Or else he went to Spain and fell in love with some Carmen Miranda or other out there, and that was that. Just a minute. Let me finish. We must kill that kind of gossip at all costs. At all costs, I say. No, not for my sake; I don't care any more what people say about me. As far as I'm concerned they can say that I went to bed with the Grand Mufti and with your great Plekhanov both at once. I couldn't care less. It's not for me, it's for him. It's not right to have all sorts of stories going around about Abrasha Pinski. It's not good for you: after all, you need a figure you can hold up as an example to your young people, without Carmen Mirandas and suchlike. In other words, you need a dedication. It doesn't matter who writes it. It could be you. Felix. Or me. Something like this, for instance: First page, QUESTIONS OF TIME AND TIMELY QUESTIONS, collected essays by Abraham brackets Abrasha Pinski, hero of the Spanish Civil War. That's right. Next page: this picture. Just as it is. Top of the next page: To Batya, a devoted wife, the fruits of my love and anguish. Then, on the following page, you can put that the book is published by the Workers' Party, and you can mention Felix's help. It won't hurt. Now, don't you argue with me, Abramek, I mustn't get upset, because I'm not a well woman, and what's more I know a thing or two about you and about Felix and about how Abrasha was talked into going off to that ridiculous war. So you'd better not say anything. Just do what you're told. Here, drink your tea, and stop arguing.

Then she sighed, shook herself, and sat down in her armchair to wait for him. Meanwhile she watched the fish. When she heard a buzzing, she leapt up and swatted the fly on the windowpane. How do they get in when all the windows are closed. Where do they come from. To hell with the lot of them. Anyway, how can the wretched creatures survive a storm like that.

She squashed the fly, dropped it into the aquarium, and sat down again in her armchair. But there was no peace. The kettle started boiling. Abramek will be here soon. Must get the room tidy. But it's all perfectly tidy, just as it has been for years. Close your eyes and think, perhaps. What about.

10

We were recovering hour by hour.

We tackled the debris with determined dedication. Buildings in danger of collapse were roped off. The carpenters fixed up props and blocked holes with boards. Here and there we hung flaps of canvas. Tractors brought beams and corrugated iron. Where there was flooding we improvised paths with gravel and concrete blocks. We rigged up temporary powerlines to essential points until the electrical system could be repaired. Old kerosene heaters and rusty cooking stoves were brought up from the stores. The older women cleaned and polished them, and for a while we all relived the early days. The bustle filled us with an almost ecstatic joy. Old memories were brought out, and jokes were exchanged. Meanwhile Felix alerted all the relevant agencies, the telephone engineers, emergency services, the Regional Council, the Department of Agricultural Settlements, the headquarters of the movement, and so on and so forth. The messages all went by jeep, because the telephone lines had been brought down by the storm. Not even our children were idle. To keep them from getting under our feet, Felix told them to catch the chickens, which had scattered all over the village when their coops had been damaged. Happy hunting cries arose from the lawns and from under the trees. Panting, red-faced gangs came running eagerly from unexpected places to block the escape routes of the clucking hens. Some of these sounds managed to penetrate the closed shutters, windows, and curtains into Batya Pinski's room. What's the matter, what's so funny, the widow croaked to herself.

By the same afternoon all essential services were operating again. A cold but nourishing meal had been served. The nurseries were light and warm once more. There was running water, even if the pressure was low and the supply intermittent. After lunch we were able to draw up a first unofficial assessment of the damage. It transpired that the worst-hit area was the group of old shacks at the bottom of the hill, which had been put up by the founders decades previously. When they had folded up the tents that they had pitched on the barren slope and installed themselves in these shacks, they had all known at last that they were settling here and that there was no going back.

Years later, when the successive phases of permanent buildings had been completed, the old wooden shacks were handed over to the young people. Their first inhabitants were a detachment of young refugees who had arrived from Europe via Central Asia and Teheran to be welcomed by us with open arms. They were followed by a squadron of underground fighters that later produced two outstanding military men. From this group of huts they set out one night to blow up a British military radar installation, and it was here that they returned toward dawn. Later, after the establishment of the state, when the task of the underground had been completed, the tumbledown huts became a regular army base. This was the headquarters of the legendary Highland Brigade during the War of Independence, where the great night operations were planned. Throughout the fifties the shacks housed recent immigrants, paramilitary youth groups, students in intensive language courses, detachments of volunteers, eccentric individuals who had begun to come from all over the world to experience the new way of life; finally they were used as lodgings for hired laborers. When Phase C of the building program was drawn up, the huts were scheduled for demolition. In any case they were already falling down: the wooden walls were disintegrating, the roof beams were sagging, and the floors were sinking. Weeds were growing through the boards, and the walls were covered with obscene drawings and graffiti in six languages. At night the children came here to play ghosts and robbers among the ruins. And after the children came the couples. We had been about to clear the site to make way for the new development when the storm anticipated us, as if it had run out of patience. The carpenters searched the wreckage, salvaging planks, doors, and beams that might be reused.

Felix's short, stocky figure was everywhere at once, almost as if he were appearing simultaneously in different places. His sober, precise instructions prevented chaos, reduplication, and wasted effort. He never for a moment failed to distinguish between essential and trivial tasks.

For seventeen years Felix had been a public servant, secretary general, chairman, delegate, and eventually even a member of Parliament and a member of the executive committee of the party. A year or so earlier, when Zetka, his wife, was dying of cancer, he had given up all his public positions and returned home to become secretary of the kibbutz. Social and financial problems that had seemed insoluble for years suddenly vanished at his return, as if by magic. Old plans came to fruition. Unprofitable sections of the farm took on new life. There was a new mood abroad. A few weeks earlier, ten months after Zetka's death, Felix had married Weissmann's ex-wife. Just two days before the storm, a small, stern-faced delegation had come to prepare us to lose him once more: with new elections coming, our party would need a strong man to represent it in the Cabinet.

The telephone was working again after lunch. Telegrams of concern and good will began to pour in from all over. Offers of help and sympathy from other kibbutzim, institutions, and organizations.

In our kibbutz calm reigned once more. Here and there police officers confabulated with regional officials, or an adviser huddled with a curious journalist. We were forbidden by Felix to talk to the press and the media, because it would be best for us to put forward a unanimous version when the time came to make our claim for the insurance.

• • •

At a quarter past one old Nevidomsky was brought home from the hospital, with his dislocated shoulder carefully set and his arm in an impressive sling, waving greetings with his free hand. At half past one we were mentioned on the news; again they stressed that it had been neither a typhoon nor a tornado but simply a limited, local phenomenon: two conflicting winds, one from the sea and the other from the desert, had met and caused a certain amount of turbulence. Such phenomena were of daily occurrence over the desert, but in settled areas they were infrequent, and the likelihood of a recurrence was remote. There was no cause for alarm, although it was advisable to remain on the alert.

Batya Pinski switched off the radio, stood up, and went over to the window. She peeped outside through the glass of the shutters. She cursed the kitchen crew who had neglected their duty in the confusion and forgotten to send her her lunch. They should know better than anyone how ill she was and how important it was for her to avoid strain and tension. Actually she did not feel in the least hungry, but that did nothing to diminish her indignation: They've forgotten. As if I didn't exist. As if it wasn't for them and their pink-faced brats that Abrasha gave his life in a faraway land. They've forgotten everything. And Abramek's also forgotten what he promised; he's not coming today after all. Come, Abramek, come, and I'll give you some ideas for the jacket and the dedication, I'll show you the havoc the storm has wrought here, you're bursting with curiosity and dying to see it with your own eyes, only you have no excuse, why should the director of the party publishing house suddenly drop all his work and come goggle at a disaster like a small child. So come, I'll give you your excuse, and I'll also give you some tea, and we'll talk about what we have to talk about.

She leapt across the room, spotting some dust on the bookshelf. She swept it away furiously with her hand. She stooped to pick up a leaf that had fallen from a potted plant onto the carpet. Then she drew Abramek Bart's letter from her dressing-gown pocket, unfolded it, and stared briefly at the secretary's signature, some Ruth Bardor, no doubt a painted hussy with bare thighs, no doubt she's shaved her legs and plucked her eyebrows and bleached her hair, no doubt she wears see-through panties and smothers herself in deodorants. God damn her. I've given those fish quite enough food for today; they'll get no more from me. Now here's another fly; I can't understand how they get in or where they hide. Perhaps they're born here. Kettle's boiling again. Another glass of tea.

11

AFTER THE embarrassing episode in the dining hall in the early forties, some of us were glad that the affair between Batya Pinski and Felix had been broken off in time. But all of us were sad about the change that took place in Batya. She would hit her child, even in the presence of other children. None of the advice or discussions did any good. She would pinch her till she was black and blue and call her names, including, for some reason, Carmen Miranda. The girl stopped wetting her bed but instead started to torture cats. Batya showed the first signs of asceticism. Her ripe, heady beauty was beginning to fade. There were still some who could not keep their eyes off her as she walked, straight and dark and voluptuous, on her way from the sewing room to the ironing room. But her face was hard, and around her mouth there played an expression of disappointment and spite.

And she continued to discipline the child with an iron hand.

Some of us were uncharitable enough to call her a madwoman; they even said of her: What does she think she is, a Sicilian widow, that cheap melodramatic heroine, that Spanish saint, that twopenny actress.

When the founders of the kibbutz moved into the first permanent buildings, Batya was among them. Zeiger volunteered to build her an aquarium in her new house. He did this out of gratitude. Zeiger was a thickset, potbellied, hirsute man. He was always joking, as if the purpose of life in general and his own life in particular was amusement. He had certain fixed witticisms, and his good humor did not desert him even when his wife did. He said to anyone who cared to listen: I am a mere proletarian, but Felix is going to be a commissar one day, when the revolution comes; I'd live with him myself, if only he'd have me.

He was a short, stocky man, who always smelled of garlic and tobacco. He moved heavily and clumsily like a bear, and there was an endearing lightheartedness about him — even when he was accidentally shot in the stomach during illegal weapon-practice in the old days. We were fond of him, especially at festivals, weddings, and parties, to which he made an indispensable contribution.

Ever since his wife left him, he had maintained a correspondence with a female relative, a divorcee herself, who lived in Philadelphia and whom he had never set eyes on. He used to call on Batya Pinski in the evenings, and she would translate the relative's letters from English into Yiddish and his comical replies from Yiddish into English. Batya had taught herself English from the novels she read in bed at night. He always apologized at the end of each visit for taking up her valuable time; but it was he who dug the flower bed in front of her new house, and raked it and mulched it and brought her bulbs and seedlings. His distinctive smell lingered in the room. Little Ditza loved to ask him riddles; he never knew the answers, or if he did he pretended not to, and she always laughed at his amazement when she told him.

One day he came with aluminum frames, panes of glass, a folding ruler, a screwdriver, and a sticky, smelly substance which he referred to as *kit* but which Batya taught him to call putty.

"An aquarium," he said, "for fish to swim in. It's aesthetic. It's soothing. And it doesn't make a noise and it doesn't make a mess."

And he set to work.

Batya Pinski took to calling him Ali Baba. Willingly accepting this nickname, he responded by calling her "the Contessa from Odessa."

It was perhaps because of this nickname that little Ditza began to address Zeiger as Pessah. Even though his real name was Fischel, we all came to call him Pessah, so that even in the kibbutz newsletter he was referred to as Pessah Zeiger.

Firmly but carefully he fitted the panes of glass into the soft bed of putty. At intervals he employed a tool that fascinated both Batya and Ditza: a diamond glass-cutter.

"How can we thank you for this beautiful present?" Batya asked when the aquarium was finished.

Zeiger pondered a moment or two, breathed out a gust of garlic and tobacco, winked to himself, and suddenly shrugged his shoulders and said, *"Chort znayet,"* which is to say, the Devil alone knows.

The fish were brought in a jar and put into the aquarium with a great deal of fuss. Ditza had invited all her friends to a "fish party," which did not please Batya. That evening Zeiger brought, in addition to the letter from his relative in Philadelphia, a small flask of brandy.

"Won't you offer me a drink?" he said.

Batya poured him a drink and translated the letter and his reply.

That evening we were celebrating the Allied victory. World War II was over, and the monster had been vanquished. We flew the Zionist and socialist flags from the top of the water tower. In the nearby British army camp there was a fireworks display, and in the small hours of the morning the soldiers came in army trucks to join in the singing and dancing. The girls of the kibbutz saw fit to consent for once to dance with the British soldiers, despite their smell of beer. The dining hall was decorated with slogans and with a large portrait of Josef Stalin in uniform. Felix delivered a passionate oration about the pure new world which was about to be built on the ruins of the defeated powers of darkness. He pledged to us all that we would never forget those who had sacrificed their lives in this struggle, here and on distant frontiers. Then he pinned the victory badge printed by the Workers' Party onto Batya's lapel, shook her hand, and kissed her. We rose to our feet, sang the Zionist anthem and the "Internationale," and danced all night. At ten past three Zeiger seized Batya's arm, dragged her almost forcibly out of the corner of the dining hall where she had been sitting silently all evening, and saw her to her room. His voice was hoarse and his white shirt was clinging to his back, because between dances he had taken it upon himself to act like a clown, as if this had been an old-fashioned Jewish wedding. When they got to Batya's door Zeiger said:

"That's it. You've had more than enough. And now, good night." He turned to go.

But she ordered him to come inside and he obeyed her. She took off his sweaty shirt. When he asked if he could wash his face, she said neither yes nor no, but instead she switched on the light in the aquarium and turned off the overhead light. He began to apologize or to plead but she cut his stammering short by pressing him to her, sweaty, steaming, unwashed, and embarrassed, and conquered him in silence.

12

IN A small village run on sound principles there are no secrets, nor can there be any.

Just before six o'clock in the morning, the neighbors saw Zeiger emerge, subdued, from Batya Pinski's door. By seven o'clock the news had already reached the sewing room. Some of us, including Felix and his wife, Zetka (who had previously been married to Zeiger), saw a positive aspect to this new development: after all, the whole situation had been unnatural and full of unnecessary tensions. Now everything would be much simpler. Martyrdoms, Mediterranean tragedies, emotional arabesques were irreconcilable with the principles according to which we guided our lives.

Even these people, however, could not accept what ensued with equanimity. Zeiger was the first, but he was not the last. Within a matter of weeks, news had spread of various peripheral characters' finding their way to Batya Pinski's room at night. She did not even turn up her nose at refugees, or at eccentrics like Matityahu Damkov. Her silent, noble melancholy had turned into something better left unnamed. And her face was becoming ugly.

Within a year or two even little Ditza was going around with soldiers and birds of passage. We were unable to devote our full attention to this unhappy episode, because the struggle to drive out the British was reaching its climax, and then regular Arab armies invaded the country; they reached the very gates of our kibbutz, and we repelled them almost barehanded. Finally all was calm again. Hordes of refugees poured in from all directions. Zeiger's relative, a middle-aged woman, also came, as a tourist, and dragged him back to Philadelphia with her. We were all sorry to see him go, and there were some who never forgave him. Felix accepted a central party position and graced us with his presence only on weekends. As for Batya, her last embers died. Ditza ran away again and again to the pioneering camps and the newly emerging settlements in the desert; again and again she was brought back. Her mother took to her room. She announced that her condition would not permit her to work any more. We did not know what this condition was, but we decided not to ask too many questions. We left her alone. We were all relieved when Ditza finally married Martin Zlotkin, the son of the well-known banker. Batya accepted the marriage and the presents of expensive furniture from the young couple calmly. It was the fish that were now in the center of the picture. The electric kettle was always on the boil. It seemed as though it was all over for her, when the matter of Abrasha's literary remains came up and it was decided to publish his collected essays along with his letters from Madrid. Just as Felix had promised at the victory celebrations: we would not forget our comrades who had sacrificed their lives. And Felix it was who, despite all his commitments, did not forget, and made the kibbutz-movement publishing house finally tackle the job. The widow waited day by day. The fish swam across the picture without blurring it. They were cold but alive, they were not subject to the law of gravity, since they could hover effortlessly in the water. Last night's storm will bring Abramek Bart; but it's two o'clock already, and he hasn't come yet. A man like him will be able to understand the delicate matter of the dedication; he won't make any difficulties.

13

BUT I can't receive him in my dressing gown. I must get dressed. I must tidy the room, if it's not tidy enough already. I must get out the best china, so that I can serve the tea properly. And open the shutters. Let some fresh air in. Freshen up the biscuits, too. But first of all, get dressed.

She went to the sink and washed her face repeatedly in cold water, as if to mortify her flesh. Then she ran her bony fingers over her face and hair in the mirror and said aloud, There, there, you're a good girl, you're lovable, don't worry, everything's all right.

She put a little makeup on and brushed her gray hair. For an instant she caught a glimpse in the mirror of the old witch the children called Baba Yaga, but at once she was replaced by a noble, lonely woman unbowed by her suffering. Batya preferred the latter, and said to her: No one else understands you, but I respect you. And the book is dedicated to Batya, a devoted wife, the fruits of my love and anguish.

Just as she pronounced these words she heard the squeal of brakes in the clearing in front of the dining hall. She leapt to the window, still disheveled because she had not had time to put the hairpins in place; she flung the shutters open and thrust her head out. Abramek Bart, director of the publishing house, got out of the car and held the door open for the secretary general of the movement.

Felix appeared from nowhere to greet them both with a warm yet businesslike handshake and a serious expression. They exchanged a few words and walked off together to inspect the damage

and the reconstruction work, which had been proceeding cease-
lessly since early in the morning.

14

SHE FINISHED getting ready. She put on her burgundy-colored
dress, a necklace, and an unobtrusive pair of earrings, dabbed a few
drops of perfume behind her ears, and put the water on to boil.
Meanwhile the blue daylight poured in through the open windows.
Children and birds were shrilling joyfully. The streaming light
seemed to dull the water in the aquarium. The old Spanish tune
came back to her lips, and a warm, deep voice emerged from her
chest. The song was compelling and full of longing. In the old days,
in the distant thirties, the Spanish freedom-fighters and their sym-
pathizers all over the world had been forever humming it. Abrasha could not stop singing it the night he left. A decade or so later,
during the Israeli War of Independence, it had acquired Hebrew
words. It was sung around the campfire among the old shacks by
pale-faced soldiers who had recently fled from Europe. Night after night it had drifted among the kibbutz buildings and had even
reached Batya Pinski:

> *The first dish to be served*
> *Is your beloved rifle*
> *Garnished with its magazines . . .*

Suddenly she made up her mind to go outside.

Bursting out among the fallen trees and broken glass, she saw the
sky peaceful and clear over the hills, as if nothing had happened.
She saw Matityahu Damkov, his bare back glistening with sweat,
mending a water pipe with silent rage. And farther away she could
see the empty spot where the wooden shacks, the first buildings of
the kibbutz, had stood. Workers were rooting among the wreckage.
A few goats grazed peacefully.

She reached the clearing in front of the dining hall at the very moment when Felix was escorting his guests back to their car. They were standing by the car, presumably running over the main points . of their discussion. Up to that moment Felix had kept his glasses in his shirt pocket; now he put them on again while he jotted down some notes, and at once he lost the look of a general and regained his habitual appearance of a philosopher.

Finally they shook hands once more. The visitors got into the car and Abramek started the engine. As he began to maneuver his way among the beams and scattered planks, Batya Pinski darted out of the bushes and tapped on the window with a wrinkled fist. The secretary general was momentarily alarmed and covered his face with his hands. Then he opened his eyes and stared at the terrifying figure outside. Abramek stopped the car, rolled the window down a fraction, and asked:

"What's up? Do you need a lift? We're not going to Tel Aviv, though. We're heading north."

"Don't you dare, Abramek, don't you dare leave out the dedication, or I'll scratch your eyes out and I'll raise such a stink that the whole country will sit up and take notice," Batya screeched without pausing to draw breath.

"What is this lady talking about?" asked the secretary general mildly.

"I don't know," Abramek replied apologetically. "I haven't got the faintest idea. In fact, I don't even know her."

Felix immediately took command of the situation.

"Just a minute, Batya, calm down and let me explain. Yes, this is our Comrade Batya Pinski. That's right, Abrasha's Batya. She probably wants to remind us of the moral obligation we all owe her. You remember what it's about, Abramek."

"Of course," said Abramek Bart. And then, as if assailed by sudden doubts, he repeated, "Of course, of course."

Felix turned to Batya, took her arm gently, and addressed her kindly and sympathetically:

"But not now, Batya. You can see what a state we're all in. You've chosen a rather inconvenient moment."

The car, meanwhile, was disappearing around the bend in the road. Felix took the time to see Batya back to her room. On the way he said to her:

"You have no cause to worry. We'll keep our promise. After all, we're not doing this just for your sake, there's no question of a personal favor to you; our young people need Abrasha's writings, they will be the breath of life for them. Please don't rush us. There's still plenty of time; you've got nothing to worry about. On the other hand, I gather you didn't get your lunch today, and for that you have reasonable grounds for complaint. I'll go to the kitchen right away and tell them to send you a hot meal: the boilers are working again now. Don't be angry with us, it hasn't been easy today. I'll be seeing you."

15

THERE WAS still the aquarium.

Now the fish could get the attention they deserved. First of all the old woman inspected the electrical fittings. Behind the tank there was concealed a veritable forest of plugs and sockets, of multicolored wires, of switches and transformers which kept the vital systems alive.

From a tiny electrical pump hidden underneath the tank, two transparent plastic tubes led into the water. One worked the filter, and the other aerated the water.

The filter consisted in a glass jar containing fibers. The water from the bottom of the tank was pumped up into the filter, to deposit the particles of dirt, uneaten food, and algae, and returned to the tank clear and purified. The aerator was a fine tube that carried air to the bottom of the tank, where it escaped through a perforated stone in a stream of tiny bubbles which enriched the water with oxygen and inhibited the growth of algae. These various appliances kept the water clear and fresh, and enabled the fish to display their array of breathtaking colors, and to dart hither and thither with magical swiftness.

A further electrical fixture without which the aquarium could not function was the heating element, a sealed glass tube containing a finely coiled electric wire. The glowing coil kept the water at a tropical temperature even on rainy days and stormy nights. The light and warmth worked wonders on the gray-green forests of water plants in the depths of which the fish had their home. From there shoal after shoal emerged to pursue a course that was unpredictable because subject to unknown laws. The quivering tails suggested a heart consumed by longing, rather than mere pond life. The fish were almost transparent; their skeletons were clearly visible through their cold skins. They, too, had a system of blood vessels; they, too, were subject to illness and death. But fish are not like us. Their blood is cold. They are cold and alive, and their cold is not death but a liveliness and vitality that makes them soar and plunge, wheel and leap in mid-course. Gravity has no power over them.

The plants and stones emphasize this by contrast. The sight of a school of swordfish swimming gently through the hollow stone arouses a grave doubt in the widow's mind. Is death a possibility, and if so, what need to wait, why not plunge in this very instant.

She presses her burning forehead against the glass. It feels as though the fish are swimming into her head. Here is peace and calm.

Breadth distracts the mind from depth. Depth also exists. It sends wave upon wave of dark stillness up toward the surface. And now the surface of the water reflects the crest-shorn palm trees.

The daylight fades and the windows darken.

Now she will close the shutters and draw the curtains. The kettle will boil again. More tea — this time in one of the china cups she has brought out specially. The fish are clustering around the underwater lamp as if they, too, can sense the approach of night.

A blue-tinged crystalline calm descends on our hills. The air is clear. The day's work is done. May she repose in peace. May the fish swim peacefully through her dreams. May she not be visited in the night by the crest-shorn palm trees. A last procession passes through the hollow stone. Darkness is coming.

1963

Upon This Evil Earth

1

JEPHTHAH WAS BORN at the edge of the desert. At the edge of the desert his grave was also dug.

For many years Jephthah roamed the desert in the company of wandering tribesmen close to the borders of the land of Ammon. Even when the elders of Israel came down to seek him in the desert and raised him to be judge of Israel, Jephthah did not leave the desert. He was a wild man. It was for his wildness that the elders of the congregation chose him as their leader. All these things befell in lawless times.

Jephthah was judge for six years. He was victorious in every war he fought. But his countenance was ravaged. He did not love Israel and he did not hate his enemies. He belonged to himself, and even to himself he was a stranger. All the days of his life, even when he sat within his own house, his eyes were narrowed as if for protection against the dust of the desert or the dazzling light. Or else they were turned inward, because nowhere around could he find.

Indeed, on the day of his victory over the Ammonites, when he returned to his father's estate and the people shouted for triumph and the daughters of Israel sang: Jephthah has slain, Jephthah has slain, the man stood as if in a daze. One of the elders of the tribe who was present thought in his heart: This man is deceptive; his heart is not here with us but far away.

His father's name was Gilead the Gileadite. His mother was an Ammonite harlot named Pitdah daughter of Eitam. He named his daughter Pitdah after her. Toward the end of his days, when he was drawing near to death, Jephthah thought of those two women as one.

His mother Pitdah had died when Jephthah was a young man. His brothers, his father's sons, drove him out into the desert because he was the son of another woman.

In the desert bitter-hearted wanderers gathered around him, and he became their leader because he possessed the attributes of lordship. He knew how to speak to them either in a warm voice or with cold malice, at will. Moreover, when firing an arrow, taming a horse, pitching a tent, the man seemed to move slowly, as if weary or sluggish, but this was deceptive, like a dagger reposing in folds of silk. He could say to a man: Rise, come, go; and the man would rise or come or go, although Jephthah the Gileadite made not a sound, only his lips moved. He spoke little because he did not like words and did not trust them.

For many years Jephthah dwelled in the mountains of the desert, and even when he was surrounded by tumultuous throngs of men he was always alone. One day the elders of Israel came down to ask him to fight for them against the Ammonites. They gathered up the hems of their robes because of the dust of the desert and went down on their knees before the wild man. Jephthah stood facing them, listening in silence, and he surveyed their broken pride as though it were a wound. Sorrow suddenly took hold of him, not sorrow for the elders, perhaps not sorrow at all, but something resembling gentleness, and gently he said to them:

"The son of a whore will be your leader."

And voicelessly the elders echoed:
"Our leader."

All this took place in the desert, outside the land of the Ammonites, outside the land of Israel, deep in the silence amid shifting surroundings: sand, mist, low scrub, white mountains, and black boulders.

Jephthah defeated Ammon, returned to his father's estate, and fulfilled his vow. He was certain that he was being confronted with a test, a test that he would withstand. As soon as he had bound his daughter he would be told: Lay not thine hand upon the girl.

Afterward he returned to the desert.

He had loved Pitdah and trusted the night sounds that filled the desert every night. Jephthah the Gileadite died in the mountains in the place which is called the Land of Tob. Some men are born and come into the world to see with their own eyes the light of day and the light of night and to call the light light. But sometimes a man comes and traverses the length of his days in gloom and at his death he leaves behind him a trail of foam and rage. At Jephthah's death his father dug a grave and over it he said:

"He judged Israel for six years by the grace of God."

And then he added:

"The grace of God is vanity."

For four days every year, the daughters of Israel go to the mountains to lament Pitdah daughter of Jephthah. An old blind man follows them at a distance. The dry desert winds snatch the tears from among his wrinkles. But all the winds cannot take away the salt, and it dries, scorching, on the old man's cheeks. To the mountains go the daughters of Israel to send forth their wailing to the desert, lands of fox and asp and hyena, wide expanses eaten by white light.

Bitter-hearted men, wanderers of the Land of Tob, hear their weeping in the night and respond from the distance with a bitter song.

2

THE PLACE of Jephthah's birth was at the edge of the land. The
estate of Gilead the Gileadite was at the far end of the tribe's patrimony. Here the desert licked at the sown land, and sometimes it
would penetrate into the orchards and touch both men and cattle.
In the morning, as soon as the sun burst over the eastern mountains, it would begin to scorch the whole land. At midday it fell like
blazing hail and smote everything with outpoured wrath. At the
end of the day the sun descended westward to burn the mountain
heights to the west. The boulders changed color and took on from
a distance the semblance of desperate movement, as though they
were being roasted alive.

But at night the land was calm. Cool breezes spread over it gently, like a caress. Dew covered the boulders. The night breeze was
merciful. This mercy was transitory, and yet it returned ever and
again, like the cycle of birth and death, like wind and water, alter-
nating hatred and longing, a shadow that came and went.

Gilead the Gileadite, the lord of the estate, was a tall, broad man.
The sun had scorched the skin of his face. He strove with all his
might to subdue his spirit, but even so he was a tyrant. His words
always left his mouth reproachfully or in a venomous whisper, as
though whenever he spoke he had to silence other voices. If he laid
his strong rough hand on the head of one of his sons, on the neck
of his horse, or on a woman's hips, they knew without looking that
it was Gilead. Sometimes he would touch an inanimate object, not
because he wished to say or do anything, but because he was smitten with doubts: the substantiality of all things suddenly filled him
with wonder. And sometimes he sought to handle things that cannot be touched — sounds, longings, smells. When night came Gil-

ead would sometimes say suddenly: Night has come. Such words are surely unnecessary. In the evening he would summon his household priest to read to him from a holy book, and he would shrink and listen. Even in trivial matters he would turn to God and ask for the birth of a bull calf or the repair of cracked earthenware pitchers. At times he would laugh for no reason at all.

All these things inspired great fear in his servants. Whenever loud hoarse laughter burst from him in the fields at midday in midsummer, the slaves laughed with him out of fear. Or sometimes in the night Gilead was suddenly overcome by a cold hatred of the cold starlight, and he would shout aloud and assemble all the men and women in the courtyard. Before their eyes he would stoop and pick up a large stone, and his eyes shone white in the dark as though he meant to hurl the stone and fell a man. Then slowly and painfully, as though the breath were being squeezed out of him, he would bend and replace the stone in the dust of the courtyard, as gently as if he were placing glass on glass, taking great care not to hurt the stone or the dust or the silence of the night, for the nights in that place were quiet, and any sounds that passed through them were like dark shadows moving silently beneath the surface of the waters.

Gilead's wife was the offspring of priests and merchants, and her name was Nehushtah daughter of Zebulun. She was white as chalk and timorous. In her youth in her father's house, she had known dreams and darkness. She was passionately fond of small objects, little creatures, buttons and butterflies, earrings, morning dew, apple blossom, cat's-paws, soft lamb's wool, slivers of light shimmering in water.

Gilead took Nehushtah to wife because he thought he detected in her signs of an inner thirst which nothing in the world could ever quench or assuage. Whenever she said, "Look, a stone," or "Look at that valley," she seemed to be saying, "Come, come." He yearned to touch this thirst the way a man may suddenly ache to feel some

idea or desire with his very fingertips. And Nehushtah followed after Gilead because she saw in him sorrow and strength.

Nehushtah longed to dissolve his strength and penetrate his sorrow and at the same time submit to them. However, Gilead and
Nehushtah were unable to do all these things to each other because,
after all, body and soul are no more than body and soul, and living
men and women are not able to plumb their depths. A few months
after she arrived at Mizpeh of Gilead she was already in the habit
of standing alone at the window pleading with her eyes, hoping
that across the wilderness and the mountains she might descry the
plains of black earth from which she had been brought here to the
desert. In the evenings she said to him:

"When will you take me."

And Gilead would answer:

"But I have already taken you."

"When shall we ride away from here."

"All places are the same."

"But I cannot endure any more."

"Who can. Bring me wine and apples and leave me, go to your
room or sit at the window if you like; just stop staring into the darkness like that."

After years went by, after she had given birth to Jamin, Jemuel, and
Azur, Nehushtah fell ill and seemed to be in the grip of a sensuous
decay. She was already white as chalk, and her skin grew ever finer.
She hated the desert that blew in at the window of her room all day
long and at night whispered to her, "Lost lost," and she also hated
the savage songs of the shepherds and the lowing of the beasts in
the courtyard and in her dreams. Sometimes she called her husband
a dead man and her children orphans. And sometimes she would
say of herself, Surely I, too, have long been dead, and she would sit
for three days at the window without tasting food or water. The
place was very remote, and from the window she could see by day
only sand dunes and mountains and at night stars and darkness.

Three sons did Nehushtah daughter of Zebulun bear to Gilead the Gileadite: Jamin, Jemuel, and Azur. She was white and her skin grew ever finer. She could not endure the man's moods. If she complained and wept, Gilead would raise his voice and shout and dash the pitcher of wine to clattering smithereens. If she sat silently at the window stroking the cat or playing with earrings and brooches on her lap, Gilead would stand and watch and laugh hoarsely, exuding a shaggy smell. At times he would take pity on her and say:

"Perhaps the king will hear of your sorrow. Perhaps he will send chariots and horses to take you to him. Perhaps today or tomorrow torches will appear in the distance and the outrunners will arrive."

And Nehushtah would say:

"There is no king. There are no outrunners. Why should anyone run. There is nothing."

At these words Gilead would be filled with compassion for her and terrible anger at himself and at what he had done to her, and he would beat his chest with his fists and curse himself and his memory. In the midst of his compassion he would suddenly despise her, or himself and his compassion for her, and he would shut himself up and hide his face. For many days she would not see him, and then one night toward the dawn, when she had despaired of him, he would come and throw himself upon her in love. In his love-making he would purse his lips like a man straining to break an iron chain with his bare hands.

He was a moody and hopeless man. At night, if the torchlight fell on his face it looked like one of the masks with which the pagan priests covered their faces. It may happen that a man traverses all the days of his life like an exile in a strange land to which he did not choose to come and from which he cannot escape.

In the winter Gilead was filled with melancholy. He would lie on his back for a day or a week with his eyes fixed on the arched ceiling, staring blankly and seeing nothing. Then Nehushtah would sometimes enter his bedchamber and fondle him with her pale fingers as if he were one of her pet animals. Her lips were as white as a sickness, and he yielded his body to them as a weary traveler yields himself to a harlot in a wayside inn. And upon both of them there was silence.

But when mounting vigor roused his body against him, Nehushtah took refuge in her innermost chamber, and Gilead would storm into the women's quarters to relieve on the maidservants the pressure of the boiling venom. All night long the quarters were alive with wet sounds and low tremulous moaning and the squeals of the maids, until the dawn, when Gilead would burst forth and rudely awaken the household priest. Cowering at his feet, he would sob: Unclean, unclean. Then, with the tears still wet on his face, he would knock the priest flat on his back with a punch, and out he would rush to saddle his horse and gallop away into the eastern hills.

In the women's quarters there was a little Ammonite concubine named Pitdah daughter of Eitam, whom the Gileadites had snatched in the course of one of their raids on the Ammonite settlements beyond the desert. Pitdah was a strong, slender girl whose eyes were shaded by thick lashes. If she directed her green-eyed gaze at her lord's lips or at his chest, if she stood facing him in the courtyard with her fingertips fluttering over her belly, he would tremble and curse the little servantgirl. Bellowing aloud, he would clasp both her hands in one of his and bite her lips until the two of them screamed together. Her hips were never still, and even when she came and stood at the stable door to inhale the smell of horses' sweat, they seemed to be dancing to a secret inner rhythm. Fire and ice sparkled green in the pupils of her eyes. And she always walked barefoot.

In time it transpired that the Ammonite woman practiced sorcery. This was disclosed by her rivals, who had seen her at night brewing herbs in the night with a gleam in her eye. Pitdah called to the dead at night and summoned them to her, because she had been dedicated from her childhood as a priestess of Milcom the god of Ammon. The trees in the orchard rustled secretively in the darkness and the doors of the house shrieked in the wind. She worked her magic in the cellars at night and the brew bubbled and boiled and the woman's shadow quivered and flickered over rotting saddles and casks of wine, on wooden threshing sledges and iron chains.

When her doings came to light, Gilead ordered her to be given a leather flask of water and sent away into the desert to the dead to whom she called at night, for it is written: Thou shalt not suffer a witch to live.

But at first light the lord saddled his horse and rode out and brought her home. He cursed her gods and struck her face with the back of his rough hand.

Pitdah blew in his face and cursed him and his people and his God. A hot green sparkle glinted in the pupil of her eye.

Suddenly they both laughed and went inside. The door closed behind them while outside the horses neighed.

Gilead's wife Nehushtah urged her three sons against the Ammonite woman because she could endure no more. She rose from her bed and stood at the window in her white robe, with her back to the room and her sons and her face to the desert, and she whispered to them, You see your mother dying before your eyes and you are silent: do not be silent.

But Jamin and Jemuel feared their father and would not raise a finger.

Only Azur, the youngest of her sons, hearkened to her and plotted against the Ammonite servantgirl. This Azur devoted all his days to the dogs of the estate. He it was who fed and watered them, taught them tricks, and trained them to go straight for the throat. In Mizpeh of Gilead they said of him: That Azur understands the dogs' tongue and can howl or bark in the dark like one of them. Azur had a small gray wolf cub that ate from his dish and drank from his cup, and both of them had sharp white teeth.

One day at the beginning of autumn, when Gilead had gone away to another field, Azur set his dogs on Pitdah the Ammonite concubine. He stood in the shade of the house and let out a guttural growl when Pitdah went past, and the dogs, with the wolf cub in their midst, darted from the dungheap and almost tore her apart.

At nightfall Gilead returned home and gave his son Azur over to a cruel slave, shriveled and shorn, to take him out to the desert, as shall be done to a murderer.

In the night the wild beasts howled, their eyes gleaming yellow in the darkness beyond the stockade.

This time, too, Gilead set out on horseback at the end of the night and brought his son back. He struck and cursed his son just as he had struck and cursed his concubine.

After these things it came to pass that the Ammonite woman cast a spell upon the boy Azur: for forty days he howled and barked and could not speak a word.

Upon her lord Pitdah also cast a dark spirit, because he had spared Azur and she did not forgive him this pardon. A brooding gloom fell on the master of the house which only lifted when he consumed large draughts of wine.

When Pitdah bore Jephthah, Gilead the Gileadite shut himself up in the cellar of the house for four days and five nights. All through these nights he clinked cup on cup, drained them both, and filled them again. On the fifth night he collapsed on the ground. In his dream he saw a black horseman with a lance of black fire, mounted on a black horse, while a floating woman who was neither Pitdah nor Nehushtah but a stranger held the reins; horse and rider followed her silently. Gilead did not forget this dream, because he believed, like some other men, that dreams are sent to us from that place from which man comes and to which he returns through his death.

When the child Jephthah grew old enough to leave the women's quarters and walk about in the courtyard, he learned to hide from his father. He would shelter in a haystack until the heavy man had passed and his sinister footsteps had receded, so that he should not find him. Until Gilead disappeared the infant would chew straw or hay or his own finger and whisper to himself: Quiet, quiet.

If the child was so absorbed in his dreams that it was too late for him to hide, Gilead the Gileadite would catch him and wave him aloft between his frightening hands and moo at him, and he smelled sweaty and shaggy, so that the child howled with pain and fear and planted his tiny teeth in his father's shoulder in a vain effort to free himself from the powerful grasp.

3

JEPHTHAH WAS born facing the desert. The estate of Gilead the Gileadite was the last of all the tribe's patrimony. At its fringe began the desert, and beyond the desert was the land of the Ammonites.

Gilead the Gileadite possessed flocks of sheep, and he also had fields and vineyards whose margins were yellowed by the desert. The house was surrounded by a high stone wall. The house itself was also built of black volcanic stone. An ancient vine sprawled over its walls. On summer days people seemed to come and go through a thicket of vines; the foliage was so dense that the stone walls of the house could not be seen in summer.

Toward morning sheep bells could be heard, and the shepherds' pipes spread vague enchantments, the water whispered quietly in the irrigation channels, and a gray light shone in the wells. There was calm toward morning over all Gilead's estate.

Within the calm rippled a suppressed yearning. The shade of large trees concealed chilly twilight.

But every night dark, impassive shepherds guarded the farmstead against bears and nomads and Ammonite marauders. All night long torches flamed on the rooftop and a pack of lean hounds lurked in the darkness of the orchards. The household priest flitted like a dark shadow along the fences in the night, conjuring evil spirits.

From his earliest childhood Jephthah knew all the sounds of the night. He knew them in his blood, sounds of wind and wolf and bird of prey, and human sounds disguised as wind and fox and bird.

Beyond the fence lived another world, which silently yearned by day and night to raze the house to the ground, gnawing slyly and with infinite patience, like a stream slowly eating away at its banks. It was unimaginably soft and quiet, softer than a mist, quieter than a breeze, and yet ever-present: powerful and invisible.

Black goats kept the boy company; he led them to pasture and watched them all day long munching the sparse grass, risking their lives on the sheer crags of the narrow strip of pasture that survived among the rocky ravines, for the place was on the edge of the desert. He was also accompanied by emaciated dogs, his brother Azur's dogs. They were rough dogs, and savagery always lurked beneath their obsequiousness. Wild birds also flocked to Jephthah, shrieking their reproaches in his ears.

Early in the morning birds screeched in the distance. In the evening, as twilight fell, the crickets shrilled as though they had an urgent, fearful message to deliver. In the dark Jephthah heard a fine stillness pierced occasionally by the cry of a fox or jackal, punctuated by a hyena's laughter.

Sometimes desert nomads raided the estate at night. In the darkness Gilead's shepherds lay in wait for the foe, who came as softly as a breath; if he slew he stole silently away, and if he was slain he died as silently. In the morning they would find a man lying on his back under the olive trees, his hand perhaps still clutching the haft of the knife that was sunk in his flesh and his eyes turned inward. Shepherd or foeman alike.

Seeing the whites of the corpse's bulging eyes, Jephthah would say to himself: A corpse turns his eyes inward, perhaps there he finds other sights to see.

Sometimes Jephthah dreamed of his own death, and he seemed to feel strong, kindly hands bearing him down to the plain. Softly, sweetly, a light drizzle touched him, and a little shepherd girl said: Here for a while we shall sit and rest until after the rain and the light.

In the summertime the vegetation ran riot in the orchards and the ripening fruit filled out with moisture. Powerful juices coursed through the veins of the apple trees. The vine shoots seemed to shudder with the pressure of pent-up sap. Goats sported wantonly and the bull bellowed and raged. In the women's quarters and in the shepherds' booths there was heavy panting; toward dawn the boy could hear in his slumber a sound like a dying beast's groans. Women also occupied his dreams: Jephthah was filled with longing for delicate forces he could not name, not silk, not water, not skin, not hair, but a yearning for a warm, melting touch, hardly a touch at all, perhaps river-thoughts, smells, colors, and not that, either.

He did not like words and therefore he was silent.

In his dreams on summer nights in his youth, he forced his way gently upstream.

In the morning, when he rose, he took the dagger and slowly, patiently tested with it everything he found in the courtyard: Dust. Bark. Wool. Stone. Water.

Jephthah did not display his father's moods. He was a strong, finely shaped boy; colors, sounds, smells, and objects attracted him much more than words or people. When he was twelve he could handle an ax, a ewe, a cudgel, or a bridle. As he did so, a controlled excitement could sometimes be discerned in him.

And now the hatred of his brothers Jamin, Jemuel, and Azur began to close in all around him. They wished him ill because he was the son of another woman, because of his haughty silence, and because of the arrogant calm that seemed at every moment to be concealing stubborn, secretive thoughts which brooked no sharing. If ever the brothers invited him to join in their games, he played with them without saying anything. If he won a contest he did not boast or gloat, but merely shut himself up in a silence which increased their hatred sevenfold. And if one of the brothers defeated Jephthah, it always seemed as though he himself had voluntarily renounced the victory out of calculation or contempt, or because he had lost his concentration in the middle of the game.

The three brothers, Jamin, Jemuel, and Azur, were solidly built, broad-shouldered youths. In their own way they knew joys and laughter. Jephthah, on the other hand, the son of the other woman, was slim and fair. Even when he laughed he seemed withdrawn. He had a habit of fixing his gaze on others and refusing to look away. A fleeting yellow spark would flash in his eyes, compelling others suddenly to yield.

Because of Pitdah's spells, or perhaps because of fear of their father, the brothers did not dare to mistreat Jephthah as they wished. They merely hissed from a distance in a whisper: Just you wait.

Once Pitdah said: Weep, Jephthah, cry out to our god Milcom, he will hearken and protect you from their whispering hatred.

But in this matter Jephthah did not heed his mother. He did not weep to Milcom god of Ammon but merely bowed low and said to his mother: As my lady mother says. As though he considered Pitdah to be the lady of the house.

She wanted to bring down on her son the blessing of Milcom god of Ammon, because she foresaw that she would die and that the boy would be left alone among strangers. And so she brewed her potions at night and fed them at night to Jephthah. When her fingers touched his cheek he would tremble.

In his heart Jephthah had no faith in these potions, but neither did he refuse to drink them. He loved their strange, pungent smell, the smell of his mother's fingers. And she would speak to him of Milcom, whom the Ammonites worshiped with wine and silk.

Not like your father's god, a barren god who afflicts and humiliates those who love him. No, Milcom loves marauders, he loves those who are merry with wine, he loves those who pour out their hearts in song, and the music that blurs the line between ecstasy and rage.

Of the God of Israel Pitdah said: Woe to those who sin against him and woe to those who worship him in faith; he will afflict them both alike with agonies because he is a solitary god.

Jephthah observed the stars in the summer sky over the estate and the desert. They seemed to him to be all alone, each star by itself in the black expanse, some of them circling all night long from one end of the sky to the other, while others remained rooted to one spot. There was no sorrow in all the stars, nor was there any joy in them. If one of them suddenly fell, none of the others noticed or so much as blinked, they simply went on flickering coldly. The falling star left behind it a trail of cold fire, and the fiery trail also faded and gave way to darkness. If you stood barefoot and strained to listen, you might hear a silence within the silence.

The household priest who taught the other brothers also taught Jephthah to read and write from the holy scriptures. Once Jephthah asked the priest why God was more merciful to Abel and Isaac, Jacob, Joseph, and Ephraim, and why he preferred them to their elder brothers, Cain, Ishmael, Esau, and Manasseh: surely all the evil in the scriptures came from God himself, surely it was to him that the blood of Abel cried from the earth.

The household priest was a corpulent man with small, anxious eyes. He was constantly shrinking from the wrath of the lord of the house. The priest replied to Jephthah that the ways of God were wonderful and who could say to God why or wherefore. At night Jephthah dreamed of God coming heavy and shaggy, a bear-God with rapacious jaws who growled at him panting gasping and panting as though he were throbbing with lust or boiling rage. Jephthah cried out in his dream. People occasionally cried out in their sleep in Gilead's house, and at the end of their cries there was silence.

Milcom, too, crept into Jephthah's dreams on those summer nights. Warm currents coursed luxuriantly through his veins as the silken fingers touched his skin and sweet juices washed through him to the soles of his feet.

Next morning Jephthah would appear solitary and withdrawn in the great courtyard, skipping from shadow to shadow, and the yellow glint had even faded from the pupils of his eyes.

When Jephthah was a boy of about fourteen, he began to be favored with signs. As he walked alone in the fields or followed the flocks down into one of the gullies, he was beset by signs, and he felt that it was to him alone that they were directed, that he was being called. But he could not discover what the signs were or who was calling him. Sometimes he fell on his knees as the household priest had taught him and struck his head on the rock and pleaded aloud: Now, now.

In his mind he weighed the love of God against the love of Milcom. He found the love of Milcom very easy, it came to him at almost no cost, like the love of a dog. You play with it for a moment and you have won its heart; it will come close, lick your hand, and perhaps even guard your sleep in the field.

But to ask for the love of God Jephthah did not dare, because he did not know what. If a momentary pride flared up inside him and he made a mental comparison, saying: I am the youngest, I am like Abel and Isaac and Jacob, sons of their parents' old age, at once he would recall that he was the son of another woman, like Ishmael, who was the son of the Egyptian woman.

One day the lord told his household that God must be approached not in the way that a butterfly approaches a flower but as it approaches the fire.

The boy heard these words and he also put them to the test.

He began to seek out dangers with which to challenge himself. He tested himself on the mountain crags, in the shifting sands, in the well. He even pitted himself against a wolf. One night he went out alone and unarmed to find the wolf and fight it at the mouth of its lair, and with his bare hands he broke the beast's back, and returned home from the test merely bitten and scratched. He was trying to court God's favor, and in the autumn he even trained himself to pass his hand through the fire without crying out.

Some of these acts were seen by the household priest, and he went and told the lord that the Ammonite was passing his hand through fire. Gilead heard the priest out, then his face clouded with rage, he gave a wild laugh, cursed the priest, and gave him a blow that sent him sprawling.

That night Gilead the Gileadite gave orders for the concubine's son to be found and brought to him. A fire was burning in the hall, because it was a cold desert night and the air was dry and biting. The walls of the hall were hung with saddles, iron chains, shields, threshing sledges, and spears of polished bronze. All these objects caught the firelight and reflected it gloomily.

Gilead fixed his gray eyes on the other woman's son and stared at him long and hard. He could not recall why he had sent for him at night, or why the dogs were barking outside in the dark. At the end of his silence Gilead said:

"My son, I am told that you pass your hand through the fire and that you do not cry out when you do it."

Jephthah said:

"That is the truth."

Gilead said:

"And why should you do such a wrong and painful thing?"

Jephthah said:

"To prepare myself, Father."

"Prepare yourself for what?"

"I do not know for what."

As Jephthah spoke to his father he looked at the broad, rough hand that rested heavily on an earthen tray. At the sight of his father's hand his own pale, thin hand filled with fear and longing.

Perhaps he imagined that his father might speak to him lovingly. Perhaps he imagined that his father might ask for his love. At that moment, for the first and only time in his whole life, Jephthah suddenly yearned to be a woman. And he did not know what. In the brazier the fire blazed and sparks of firelight glowed dully on the bronze weapons hanging on the walls, and in the lord's eyes, too, a certain spark gleamed.

Gilead said in a whisper:

"Very well, put your hand in the fire and let us see."

Jephthah looked entreatingly into his father's face, but Gilead the Gileadite's face was hidden in the flickering light and shadow, for the tongues of fire in the brazier were darting restlessly hither and thither. The boy said:

"My father's word is my command."

Gilead said:

"Put your hand in now."

Jephthah said:

"If you will love me."

As he put out his hand his teeth showed as if he were laughing, but Jephthah was not laughing.

Suddenly his father shouted:

"My son, do not touch the fire. That is enough."

But Jephthah did not want to hear, and he did not avert his eyes. The fire touched the flesh, and beyond the fence the desert stretched to the most distant hills.

After this episode Gilead said to Jephthah his son:

"You are tainted as your father is tainted. And yet I cannot bring myself to hate you."

Then the lord poured wine from the earthen pitcher into two rough cups and said:

"Jephthah, you will take wine with me."

And because neither the man nor the boy could trust words or liked words, half the night passed before either of them spoke another word.

Finally Gilead rose to his feet and spoke.

"Now, my son, go. Do not hate your father and do not love him. It is an ill thing that we must be each of us son to a father and father to a son and man to a woman. Distance upon distance. Now, don't stand there staring. Go."

4

AFTER THESE things it sometimes happened that father and son rode out together toward dawn in the open country. They would cross the bed of the ravine and mount the slope that led up to the expanse of broad sands, and very slowly, as though riding in a dream, they would traverse the parched plateau. Stubborn, forlorn shrubs sprouted here and there among the crevices of the rock. They seemed less like plants than like the loins of the barren boulders. A baneful white light beat mercilessly down. When they had ridden far away, a fitful conversation might flare up between them.

Gilead might say:

"Jephthah, where do you want to go."

And Jephthah, his eyes narrowed against the brutally blazing light, would reply, after a silence:

"To my own place. Home."

Then Gilead, with a hint of a smile fleeting across his stony face, would ask:

"Well, why don't we turn around and ride for home."

And Jephthah, himself almost smiling, his voice remote and abstracted:

"That is not my home."

"Then where is your home, what home do you want to go to."

"That, Father, is what I do not yet know."

• • •

After this exchange, silence would close in once more. But now they were both within the same silence and not in two separate silences. The boy would be full of love, and lovingly he would stroke his horse's mane. Once, when they came to the valley of black basalt, he asked his father:

"What is the desert trying to say, what thought is the wasteland, why does the wind come and why does it suddenly drop, with what sense must a man hear the thronging sounds, and with what sense may he hear the silence?"

To which Gilead replied:

"You for yourself. I for myself. Every man for himself."

And after a moment he added, this time with a shadow of compassion in his voice:

"There is a lizard. Now it has gone."

And with that they both relapsed into their shared silence.

As they rode back to the farm, Gilead the Gileadite might stretch out his broad, rough hand and suddenly hold his son's bridle for a moment or two. And they rode close together.

Then he would let go as they came through the fence. Jephthah would be dismissed to join the other youngsters in the farmyard, while Gilead would go into the house.

During the last winter Pitdah sometimes came to Jephthah's bedroom at night. Barefoot, she would come and sit on the edge of his bed, whispering spells. She was given to laughing suddenly, a soft, warm laugh, until the boy could no longer contain himself and laughed along with her, without making a sound. Or else she would sing him gentle Ammonite songs about the vast expanses of water or the buck in the vineyards or about suffering and grace.

She would take his hand in hers and draw his fingers slowly up her arm slowly over her shoulder slowly around her soft neck. And she would entice him to Milcom god of pleasure, whispering rapid strange words, the secret of his own flesh and everything of which flesh was capable. And she also entreated him to flee from the desert to the places of shade and water before the desert succeeded in parching his blood and his flesh.

Jephthah had never set eyes on the sea in his life, he did not know its smell or the sound of its waves in the night, but he called his mother, Sea, sea.

One night, after she had left him, Jephthah had a dream. The bald, shriveled steward came and sheared a ewe closely, then sheared her again until her skin showed pink and sickly, crisscrossed with countless veins, and the servant sheared her yet again and slaughtered the ewe, not by the throat but by the belly, and black blood gushed and bubbled and stuck to Jephthah's skin in his dream and then God came heavy and iron-shouldered clad in a bearskin and he was hot and parched. On a carpet of vine leaves Milcom lay wrapped in silk and jewels, and Jephthah saw God force his way into the silk as a ram forces his way with bloodshot eyes into a ewe stooping submissively as if stupefied by the powerful rage unleashed against her.

Jephthah woke from this bad dream drenched in sweat. He opened his eyes and lay trembling feverishly and saw darkness, and he closed his eyes and again saw nothing but darkness and he started to whisper a prayer which he had learned from the household priest and still he saw darkness and he tried singing his mother's songs but still the darkness did not release him and he lay on his bed as though petrified because he imagined that while he was dreaming they had all, his father and mother, the priest and the maidservants, the sheep and the shepherds and his stepbrothers and the farmdogs and even the wandering nomads outside, been carried off dead and he was left all alone by himself and outside in the dark the desert stretched to the ends of the earth.

One night at the end of that winter Pitdah died. The maidservants said, The Ammonite whore has died by her sorcery. So she was buried on the following day in the plot reserved for outcasts.

On the horizon at the end of the plain that morning a gray sand-storm rose up tall and furious in the distance, and all the air was filled with dust and the smell of a gathering tempest. All the land was covered with a fine ash. And meanwhile the household priest tossed earth onto the dead woman's grave and uttered a dark oath: Leave us now and go to the accursed place from which you were taken and do not return to us either in the dark or in a dream, lest the curse of God pursue you even in your death and the demons of destruction hound you. Go, go, accursed one, go and never return, and let us have rest. Amen.

At the sound of these words the boy Jephthah picked up a small stone and touched his lips with it, and suddenly he pleaded out of the depths: God love me and I will be your servant, touch me and I will be the leanest and most terrible of your hounds, only do not be remote.

After the burial the sky closed in. Massive, dark shapes sped in succession on the wind, as though sent to crash against the wall of mountains to the east or to break through that same mountain wall. Later still, white flashes struck and then the low thunder rolled. The house built entirely of black volcanic stone stood in the midst of the storm looking as though it had already been burned.

Jephthah returned from the burial ground and entered the house. Pressed against the dark wall in the shadow of the entrance hall stood his three half-brothers, Jamin, Jemuel, and Azur, as though awaiting his return. He passed between them in the narrow hall, and their chests almost brushed his shoulders as he passed, yet not one of them moved or stirred. Only the wolflike look in their eyes groped at Jephthah's skin as he passed between them in the entrance to the house. He did not speak and the brothers did not speak to him, they did not even speak to one another, not a whisper passed among them. All day long the three of them paced up and down the passages of the house; every footfall gave an impression of supreme delicacy, even though the brothers were generally clumsy men.

Jamin, Jemuel, and Azur paced up and down the house on tiptoe all day long, as though their brother Jephthah were dangerously ill.

Toward evening their mother Nehushtah left her bed and her bedchamber and went to stand at a window. But contrary to her habitual custom, she did not look through the window to see what was outside, but stood with her back to the window and her eyes on the orphan boy. With a chalk-white hand Nehushtah daughter of Zebulun stroked her hair. She said to her sons:

"From now on he, too, is an orphan cub."

And the sons said:

"Because his mother is dead."

She added in a whisper:

"You are all large and dark, but one of you is quite different, fair and very thin."

And Jamin, the eldest, said:

"Thin and fair, but not one of us. The night is falling."

That same night Nehushtah his stepmother suddenly came to see Jephthah in his room on the rooftop. She opened the door and stood barefoot in the doorway, just as Pitdah used to come barefoot, but between Nehushtah's white fingers there was a white candle, and its flame was trembling violently. Jephthah saw her wan smile as she came close to his bed and passed a cold, damp hand across his brow. She whispered to him:

"Orphan. Go to sleep now, orphan."

He did not know what to say to her.

"You are mine now, thin little orphan cub. Go to sleep now."

With her fingertips she touched the curls on his chest for a moment. Then stopped.

When she left the room the stepmother blew out the lamp. She took both the lamp and the candle out with her when she went. It was dark.

All night long the storm raged outside. The wind hurled itself drunkenly against the walls of the house. The pillars groaned and the wooden ceiling whistled and creaked. In the yard the dogs went mad. The terrified cattle moaned and wailed in the darkness.

Jephthah stood watching at the door until dawn in case they came. He gripped his knife between his teeth. He imagined that beyond the door he could hear soft footsteps padding up and down, the whisper of cloth rubbing against stone, a rustling sound on the topmost stair. And outside a hyena laughed, a bird screeched, iron clanged at the edge of the shadows. The house and the farm stood strange and sinister.

At first light Jephthah slipped out through the window of his room and shinned down the vine with his knife between his teeth. He stole bread, water, a horse, and a dagger from the empty farmyard and fled to the desert to escape from Jamin, Jemuel, and Azur his brothers, his father's sons.

Gilead the Gileadite, the lord of the property, had not appeared at the graveside of his servant Pitdah in the plot reserved for outcasts, nor after the burial, in the evening or the night.

The sun rose and the storm ceased. The desert sand drank up all the puddles of water and once more became arid and brilliant in the terrible light.

The whiteness of those wide expanses rose uncompromising and merciless.

Only in the crannies of the rocks did a little water still remain, dazzled by the blinding sunlight. For a moment Jephthah imagined that the hollows of the stones were clutching the remains of last night's lightning. He had seen all these sights before in his dreams. Everything, the mountains, the sand dunes, the wind, and the dazzle, everything called out to him, Come, come.

After a few hours, when his horse had carried him well away from his father's house, his mind suddenly cleared. To the Ammonites. It was time for him to go to the children of Ammon. With the Ammonite bands he would return when the right time came and set fire to the whole farm. As the fire consumed everything, Jephthah the Ammonite would emerge through the flames carrying the unconscious body of the old man in his arms. He would lay him down among the embers and ashes and crouch over him to give him water and dress his wounds. When Gilead had lost his wife, his farm, and his sons, what would he have left except his last son, who had saved his life.

And then they could both set out together to look for the sea.

The following night, by the light of a clay lamp, the household clerk wrote in the household records: Jephthah shall have no inheritance in his father's house because he is the son of another woman. And the household clerk wrote further in the household records: Darkness and wrath surely beget wrath and darkness. This whole affair is evil: evil is he who has fled and evil are those that remain. Evil will also be our latter end. May God forgive his servant.

5

JEPHTHAH DWELLED for many days among the Ammonites in the city of Abel-Keramim. From his childhood he spoke their language and knew their laws and their songs, because his mother had been an Ammonite woman who was snatched by the Gileadites when they raided the Ammonite settlements beyond the desert.

Indeed, in Abel-Keramim he also discovered his mother's father and all her brothers, who were great men, and they adopted Jephthah and took him into the palaces and temples. The Ammonite princes honored and exalted Jephthah, because the sound of his voice was cold and lordly and a yellow glint sometimes appeared in his eye, and also because he was very sparing in his use of words.

They said:

"This man was born to be a leader."
And they also said:
"Truly it seems that this man is always at rest."
And also:
"It is very hard to know."

When shooting arrows or carousing, Jephthah sometimes seemed to those around him to be moving slowly, almost wearily or with a slight hesitancy. How deceptive this was: like a knife reposing between folds of silk.

He had the power to say to a stranger: Rise, come, go; and the man would rise or come or go, although Jephthah made not a sound, only his lips moved. Even when he turned to one of the elders of the city and said, Now speak, I am listening, or, Do not speak, I am not listening, the elder felt an inner compulsion to reply; Yes, my lord.

He was loved by many women in the city of Abel-Keramim. Like his father Gilead before him, he was endowed with powers of sadness and powers of silent dominion. Women longed to dissolve the power and penetrate the sadness and also to submit to them. At night, between the silken sheets, they whispered into his ear: You stranger. When his skin touched theirs they would cry out. And he, mute and remote, knew how to extract from them a gushing melody, as well as slow, tormented tunes, a fervent arching and swelling beyond endurance, patiently sailing upstream night after night to the very limit of the soul.

In those days Gatel ruled over the children of Ammon. He was a boy king. When Jephthah came before King Gatel the king looked at him as a sickly youth looks at a racing charioteer, and asked him to tell him stories: let the stranger tell the king stories to sweeten his sleep at night.

And so Jephthah sometimes came to King Gatel at the end of

the day to tell him about rending a wolf barehanded, about the wars of shepherds and nomads, about whitening bones in the desert at midday, about the terror of the night sounds that rise from the desert at the middle watch.

Sometimes the king would plead, More, more; sometimes he would implore, Don't leave me, Jephthah, sit here till I fall asleep, because of the dark; and sometimes he would suddenly burst out laughing feebly like a haunted man, unable to stop unless Jephthah laid a hand on his shoulder and said to him: That's enough, Gatel.

Then the king of the Ammonites would stop laughing and turn his pitiful blue eyes on Jephthah and beg, More, more.

In the course of time King Gatel made Jephthah his confidant and was always watching attentively for the yellow spark which did or did not glint in Jephthah's eye.

The elders of Ammon looked askance on all this: A young slave has come to the city out of the sand dunes, and now the king is under his spell, and must we watch and say nothing.

King Gatel was an assiduous reader of the chronicles of ancient times. He had set his heart on being like one of those mighty kings who had brought many lands under their dominion. But because he loved words with all his being and always paid more attention to the words in which his chronicle would be written than to the victorious deeds themselves, he was smitten by serious doubts about even simple questions. If he had to select a new groom, or order the construction of a new turret, or in general to choose between two different courses of action, he would torment himself with doubts all night long because he could always see both sides of the problem.

If ever Jephthah deigned to hint which was the better course or which would end badly, Gatel would be overcome with gratitude and affection, of which he was unable to express to Jephthah even the smallest part, because it is the way of words to delude the man who courts them.

He would say:

"Let's ride to Aroer or Rabbat-Ammon to see if the figs are ripe yet."

Then he would add:

"Or perhaps we shouldn't, because the stars do not favor a journey today."

Or else:

"I had a pain in my ear and in my knee all night. And now I have a toothache and a bellyache. Tell me another story about that boy you told me about, the one who could speak the language of the dogs. Don't leave me."

And so it came to pass that King Gatel fell in love and confusion, and would stamp his foot with longing if Jephthah did not come to the palace in the morning. And within the palace a secret enmity was hatched. People said to one another:

"This will lead to no good."

Abel-Keramim was a large and happy city. Its wines flowed abundantly, its women were round-hipped and sweet-scented, its servants were eager and merry, its maidservants were easygoing, and all its horses were swift. Chemosh and Milcom had showered the city with delights. Every evening the trumpets sounded for banquets, and at night sounds of players and musicians rose up and rows of torches blazed in the squares of the city until morning light appeared and the caravans set out through the city gates.

Jephthah did not stand aloof from the pleasures of Abel-Keramim. He tried everything and saw everything, but he touched it all with his fingertips only, because his heart was far away and he said to himself: Let the Ammonites play before me. Three or even four women flocked to him in the same night, and Jephthah loved to revel with them and enjoy them one by one while they enjoyed each other in unison and he would enter among them a scourge of lust a rod of rage and sometimes after all the sound and fury they would sing him Ammonite songs about expanses of water or bucks in the vineyard or suffering and grace while he lay back among them awash on a sea like a dream-swept child. At first light he would say to them all, Now, go, that's enough. And he would sit at the window watching the fingers of light and the pallor of the mountains and the distant conflagration and finally also the sun.

The summer came and went. The autumn winds snatched at the treetops. Old horses suddenly reared and whinnied. Jephthah sat at the window and remembered his father's house. He suddenly longed to be sitting in the stable with the household priest and his three brothers Jamin, Jemuel, and Azur while the priest read to them from a holy book and outside the water ran in the channels, the orchards were cloaked in wintry sadness, and the scent of autumn rose from the vineyards as the vine leaves fell. The longing pierced and stung him with the sharpness of an arrow until his soul was writhing in torment.

He rose and stood at the window while, behind him on his couch, one of the beautiful women lay sleeping, her hair covering her face, breathing peacefully. It sounded to him like a soft evening breeze, and all of a sudden he could not remember who she was, or even whether he had already been with her or if he still had to go to her, and why.

Jephthah sat down on the end of the bed and began singing his mother's songs to the sleeping woman. But his voice was rough and the song came out bitter and rasping. He reached out and touched her cheek with his fingertips, and she did not wake up. He rose and returned to the window and saw dark clouds hurrying eastward in a panic, as though something were happening beyond the eastern horizon and he must arise and go there at once, now, before it was too late. But he did not know what the place was or why it might be too late or who it was who was calling him to go, and he only said to himself:

"Not here."

And then Jephthah also thought: My brother Azur is not Abel

and I am not Cain. O Lord of the asp in the desert, do not hide yourself from me. Call me, call me, gather me to you. If I am not worthy to be your chosen one, take me to be your hired assassin: I shall go in the night with my knife in your name to your foes, and in the morning you may hide your face from me as you will, as if we were strangers. You are the lord of the fox and the vulture and I love your wrath and I do not ask you to lift up the brightness of your countenance toward me. Your wrath and barren sorrow are all I want. Surely anger and sadness are a sign to me that I am made in your image, I am your son, I am yours, and you will take me to you by night, for in the image of your hatred am I made, O lord of the wolves at night in the desert. You are a weary and a desperate God, and whomsoever you love, him will you burn with fire, for you are jealous. I say to you cursed be your love, O God, and cursed be my love of you. I know your secret for I am in your secret: you paid heed to Abel and his offering but in your heart it was Cain, Cain, that you loved, and therefore you spread your wrathful care upon Cain and not upon his simplehearted brother. And you chose Cain and not Abel to be a fugitive and a vagabond upon the face of this evil earth, and you set the seal of your image upon his brow to wander to and fro in all the land and to stamp your seal the seal of a barren God upon people and hills, O God of Cain, O God of Jephthah son of Pitdah. Cain is a witness and I am a witness to your image, O lord of the lightning in the forest of the fire in the granary of the howling of maddened dogs in the night, I know you for you are in me. I the son of the Ammonite woman loved my mother, and my mother clove to my father out of the depths, and out of the depths my father cried to you. Give me a sign.

The city of Abel-Keramim stood at the crossroads of the caravan routes, and as dusk fell long lines of caravans from afar passed under its gates, laden with all the riches of Egypt, spices and perfumes and copper from Assyria, glassware from Phoenicia, fragrant game from the land of Edom to the south, from Judea grapes and olives, wines from the Euphrates, silk from Aleppo, little blue-eyed boys from the blue isles of the sea, Hittite harlots, bracelets, myrrh, and concubines; by nightfall everything was gathered within the walls, the heavy gates were barred, and the whole city was filled with torchlight and tumult. Sometimes the golden domes caught flashes of light and seemed to sparkle with blood and fire and all the temples overflowed with strains of ecstatic music.

Jephthah wallowed in wine, women, and court life. Despite all this luxury, his visage appeared as if scorched by fire. On his couch at night he was caressed by the fairest women of the city; they sipped his wintry powers like dazed birds. Their lips fluttered among the hair of his chest and they whispered to him: You stranger. He said nothing, but his eyes turned inward because nowhere around could they find.

In the course of time jealousy began to swell in the city. The notables of Ammon were jealous because of their wives and daughters, and also on account of the king. The elders said in their council: Ammon serves King Gatel, and King Gatel is like a woman in the hands of Jephthah the Gileadite, and this Jephthah is not one of us but belongs only to himself.

These words even reached the ears of the king, who already despised himself for his love of Jephthah. Sometimes at night he would say to himself, Why do I not have this fair-haired man killed.

But he hesitated, because he could see both sides of the question.

When the words of the elders reached his ears, and rumor whispered that the king was like a harlot before the stranger, his eyes brimmed with tears. All the days of his youth he had dreamed of waging great wars like one of the mighty kings of old, but he did not know how to make war, and whenever he so much as set foot outside his palace the sunlight made his head reel and the very smell of a horse always made his teeth chatter. Therefore he summoned Jephthah one day and said to him: Take men, chariots, and lances, take horses and horsemen, take priests and magicians, and go to the land of Gilead to conquer the land into which your mother was carried to servitude. If you refuse to go that will prove that the elders are right, that you are not one of us but a stranger. I am the king and I have spoken. Fetch me a glass of water.

That night Jephthah dreamed of the desert. In his dream he was climbing a crag in the desert and was trapped halfway up the rock face, because it was as smooth as Sidonian glass and he could neither climb up nor go down but only close his eyes, because beneath his feet there was a sheer drop onto the sharp white rocks far below. The wind howled all around him like a wild beast. Just then he felt a woman's hand caress his back, and her touch weakened his grip on the rock face, and he yearned to give up and to go to where she was calling him. In the depth of the cave there was a damp wind and the light was grim and lurid, but the woman was there at his side and there was stillness, cool water, and rest.

When he woke up in the morning he knew that his stay in the land of Ammon was at an end and that the time had come for him to leave. Outside the city reached up toward heaven with all its palm trees and gold-domed towers. When the morning light touched the gold the whole city began to blaze. This was a sadness Jephthah had not expected. He had innocently supposed that a man could simply get up and go without looking back. He almost changed his mind. It was as if the city were clutching at his robe with sharp claws of longing and would not let him go.

But King Gatel sent urgent word: Where is my war, I have waited a whole day now and there is no war or anything, what are you waiting for, Jephthah.

Jephthah delayed no longer.

He rose and fled to the desert.

He did not go alone, but took with him the daughter whom one of the women had borne to him.

Pitdah was seven years old when she was taken out of the city into the desert on the back of her father's horse. She was an Ammo-

nite, like her mother. She had passed her childhood among maidservants, eunuchs, and silks. Jephthah had lived in Abel-Keramim
for ten years.

When they left the city by the Dung Gate Pitdah laughed for
joy, for she loved riding; she fondly imagined that she was being
taken out into the desert for a day's ride and that at evening she
would be brought back to her mother and the cat. But when the
first night broke on her in the wilderness, she was alarmed and began to scream and stamp her feet, and she cursed her father and
even kicked the horse with her strong little legs. Her mouth, pursed
with rage, was a pitiful spectacle.

She did not stop screaming until the sounds of the desert
soothed her to sleep.

In the morning Jephthah gave her a little pipe he had made
from a reed. Pitdah could play the songs of Abel-Keramim which
the harlots and concubines sang in the squares of the city at night.
Some of them were the same songs his mother Pitdah had sung to
him. As she played Jephthah could hear the water running in the
channels in the orchards on Gilead's farm. His heart went out to
her whenever she said the word Father. And he rode very slowly,
and to take her mind off the heat and the discomfort of the journey he told her story after story, about the barehanded slaying of
the wolf and about his brother Azur who could understand the language of dogs. That day Jephthah used more words than on any
other day in his whole life.

After a few days Pitdah stopped asking for her mother and her
home. He revealed to her that their goal was the sea. When she
asked what that might be, he replied that the sea was a vast hilly
land where the hills were made not of sand but of water. When she
asked him what was there he replied that perhaps there was peace.
And when she wanted to know why the earth did not soak up the
sea in an instant as it soaks up all water, he did not know what to
answer and only said:

"Now cover your head from the sun."

Pitdah said:

"When will we reach the sea like you said."

Jephthah said:

"I don't know. I've never been there. Look, Pitdah, a lizard; now it's gone."

Sometimes when she looked up at her father there was a tired light in her eyes. She might have been sick from the sands and the sun, or perhaps she was merely alarmed. At night he would enfold her in his cloak to protect her against the biting cold.

When the moon began to wane, Jephthah and his daughter arrived at a cave in the mountains in a place called the Land of Tob. There was a spring there, and several oak trees which cast a deep, soft shade. Beside the spring there were some mossy stone troughs, where desert nomads gathered to water their mangy flocks. They pitched their black goat-hair tents on the slope of the hill. That was where Pitdah learned to collect sticks and to make a fire at the entrance to the cave. Jephthah would go hunting and bring back a roebuck or a tortoise, which he would roast in the fire.

At night they saw a hollow moon rolling gently along the line of mountain peaks as though cautiously testing the surface of the desert before flooding it with silvery pallor. In the moonlight the jagged mountains looked like thirsty jaws.

Early in the morning Pitdah would go down to the troughs to fetch water, and, returning barefoot to her father, she would wake him up by splashing handfuls of cold water in his face. After he was up she played on her pipe, while Jephthah sat silently absorbing the music as though it were wine.

The desert nomads who roamed the Land of Tob were all malcontents or outcasts. Jephthah joined them. Cadaverous women hugged the girl and fussed over her all day long, because in the Land of Tob no child was ever born. Its inhabitants wandered restlessly between the desert plains and the mountain ravines. Sometimes the Land of Tob was raided, either by Ammonite troops or by bands of Israelites bent on killing the nomads. These nomads were desperate men: some were killers and some were fleeing from killers; some were haters whose hatred the settled lands could not contain, others were hated men with hounds on their heels; there were also soothsayers, and dreamers who lived on roots and herbs so as not to increase suffering in the world.

Above the land there stretched a sky of molten iron; the earth was copper-colored, parched and cracked. But the nights in the Land of Tob were powerful and heady like black wine. A blessed coolness descended calmly over all each night, bringing relief to the outcasts, to the mangy flocks, and to the desperate wasteland itself.

One day Jephthah and his daughter were brought before the chieftain of the nomads.

He was a lean, shriveled old man; his face was like aged leather, and only the line of his jaw retained a vestige of strength or ruthlessness. Jephthah stood before him in the gully of a lifeless riverbed. He was silent because he chose to hear first the words that the old chieftain would address to him. The old man, too, sprawled drowsily on his gray camel, waiting for the stranger to speak. For a long while they were both silent, each testing the strength of the other's silence with stubborn patience, while a circle of thin women surrounded them at a distance.

The chieftain sat like a lizard in the sun, without flickering an eyelid. In front of his camel Jephthah stood rooted to the spot with a face of stone. At his feet his daughter Pitdah scrabbled and burrowed in the sand, trying to discover where the ants came from. Everything was still. Only the shadow of the two men, the one mounted on his camel and the other standing on his feet, moved gently, as the sun climbed higher into the white sky. It was a long silence. Finally the old man spoke, in a parched voice:

"Who are you, stranger?"

Jephthah said:

"I am the son of Gilead the Gileadite, my lord, by an Ammonite servant woman."

"I did not ask your name or your father's name; I asked, who are you, stranger."

"I am a stranger, as you say, my lord."

"And why have you come to this place. You have been sent by the Ammonites or by the Israelites to spy on us and to betray us to our mortal foes."

"I have no part in Israel, or any inheritance among the children of Ammon."

"You are a desperate man, stranger. I can see that your eyes are turned inward like the eyes of a desperate man. Whom do you worship."

"Not Milcom."

"Whom do you worship."

"The Lord of the wolves in the desert at night. In the image of his hatred am I made."

"And the girl."

"My daughter Pitdah. And she is growing more like the desert every day."

"You are a warrior. Come out with us to kill and plunder, like one of these young men. Come out with us tonight."

"I am a stranger, my lord. I have lived out my life among strangers."

6

JEPHTHAH FOUND favor among the wandering men of the Land of Tob.

In the course of time he fought with them against their attackers and joined them in several raids on the settled lands, for these nomads hated all house dwellers. They slipped by night through the fences of the farms and flitted like ghosts within. The slain died silently and the killers stole as silently away. They came with knives or daggers. And with fire. By morning charred embers smoked in the ruins of the farm, in the land of Ammon or of Israel. And Jephthah rose ever higher among them because he was endowed with the attributes of lordship. He had the power to impose his will on others without a movement, by his voice alone. As always, he spoke little, because he did not love words and he did not trust them.

One night the Jephthahites stole into the farm of Gilead the Gileadite, on the border of the land of Gilead, at the edge of the desert.

Shadowy shapes scurried along the paths of the estate, among the dark orchards and the dense foliage of the vineyards, to the door of the house that was built of black volcanic stone. But Jephthah did not allow the house to be burned with its inmates, because a sudden longing rose within his hatred and he recalled the words his father had spoken on a faraway night and a faraway day. You are tainted as your father is tainted. You for yourself. I for myself. Every man for himself. There is a lizard; now it has gone.

He knelt on all fours and drank from the irrigation channel. Then he gave a shrill birdlike whistle, and his men gathered and slipped away into the wasteland without setting fire to the farm.

The nomads raided Ammon and Israel alike. Every man's hand was against them, and anyone who found them would slay them. They slept all day in crevices, crannies, and caves, with the dark shapes of their meager flocks scattered in the shade of the oak trees beside the mossy rock-hewn troughs. Lean black-robed women watched over the flocks by day, while the sun dissolved everything with its white-hot hatred. And by night the nomads emerged from their hiding places to raid the settled lands. On their return they sang a bitter song, like a long-drawn-out wail. Occasionally a man would let out a shout in the middle of the song, and suddenly fall silent.

• • •

Pitdah, too, found favor in the eyes of the nomads. She was a darkly beautiful girl, and her movements were always dreamy, as if she were made of a fragile substance, as if even the ground beneath her feet and the objects between her fingers were all longing to break and she had always to be careful.

The bitter women adored Pitdah, because no child was ever born in the Land of Tob. She would play her pipe to the hillsides and the boulders even when there was no one to hear her. Whenever Jephthah heard her playing in the distance, it seemed to him like the sound of the wind in the vineyards on his father's estate, the plashing of the water as it ran in the channels in the shade of the orchard. Pitdah dreamed even when she was awake, and Jephthah's heart went out to her if she told him one of her dreams or if she suddenly said to him: Father.

He loved her savagely. But he was careful whenever he stroked her hair or hugged her shoulder because he would recall how his father Gilead had held him when he himself was a small boy. He would say:

"I shall not hurt you. Give me your hand."

And the girl would reply:

"But I can't help laughing, because of the way you're looking at me."

He loved her savagely. Whenever he chanced to think of a strange man coming one day to take Pitdah away from him, his blood rebelled in his veins. Some short, fleshy man might clasp Pitdah in his hairy arms, reeking of sweat and onions, licking and biting her lips, groping downwards with clumsy fingers toward her delicate recesses. At the sight of his bloodshot eyes she laughed aloud, and he cooled his burning brow with the flat of his dagger and whispered to her: Play, Pitdah, play; and he sat listening to the music like a man going blind until the rage subsided and only a dry sadness remained like a taste of ashes in his throat. Sometimes the power of his love made Jephthah bellow wildly like his father Gilead before him, and sometimes he yearned to be able to brew her potions in the night and conjure away the threatening evil.

Jephthah and the nomads could see her growing before their eyes. When she was not gathering firewood or watering the flocks with the gaunt women, she would sit in a gully playing with pebbles from the brook, building towers, walls, castles, turrets, and gates, and suddenly she would destroy them all with glee and burst out laughing. She would also weave wreaths of thistles, when the thistles were in flower. She seemed to be in a dream, and her rounded lips were slightly parted. Sometimes she would hold up in her sun-darkened hands a whitening bone she had found, and sing to it, and blow on it, and even touch it to her hair.

She knew how to carve little figures from branches of shrubs, a galloping horse, a resting lamb, a black old man leaning on a stick. Sometimes odd occurrences that were no laughing matter made Jephthah's daughter laugh warmly. If a woman was tying bundles onto a camel and the camel was startled and all the bundles fell off, Pitdah would erupt in soft, low laughter. Or if one of the nomads stood with his back to her and his head bent motionlessly forward, as if he were sunk deep in thought as he pissed among the rocks, she would laugh uncontrollably and would not stop even if the man lost his temper and shouted at her.

If one of the men suddenly stared at her sideways, with gaping eyes and parted lips and the tip of his tongue protruding between his teeth, Pitdah would laugh aloud. And if Jephthah caught sight of the man staring at his daughter and his eyes began to flash cold rage, Pitdah would move her eyes back and forth between them as though drawing a line, laughing louder than ever. Even when he shouted, That's enough, she could not stop laughing; sometimes she would infect him with her laughter and he could not stop, either. The young nomads interpreted all this as a sign of happiness, but the women considered it something that would not end well.

The nomads' wives taught Pitdah to weave and cook and milk goats, and to tame a stubborn billy goat. The girl could do all these things easily, and her thoughts always seemed to be far away.

Once she said to her father Jephthah:

"At night you go out to fight and you win, and in the daytime you sleep, and then even the flies on your face are stronger than you are."

Jephthah said:

"Everybody has to sleep."

Pitdah said:

"Snakes never sleep; they can't even close their eyes, because they have no eyelids."

Jephthah said:

"It is written in the holy writings that the snake is more cunning than any other beast of the field."

Pitdah:

"How sad to be more cunning than any other beast of the field. And how sad never to sleep and never to close your eyes and dream at night. If the snake was really cunning, it would find a way to close its eyes."

"What about you."

"I love watching you sleeping on the ground after your night fights, with the flies walking all over your face. I love you, Father. And I love myself, too. And the places where you never take me, where the sun sets in the evening. You have forgotten the sea, but I remember. Now, put this cloak over your head and moo, and I'll watch you and laugh."

In his dreams Jephthah saw a procession of princes and powerful men coming to ask him for his daughter's hand. Their faces were crooked; like dogs they must be chased away with a stick or a stone, because Pitdah was not for them. Very slowly and heavily his father Gilead appeared in Jephthah's dreams, and he, too, put out his broad, rough hand to touch Pitdah and she ran away from him and hid behind the troughs and he ran after her and Jephthah cried out in his sleep. Or else the boys appeared, Azur and Jamin and Gatel and Jemuel, and they surrounded Pitdah in his dream with hundreds of white fingers to tear off her clothes and she laughed with them and he screamed at the sight of them because they had no eyelids and their eyes were wide open and gaping at her not closing not blinking and they closed around her and he woke up with a cry and found that he was holding the dagger and his hand was shaking.

Touch me, O God, you have not touched me yet, how long shall we wait for you. Reach out for me with your hand and with fingers of fire. Here I am before you upon one of the mountains, holding the lamb for a burnt offering, and behold the fire and the wood, but where is the knife. I shall desire your shadow all the days of my life. If you appear in the mountain I shall be burning dust. If you shine forth in the crescent moon or in the reflection of the moon in water, there your servant will be in the white sands or in the depths of the water. If the dogs howl and pour out their hearts in their howling, that is a sign that you are loving and wrathful. Send me your wrath, O God, and let me be touched by it, surely you are a solitary God and I, too, am all alone. You shall have no other servant before me. I am your son and I shall bear witness all my life to your inscrutable terrors, O Lord of the wildcat stalking the lifeless riverbeds by night, night after night.

In the course of time Jephthah became the chieftain of the nomads. He spoke little, and when he did speak his voice was very soft. Anyone who wanted to hear him had to lean toward him and listen attentively.

At that time the king of Ammon invaded the land of Israel. He conquered all the cities and farms and made slaves of their inhabitants. Some managed to escape, but the rest were under the sway of

King Gatel. The king never left his palace, but passed his time filling scroll after scroll with orders for his generals, and also writing the *Book of the Wars of King Gatel*.

One day Jephthah's three brothers, Jamin, Jemuel, and Azur, came to the desert to the Land of Tob, to the place where Jephthah dwelt. They were fleeing from the Ammonites and they had come here because Jephthah's fame had spread all over the land, as he and his nomad band, the Jephthahites, snapped at the heels of the Ammonite army, robbing the caravans and flouting the king's guards like a bird playing with a bear.

Jephthah did not conceal his identity from his brothers. But neither did he fall on their necks and weep. With the passage of the years his two eldest brothers had become even coarser. Jamin, the eldest, was now a heavily built, corpulent man who resembled neither his father nor his mother but looked more like the household priest. Jemuel could not rid his face of an obsequious smile accompanied by a lecherous wink, which seemed to be saying, Come over to my house, my friend, and let's have an orgy. Only the youngest brother, Azur, had developed the speed and sharpness of an arrow in flight; he resembled his half-brother the son of the Ammonite woman, rather than the two sons of Nehushtah daughter of Zebulun.

When the three brothers had bowed down and prostrated themselves before the nomad chief, Jephthah said:

"Rise, fugitives. Do not bow down to me. I am not Joseph and you are not the sons of Jacob. Stand up. At once."

Jamin, the eldest, spoke as though reading from a written text:

"My lord, we have come to tell you that the Ammonite foe has conquered your father's estate. And now our father is an old man and cannot fight against them. We, your servants, say to you: Arise, Jephthah, rescue your father's house and your father's land, for only you and no other can defeat the Ammonite serpent."

They pleaded with Jephthah and Jephthah said nothing. He

merely ordered that they be accepted into his band. Day by day they said to him: How long will our lord tarry. He did not answer them and he did not rebuke them. In his heart he said, O God, grant me a sign.

The Jephthahites harried the armies of Ammon. Fear and panic seized the city of Abel-Keramim at night because of the Jephtha-hites who raided the caravans. Jephthah's men were as swift and cunning as their lord. His footsteps at night were like a breeze or a caress. He sent silent-knived assassins by night to the Ammonite captains. Gatel's soldiers were seized by terror whenever they heard at night the sound of a breeze or a wolf or a bird of prey, lest it be Je-phthah's nomads in the night making the sound of bird or wolf or breeze. The Jephthahites penetrated the walls of Rabbat-Ammon and infiltrated the squares of Abel-Keramim and its temples: they entered the city by day with the caravans, disguised as merchants, by night they sowed panic, and in the morning they were borne away by the wind and were no more, and time and again Gatel sent forth his army to pursue the wind. In the book of his wars King Ga-tel wrote:

"Surely this is the way of the fainthearted, to strike and to flee. Let them come by the light of day, let us meet face to face, and I shall crush them and have peace."

But the Jephthahites did not choose to come by daylight. Day by day the lord of the nomads went out and stood alone on the hill, with his back toward the camp and his face toward the wilderness, as though waiting for some sound or scent.

Then King Gatel sent word to Jephthah:

"You are an Ammonite, Jephthah. We are brothers. Why are we fighting each other? If you choose, come and I shall place you in my second chariot, and none shall lift up hand or foot without your word in all the cities of Ammon and of Israel."

By the hand of his adjutant Azur the nomad chieftain sent back word to Gatel king of Ammon saying:

"Gatel, I am not your brother or your father's son. You know that I am a stranger. I do not fight for the Israelites, I fight for one you do not know. In his honor I shall put you to the sword and your enemies, too, for I have been a stranger all the days of my life."

7

PITDAH DREAMED a dream one night in her tent in the Land of Tob. In her dream she was a bride in a bridal gown. The maidens were dancing around her with lyres and timbrels, and there were bracelets on her arms.

When she told her father about this dream he flew into a panic. He shook her by the shoulders and whispered frantically: Tell me who was your bridegroom. As he pleaded with her his hands twisted her shoulders violently, and she suddenly started to laugh, as she often laughed, without cause. Then he slapped her face wildly with the back of his hand and shouted: Who was your bridegroom.

Pitdah said:

"You are looking at me like a murderer."

"Who was it, tell me who it was."

"I couldn't see his face in the dream, I could only feel his hot breath on me. Look at you, you've got foam on your lips, leave me alone, go and wash your face in the brook."

"Who was it."

"Don't you hit me again or I'll laugh aloud and the whole camp will hear."

"Who was it."

"But you know who my bridegroom is. Why did you shout at me, why are you trembling so."

• • •

She stood laughing and he stood facing her wearing a dazed look. His eyes were closed and his lips said to him: Of course I knew, why was I so startled. They were still standing there when the elders of Israel rode down to prostrate themselves at Jephthah's feet.

He opened his eyes and saw them coming, and he also saw his father Gilead riding with them. He was just as broad and heavy and ugly as in the old days, only his beard had turned gray.

The elders of Israel raised the hems of their cloaks because of the dust of the desert. They fell flat on their faces before the chief of the nomads. Gilead alone did not bow or prostrate himself before his son. Then a delicious bubbling joy began to course through Jephthah's veins, such a joy as he had never known before and would never know again.

With an effort he controlled his voice as he addressed the elders:

"Arise, elders of Israel. The man to whom you are bowing down is a harlot's son."

But they remained on their knees and would not stand up; they merely looked at one another, not knowing what. At the end of the silence Gilead the Gileadite said:

"You are my son, who will save Israel from the Ammonites."

Jephthah contemplated their broken pride distantly as though it were a wound. Then he was touched by sorrow, not the sorrow of the elders, perhaps not sorrow at all, but something that was not far removed from gentleness, a taste of scorched earth. Gently he said to them:

"I am a stranger, O elders of Israel. No stranger should go before you in your wars, lest the camp be unclean."

At this the elders rose. They said:

"You are our brother, Jephthah, you are our brother. See, today we have made your father Gilead judge of Israel and you, our brother, shall be the captain of our army, you shall fight for us against the Ammonite; as captain of your father's army you shall be our commander, you shall have power over all your brothers, Jephthah, because from your earliest youth you have known the skills of war. To this day the story is told around the shepherds' campfires how you tore a wolf with your bare hands."

"But surely you hate me, elders, and when I have crushed the Ammonite for you you will chase after me like a rebellious slave and my father here will put me in irons because he is the judge of Israel and I am a stranger, a nomad and a harlot's son."

"You are my son, Jephthah. You are my boy who put his hand into the fire without crying out and who tore a wolf with his bare hands. If you come back and fight the Ammonites for us I shall bless you before all your brothers, and you shall be the one who leads the people out and brings them in all the days of my life."

"Why do you not leave me alone, elders. And you, too, judge of Israel: stop pleading with me. You are not children: why are you playing these games. Go while you can and save your hoarheads, and take your priests and all your scribes with you. Only leave me alone. I can see through your plot. Jephthah will not be the warhorse of Israel, and this old man will not ride on my back."

Then Gilead the Gileadite spoke, with lips pressed tight together as though he were straining to break an iron chain.

"Your father will not judge Israel. You shall fight and you shall judge."

The elders were silent; their tongues failed them at the sound of these words.

Jephthah spoke quietly, like a fox, and as he spoke the yellow spark glimmered in his eye.

"If you are really and truly appointing me to be judge of Israel this day, then swear to me now in the name of our God."

"As God hears and witnesses: you shall be judge."

"A whore's son shall be your leader," Jephthah said, and he laughed so loudly that the horses were alarmed.

And the elders soundlessly repeated:

"Our leader."

"Then clap this old man in irons at once. The judge of Israel commands you."

"Jephthah, my son —"

"And cast him into the pit. I have spoken."

The following day Jephthah inspected his army and appointed captains and commanders. He dispatched his brothers Jamin and Jemuel to assemble speedily all the fighting men among the tribes of Israel. And he sent his adjutant Azur the Gileadite with a message to Gatel king of Ammon:

"Get out of my land."

At nightfall on the following day, the judge of Israel commanded a large tent of honor to be pitched in the middle of the camp, and he ordered his father Gilead to be brought up from the pit and installed in this tent and furnished with wine and servant girls. To his daughter Pitdah he said: If the old man dashes the wine pitcher to the ground and smashes it, tell the servants to hurry and bring him a fresh one quickly. If he breaks the second let them fetch him another, because this old man sometimes takes a fancy to the sound of breaking glass. Let him smash to his heart's content. Only do not dare to enter the tent yourself; stop laughing now. Go."

Gatel king of Ammon was driven to distraction by the Jephthahites who picked off his soldiers by day, and by night seemed to be swallowed up by the earth. He sent his army after them, but it was like chasing the wind. He became a laughing stock in Moab and in Edom a byword: the fly bites and the bear dances.

Gatel sent Jephthah a message by the hand of Azur his adjutant: Leave me alone, Jephthah. You are an Ammonite; why should you harm me; surely I loved you deeply. But Jephthah knew Gatel's mind, he knew that he had set his heart on being like one of the mighty kings of old but that even the smell of horses in the distance was enough to make him feel giddy. Calmly the judge of Israel waged a war of words with the king of Ammon by means of envoys who passed to and fro: to whom did the land really belong, whose forefathers had settled it first, what was written in all the chronicles, who was in the right and who had justice on his side. Eventually Gatel came to imagine that it was a war of scrolls that he had to wage, and he multiplied scroll upon scroll.

The elders of Israel came to the judge's tent saying: In God's name, go, the time is passing, the Ammonite is devouring all the land, if you delay longer what will there be left to save for us. Jephthah listened and said nothing. The elders spoke further to the judge: Send word to the Edomite and to the Arab, send to Egypt and to Damascus, we cannot manage alone, for Ammon is too strong for us. And still Jephthah said nothing.

But to himself he said:

"Grant me but one sign more, O God, and I will offer you their carcasses strewn upon the field as you love, O Lord of the wolves in the night in the desert."

One night Pitdah saw another dream. Her bridegroom came in the darkness and said to her in a still small voice: Come, my bride, arise, for the time has come.

In the morning Jephthah listened to her dream, and this time he was silent but his face grew very dark. He had been stalked by dreams all the days of his life. And like his father Gilead before him he believed that dreams come from that place from which man comes and to which he returns through his death. To himself he said: Now is the time. And the girl laughed aloud.

One hour later the trumpet sounded.

All the camps assembled on the rocky slope, and the sun played on the lances and shields. The elders of the tribes were in a panic, searching for the right words to prevent him from launching their whole force against the walls of Ammon in one swoop, for great was the strength of Ammon, and Israel might never recover from this disaster; surely the wild man had resolved to dash the head of Israel against the stone walls of Ammon. But the judge of Israel rose and left the tent in the midst of their entreaties and stood at the entrance facing the troops, and this time his daughter Pitdah was standing at his side. He placed his hand on her shoulder and the voice of his dead mother seemed to ring in his voice as he said: O God, if you will surely deliver the children of Ammon into my hand, then it shall be that whatever comes forth from the doors of my house to meet me when I return in peace from the children of Ammon shall surely belong to God, and I will offer it up as a burnt offering—

"He will deliver the children of Ammon into your hands. Now, you, my maidens, make ready my bridal gown," said the darkly beautiful girl. The people cheered and the horses neighed, and she laughed and laughed and never stopped.

Jephthah the Gileadite emerged from his hiding place in the Land of Tob and pounced on Ammon to raze its walls to the ground, for great was the strength of Ammon. Sweeping through the villages, he toppled the towers and fired the temples, flattened the turrets and shattered the golden domes and gave the wives, concubines, and harlots as food to the fowls of the air.

By the time the day reached its heat Gatel had been put to the sword and Ammon had been smitten from Aroer until you come to Minnith, even twenty cities, and as far as Abel-Keramim, with a very great slaughter, and by nightfall Ammon was defeated and Gatel was slain and still Jephthah was silent.

8

THE DAYS of a man's life are like water seeping into the sands; he perishes from the face of the earth unknown at his coming and unrecognized at his passing. He fades away like a shadow that cannot be brought back. But sometimes dreams come to us in the night and we know in the dreams that nothing truly passes away and nothing is forgotten, everything is always present as it was before.

Even the dead return home in the dreams. Even days that are lost and forgotten come back whole and shining in dreams at night, not a drop is lost, not a jot passes away. The smell of wet dust on an autumn morning from long ago, the sight of burned houses whose ashes have long since been scattered by the wind, the arched hips of dead women, the barking at the moon, on a distant night, of remote ancestors of the dogs that are with us now: everything comes back living and breathing in our dreams.

As if in a dream Jephthah the Gileadite stood at the entrance to his father's estate, within the fences of which he was born, in the shadows of whose orchards he had first felt the touch of a hand, and from which he had fled for his life many years before: not a drop was lost, not a jot had passed away. The fences and orchards stood before him as of old, and the vine still covered all the walls of the house so that the black volcanic stones could not be seen through its embrace. And the water ran in the channels and beneath the trees there was cool dark longing.

Like a man possessed by a dream Jephthah stood looking up to the house, only half-seeing the darkly beautiful one coming out to meet him with songs. And after her came the maidens with timbrels and the shepherds with pipes and his father Gilead, a broad, bitter man. And Jamin, Jemuel, and Azur were also on the path, and their mother Nehushtah daughter of Zebulun could be seen all white in a white dress through the window with pale laughter on her lips. And all the dogs were barking and the cows were lowing and the household scribe and the household priest and the bald-headed steward, all as in a dream, nothing was left out.

And the maidens followed after her, dressed in white and playing their timbrels and singing: Jephthah has slain, Jephthah has slain;

and the people cheered and the torches blazed over all of Mizpeh of Gilead.

As she came out she seemed to be floating, as if her feet disdained to touch the dust of the path. As a gazelle comes down to water so Pitdah came down to her father. Her bridal gown gleamed white, her eyelashes shaded her eyes, and when she looked up at him and he heard her laughter he saw fire and ice burning with a green flame in her pupils. And the maidens sang: Jephthah has slain slain slain, and Pitdah's hips moved restlessly as though to the rhythm of a secret dance and she was slender and barefoot —

Drowsily the judge of Israel stood facing the entrance to his father's estate. His face was parched and weatherbeaten, and his eyes were turned inward. As though he were deathly tired. As though in a dream.

The cheering of the people grew louder as Gilead was carried out on a litter by Jamin, Jemuel, and Azur, and the troops shouted: Happy is the father, happy is the father. The whole of Mizpeh of Gilead was lit up by torches, and the noise of the timbrels was a riot of joy.

Beautiful and dark was Pitdah as she placed the victor's wreath on her father's head. Then she put her hands silently over his eyes and said:

"Father."

As his daughter's fingers touched his eyelids, Jephthah felt like a sunbaked boulder in the desert that is suddenly splashed with cold water. But he did not want to wake from his slumber.

He was tired and thirsty, and his unwashed body was still smeared with blood and ashes. For a moment he missed the city he had burned that day, Abel-Keramim, reaching up to heaven with its many towers topped with golden domes, the sun touching the gold in the mornings, and the sickly boy king pleading with him: Jephthah, don't leave me, tell me a story because of the dark, and

the caravans coming in through the gates of the city in the evening
twilight with the music of camel bells, and women's lips fluttering
on the hair of his chest and whispering: Stranger, and the lights at
night and the music, and his sword piercing the throat of the ailing
king and emerging steaming from the back of his neck, and Gatel
saying with dying lips: What an ugly story, and the city in flames
and burning women throwing themselves off the rooftops and the
smell of roasting flesh and the screaming—

Silently he stood without moving at the entrance to his father's
estate, and his eyes were closed.

Then the old man Gilead raised his hand to silence the sing-
ers and players, and the cheering crowds so that the judge of Israel
could speak to the people.

All the people stopped to listen. Only the torchlight trembled
in the silent breeze.

The judge of Israel opened his mouth to speak to the people,
and suddenly he collapsed on the ground, howling like a wolf that
has been pierced by an arrow.

My lady mother, his lips said. And one of the elders of the tribe
who was present thought in his heart: This man is deceptive; he is
not one of us.

9

SHE ASKED him for two months, and he, as though he had forgotten everything, said to her:

"Leave this place, go to another country and never come back to
me."

The girl laughed and answered:

"Put this cloak over your head and eyes and moo, and we'll
watch you and laugh."

And he, lost among his longings, said:

"Look, Pitdah, on the fence, there's a lizard. Now it's gone."

• • •

For two months she wandered in the mountains and her maidens followed after her. The shepherds fled at their approach. If she passed through one of the villages, the villagers hid indoors. Silently they went clad in white along moonswept ravines. What was the message of this ghostly pallor, dead silver light on dead hilltops. No wild beast touched them. Olive trees twisted with age did not dare to scratch their skin. Their footfall was muffled by the dust like the rustling of leaves in the breeze. With what sense must one listen to the many sounds, and with what sense listen to stillness. Man and woman, father, mother, and son, father and mother and daughter, a pair of brothers, winter, autumn, spring, and summer, water and wind, all are merely distance upon distance, and whether you scream or laugh or remain silent, everything without exception will be absorbed into the stillness of the stars and the sadness of those hills.

Pitdah was dark and beautiful as she walked and laughed in her bridal wreath, and wretched nomads who saw her from a distance said: She is a stranger, the daughter of a stranger, no man may approach her and live.

When two months had passed she returned. Jephthah had set up an altar on one of the mountains, and the fire and the knife were in his hand. In later times the wandering tribesmen would speak around their campfires at night of the great joy they had both shown, she a bride on her marriage couch and he a youthful lover stretching out his fingers to the first touch. And they were both laughing as wild beasts laugh in the dark of night, and they did not speak, only Jephthah said to her, Sea, sea.

You have chosen me out of all my brothers and dedicated me to your service. You shall have no other servant before me. Here is the dark beauty under my knife; I have not withheld my only daughter from you. Grant me a sign, for surely you are tempting your servant.

Afterward the night beasts shrieked among the rocks and the barren desert stretched to the tops of the distant hills.

10

SIX YEARS did Jephthah the Gileadite judge Israel. He sank up to his neck in blood, and he provoked Gilead against Ephraim to destroy Israel, just as he had spoken in his youth to Gatel king of Ammon saying: I have no part in Israel nor any inheritance among the children of Ammon; I shall put both you and your enemies to the sword, for I have been a stranger all the days of my life.

And after six years he tired of judging and returned alone to the desert. No man approached him, for there was a deathly fear upon all the nomads of the Land of Tob. Only his half-brother Azur would come down and leave him bread and water at a distance. And the lean hounds always came down with him.

For a whole year Jephthah dwelt alone in a cave in the Land of Tob. He studied all the night sounds which came up from the wilderness when the desert bristled, until he could utter them all himself, and then he decided: Enough.

In the chronicle of the household the household scribe wrote:

And after him Ibzan of Beth-lehem judged Israel. And he had thirty sons and thirty daughters.

1966
1974–75